# THE MAN OF GLASS

ALSO BY DONALD ZOCHERT

*Another Weeping Woman*
*Murder in the Hellfire Club*
*Laura: The Life of Laura Ingalls Wilder*
*Walking in America*
*Books and Readers in Old Milwaukee*

# THE MAN OF GLASS

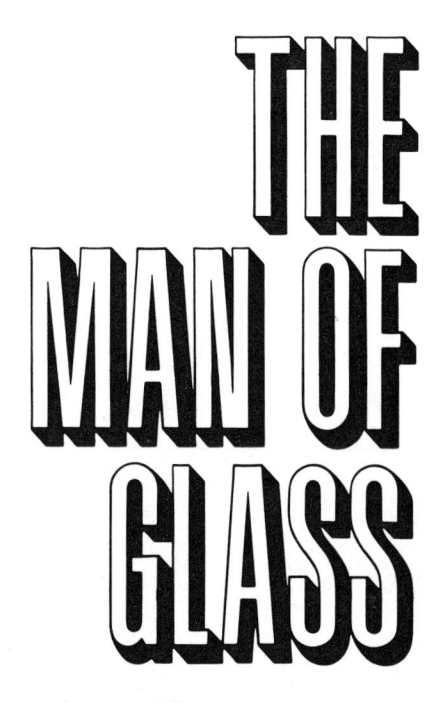

A NICK CAINE ADVENTURE

**DONALD ZOCHERT**

HOLT, RINEHART and WINSTON
New York

Copyright © 1981 by Donald Zochert

All rights reserved, including the right to reproduce this
book or portions thereof in any form.

First published in January 1982 by Holt, Rinehart and Winston,
383 Madison Avenue, New York, New York 10017.

Published simultaneously in Canada by Holt, Rinehart and
Winston of Canada, Limited.

Library of Congress Cataloging in Publication Data

Zochert, Donald.
  The man of glass.

  I. Title.
PS3576.023M3       813'.54      81-47466
ISBN: 0-03-056222-8            AACR2

First Edition

Designer: Helene Berinsky

Printed in the United States of America

10 9 8 7 6 5 4 3 2 1

*For Nancy*

No one dies when he should.
—E. M. Cioran.

# PART ONE

# 1

When the phone rang in the middle of the night and the man said hello, I knew right away who it was. A voice from the past. Another broken promise. All it took was one word and I got the whole picture.

I reached under the pillow and touched the cold steel barrel of the Margolin Special. For luck.

"Caine?" he asked again.

I let him wonder.

"Is this Nick Caine?"

"Maybe not. It's almost five o'clock in the morning."

"Caine, I'd recognize your voice anywhere."

We were even. But I could hardly hear him. Either he had a bad connection or he was calling from very far away. I voted for the latter. He had very good connections.

"Caine, I know what time it is. It's late. I know what I promised. I'm sorry. But I need your help. I need to see you. Now."

There was an edge of something ugly in his voice. It took me a moment to recognize it, because I had never heard it there before. It was fear.

"Caine?" he asked suddenly.

"Yes."

The words came quickly, through his teeth. "I made a mistake, Caine. The man of glass. I overestimated the power of guilt. Caine?"

"Yes. I'm here."

"This is a confession, Caine. I'm not usually wrong about people." The line crackled with static. He sounded even farther away than before. "I can't hear you very well. I can't speak very loudly. Are you alone? Is anyone there with you?"

"I'm alone."

"Good. Do you still have that little number designed by a blind man—the Margolin Special?"

"Yes. I have it."

He sounded relieved. "You remember how to use it?"

"No."

It stopped him.

He hesitated again, and I pictured that unforgettable horseface of his. The deep lines of resignation, the air of sadness, the closely cropped white hair, the heavy flesh that was always waxy and pale from too much of a bad thing—too many years spent in the dark, too many private pains he could tell no one about. Too many broken promises. He had always been an old man. An old man with one redeeming feature. He had the black, burning eyes of a saint.

"You haven't forgotten everything, Caine," he said finally.

"I've tried to."

He sighed. It wasn't what he wanted to hear. His voice was suddenly very tired. "My back's against the wall, Caine. I'm in a corner. I need your help. I believe you were once in that position yourself?" He let it hang there, a long-bladed knife poised above the past.

"Caine?"

The line snapped with static again.

"Caine?"

He was clinging to my name like a drowning man being carried out to the night sea by a tide he hadn't calculated on. Only one thing was wrong. He calculated on everything.

"Caine? This is between you and me. No one else. Stay where you are. It will be more convenient for me to—"

Another burst of static put a period in his sentence where he least expected it. The line went dead.

I reached across the bed and put the phone down.

I gave him a minute.

Then I gave him two minutes.

I leaned over and killed the light and reached under the pillow. At the end of three minutes I was wide awake. It was a hell of a way to start the day but I knew I didn't have to wait any longer.

He never called back.

Morning was coming down Delgany Street, ready or not. You don't get a choice.

The street was deserted. Nothing had changed. Everything was different. A few loose sheets of scrap paper danced down the sidewalk from in front of the Pee Wee Lounge, up at the other end of the block. They were ghosts in the morning light.

The Pee Wee used to be the Down Home, a hot little country bar with nickel beer on Thursday nights and Dolly Parton look-alike contests. Now it was the Pee Wee. What else is new? The place changed hands every six months, like hard times and easy women. Now they had drink-alongs. The pick-me-ups all had two legs. The pickup trucks and the cowboys and the peroxide pretties were gone. In their place were slick little creeps who learned everything there was to know by watching commercials on TV. They showed up straight from the office with their stylish attache cases and their stylish secretaries and their stylish $700 suits. I didn't like their shoes either. Too stylish. I'd been in the Pee Wee once and I'd watched them do isometric exercises with their faces and run through all the jokes they'd heard on television and I'd decided once was more than enough.

Across the street from the Pee Wee, Michael Moro's disco was on its way back to being just another abandoned warehouse. People had stopped dancing. Plywood panels covered

**5**

the doors and windows. The sign said "Lost Our Lease." Michael Moro was merely trying to put a shine on a bad apple. The joint didn't jump anymore. The beautiful people didn't come around. Not on Delgany Street.

Delgany Street is too quiet for the beautiful people. It's not a street to play let's-pretend on. Warehouses, parking lots, broken glass, the Pee Wee, one old brick factory that manages to manufacture a terrible smell from plastics on days when the wind is from the wrong direction, as it usually is. And, of course, the old restored Victorian bordello where I try to stay out of harm's way. Now and then a magnificent old lady with silver hair and too much lipstick raps politely at the door and asks to see the joint one more time before she dies. She gets the grand tour. The house was left to me long ago in someone's will, I don't remember whose. I think it was an uncle, call him Sam.

I cased the street and saw that it was empty and then I went into the kitchen and poured myself a stiff drink. It looked like milk and probably was. Then I went back to the window in the study and watched the street.

The big neon sign over the Pee Wee blinked on and off up the block, measuring the slow, boozy pace of the real world. Fluorescent light bleeding into the thin air. Part of the neon tubing was burned out. I knew the feeling. It wasn't the best of times.

It had been a long dry summer.

It had been a summer of strange noises in the night—the thunder of storms that never came, the muffled sound of mountains shifting their weight under massive flanks of stone. You turned over in your bed at night, alone, which made it worse, and you noticed that you were sweating, and you tried to go back to sleep. But you couldn't.

Everything stuck to you. The sheets, the darkness, the past you'd just as soon forget, the dreams that wouldn't go away, all the promises you'd made and never kept. The best you could do was wait for morning to come and hope it wouldn't bring a call from a man who was calling in all his cards. The dealer. The best you could do was try to keep your distance, and survive.

If you were lucky, you had a Margolin Special tucked away under your pillow. But that was unlikely. Only three had been made. If you were smart, you didn't open your mouth. Too much dirt and grit floating around in the yellow air. It wasn't healthy. So you kept to yourself.

I was lucky and I was smart. I kept to myself.

The sky was yellow most of the time, except in the evening. In the evening the air became very still, and the birds grew quiet, and over the mountains to the west the sky slowly turned the color of blood. It stayed that way for a long time after the sun went down.

A lot of people went into the mountains to try to get away from it all. All they found was more people, and no place to park. The ones who stayed behind killed one another. Why not? It helped pass the time.

One morning a young man with a pleasant brown face was found hanging upside down from a tree in one of the city's parks. His feet were suspended by a thick rope. A ten-inch knife blade of Sheffield steel was embedded in his belly. A thin nylon climbing cord had been knotted tightly around his neck. His hands had been hacked off at the wrists. He didn't bleed much because he was already dead when they strung him up. They had killed him twice.

His name was Hernando Cortez, something like that. No one knew where he came from. No one knew where he was headed or who decided he wouldn't get there. That day it was 102 degrees in the sun. They didn't measure the temperature in the shade. There was no shade. The leaves had all been burned off the trees.

The cops knew their job and did it. They cut him down before the rush hour started. That way, traffic went smoothly. Everyone got to work on time. The Gross National Product didn't fall as much as everyone thought it would.

The cops that day went back to their business, which consisted of telling schoolkids how to ride their bicycles, and keeping the traffic moving along the main streets and freeways, and making the rounds of the pornographic bookshops in the afternoon just to check up on business and see what was new. Business was good. Nothing was new. Then they went home to their wives, all of whom they'd met in high school; had supper just the same, all of which they'd had before; listened to the kids fight; watched the wife fall asleep in front of the TV; and went to bed—where they also found nothing new. When they woke up the next morning they felt just the same as always. Not very well. The newspapers were telling us what a privilege it is to live in Denver. South wind. High near a hundred. The market? Mixed.

Forget about Hernando Cortez, if that was his name, which I doubt. A very small thing. One life less, lost on the road to Cibola.

Another day a young man with thick, greasy glasses and skin of the same persuasion walked into a local department store with socks on his hands. A blue sock on his left hand, a black sock on his right hand. He checked out the bras and the slips and the lingerie, whether for himself or his cutie not stated. Then he strolled up to a saleslady, put one arm around her neck from behind, and started rearranging her face with an old-fashioned straight razor, which he had in his left hand. It's funny how people overlook these things. A couple of people noticed the socks on his hands. They figured he had a rash. No one noticed the straight razor.

He didn't say good morning. He didn't announce his line of thought, if he had one, which I doubt. He just carved, pulling straight back on the wet and glistening blade. A stockboy saved the woman's life. She didn't thank him. The doctors put her face back together again, because they're miracle workers, but she could no longer smile. Or laugh. She could still cry, however. She wasn't much to look at to begin with, the doctors said. We're only human. We're not God.

You get the idea. Who needs particulars?

There was something dead and dangerous in the air, a kind of decay and defeat that soaked into the bone. Everyone felt it. The mailman who dumped all his mail in somebody's garbage can and crawled into a relay box and wouldn't come out, not even when the firemen showed up and turned their hoses on him and laughed at all his tears. The computer programmers felt it, and the space salesmen, and the junior accountants, and the punk shoe salesmen who got their kicks by showing lady customers something in a pump with their pants undone. The kids felt it too, the secondhand children with nothing to do except be bored, with no dreams of their own, no feelings except the approximation of music that poured from the little black-and-silver boxes they held pressed to their heads like blocks of sandpaper, trying to smooth out the rough edges of their lives.

Even the lawyers felt it, and the lawyers usually didn't feel anything.

No act had any consequences. Nothing was connected. There were too many people. There was nowhere to go. Everything people did, they'd done before. All they had to look forward to was yesterday.

I try to stay out of it.

I'd gone up to the mountains myself for a while, out through the alleys of quaking aspens at One-Woman Pass and down into an empty little valley where the streams are usually full of starving trout and the only sound you hear is at night, the sound of the stars whispering to one another in the trees right above your head, the deadly mechanical hum of distant galaxies that don't give a damn either.

I had company on that occasion. A girl with gold-flecked eyes and a turned-up nose and hair the color of honey. A girl who didn't like to say good-bye. You don't need to know her name. All you need to know is that she wasn't afraid of the dark anymore. We listened to the stars and couldn't catch what they were saying. And didn't care. We fished a little in the feeders and caught nothing. I cared, she didn't. Whatever else we did was more than enough. When we came down from the mountains, the girl who didn't like to say good-bye said good-bye.

That left me alone in the old Victorian house on Delgany Street.

There are some things I like. Naps in the afternoon. Fishing for trout. Flying the old sailplane, a Libelle, that I keep down at Clearwater. People who don't bother to bother me. A good woman who's not afraid of the dark. Or the light. Watching old movies on TV. Not necessarily in that order. There are a lot of things I don't like. People who know where you're coming from. People who hear what you're saying. People who know where it's at but don't know what to do with it. People who are into things they shouldn't be into. People who have more than one suit. People who have more than one necktie. Don't get me started. Frank Gifford gets on my nerves. So does Pat Summerall, only more so.

As for alone, put me down as undecided. It's better if you have someone to share it with.

There was no one to share it with that morning when the phone rang and I answered it and heard a voice from the past, the voice of a man who'd once promised never to get in touch with me again. "You've got a lot to forget," he'd told me. "I'll try," I'd said. But there are some things you don't forget.

I stood at the window in the study, looking the wrong way for trouble. Maybe he was playing the same old game. He played it well. Give you the answer, let you find the question.

The answer was easy: Bradley Saltonstall.

The last time I'd seen him was four years before. Four years of silence, bridged only by memory. He was sitting behind a very cluttered desk in a very small townhouse outside of Washington, somewhere in Maryland. No number on the door, no nameplate on the desk. Saltonstall knew who he was. So did everybody else. We'd spent a few months together in that little townhouse somewhere in Maryland—Salty and myself and a few other people who thought they were funny and liked to stay up half the night proving it.

"Where the hell are we?" I'd ask, while they tried to figure out what their next question was going to be.

"Somewhere in Maryland," they'd say.

You see what I mean about being funny. They kept a lot of flowers around that I could never remember the name of, and nobody went out for milk and the paper, everything was brought in, and they asked a lot of interesting questions. All except Bradley Saltonstall. He asked answers. Smiled his plug-ugly smile. Waited for you to come up with the right question. "This way we learn about each other," he'd say. I was only passing through. I was on the road to my own Cibola, just like Hernando Cortez, if that was his name, which I still doubt. But Saltonstall was very attentive. He fixed those burning black eyes on you and ran one hand through his short white hair and asked the answer again. He smiled when you got the question right.

He was an old man put together with slabs of granite and no clay but patience. A man without fear. He didn't get up to say good-bye that last day we spent together. He couldn't. He'd been in a wheelchair for twenty years.

So now I had the answer, that was easy enough. But I didn't have the question. A man without fear, suddenly afraid. A promise never to get in touch with me again, a promise broken.

Narrow it down to generalities:

*The man of glass.*

I'd never heard of him. Maybe he was the question. Maybe he was the answer. Maybe not. At five o'clock in the morning, and nothing in the house except something that looked like milk and probably was, one question was one question too many. Questions were out of the question.

I was still chewing on it when I heard the morning paper hit the front door with a soft thud. It reminded me of something important. I don't get the morning paper.

I went back into the kitchen, took the Margolin Special down from the top of the refrigerator where I'd left it, removed the safety, walked back down the hallway to the front of the house, slipped the gun into my back pocket so it wouldn't bother anybody, such as the paperboy, and opened the front door.

It's a good rule. Expect nothing. Be prepared for anything.

Delgany Street was still empty.

The morning sky was starting to turn pink over the deserted warehouses and empty parking lots to the east. I could feel the heat beginning to rise from the sidewalk.

The man who had tried to knock on my front door couldn't feel anything. Not anymore.

He was wearing an expensive business suit but he had no business being there. He was sprawled backward on the porch steps, his head turned toward the curb. His arms were thrown back helplessly. His hands were relaxed. They were empty.

There was an ugly purple welt high on his left cheekbone where somebody's bullet had kissed him good morning and straightened his tie. On the other side, part of his face was missing.

It didn't matter.

Enough was left to tell me what I wanted to know.

I'd never seen him before in my life.

# 2

Dr. Lew Diamond winced and took another deep breath.

"I spent the night with a beautiful woman."

"Congratulations."

"In a doughnut shop. One of those all-night joints. On Colfax."

Dr. Lew Diamond is chief of homicide, Denver police. He was standing on the top step of my porch. I looked beyond him at the grimacing sergeant who was down on his hands and knees, scrubbing up blood from the sidewalk. The ambulance had already carried Humpty Dumpty away. No one was going to put him back together again.

"Who was he?" Diamond asked.

I took a guess: "Harry Truman?"

"We had a real nice talk," Diamond added. "Neil Simon, Bob Fosse, Harry Warren. Especially Harry Warren. You never heard of Harry Warren. 'You'll Never Know.' 'You're My Everything.' 'By the River Sainte Marie.' 'Jeepers Creepers.' Hell, he's only the greatest composer who ever lived. His real name? Guaragna. He's a Calabrian. Ever meet a Calabrian? Wonderful people. Nicest people in the world." He took another deep breath. "A real nice suit. Expensive. But no identification. Don't try to tell me somebody rolled him. He had cash on him. This is murder in the worst degree. And you never saw him before?"

I got a word in edgewise: "Never."

Dr. Lew Diamond's eyes rolled skyward. The shade of pink was about the same, the sky and Diamond's eyes. He looked as though he'd been up all night with a beautiful woman. In a doughnut shop.

"Her name is Suzanne Leeds," Diamond said, "and she's a hoofer, as you used to say. The point is, she's heard of Harry Warren. I thought I was the only one left. 'Naughty But Nice.' 'Chattanooga Choo-Choo.' 'Lullaby of Broadway.' 'Hard to Get.' 'You're Getting to Be a Habit with Me.' She has terrific legs, Nick. Red hair and etcetera, although I can't swear about the etcetera. I think those dancers shave it. Why do you suppose he picked *your* steps to die on? Convenience?"

"You're the cop. You tell me."

Dr. Lew Diamond tried to smile. But he was too tired.

"She's at the Paramount for six weeks, Nick. *Kickin' Up a Storm.* The road company. She's in the kick line, third from the left. Hell, you can't miss her. Not if you start counting from the left. She's a well-formed woman. Short, but she looks a lot taller. It's the legs, of course. Gams, as you used to say. Dancer's legs. I suppose you noticed. There's a very small bruise about an inch above the entrance wound, on his temple. As though he were slugged first, then shot."

"I noticed."

"You did?"

"Yes."

Diamond scratched his head.

"It's her second marriage, Nick. The first guy turned out to like boy dancers better than girl dancers. Her current husband is quite a bit older than she is. I get the idea he's a real croaker, but she won't say. It's apparently a sensitive subject. His name is Bernard Rococco and he's in futures. You know what that is? Me either. But the guy's loaded. If you're in futures, you're automatically loaded. Me? I'm in the present, Nick. There's no goddamned future in it. Not when you spend the night with a beautiful woman and she tells you that somebody is trying to kill her husband."

Dr. Lew Diamond finally forced a smile onto his thin, tired face. I knew he didn't mean it. Dr. Lew Diamond was very serious when it came to the subject of murder.

"Sorry," I said. "I'm busy. A man has just been murdered on my front porch."

"You're right. I want you to talk to her. She's nuts about the guy, Nick. She may be just plain nuts. I don't know. Sniff around. See what you think. I was planning to stop by and see you today anyway. I'd just dropped Suzanne off at her hotel when they paged me for this. An unhappy coincidence. I'll tell you the truth, Nick. I don't like standing out here like this. You've got a very dangerous porch."

I let him in.

Dr. Lew Diamond is the best cop I ever saw. Every so often he pays me a visit on Delgany Street. Borrows a book, has a little lamb shashlik or zatsivi, tries to get me to do his dirty work for him. Such as thinking.

"I like Greek food," he told me once.

"It's not Greek, Lew."

"I like it anyway. The shashlik tastes like chicken."

Dr. Lew Diamond headed for the big leather recliner in the study and reclined. For a long time he said nothing. That made two of us. He was tired. I wasn't. I didn't like the idea of a stranger getting his last hurrah on my front steps. I didn't like the idea of the chief of detectives stepping over the stillwarm body to try to rope me into a wild-goose chase involving a redheaded hoofer with nice gams, as I used to say, whose husband was in danger of dying prematurely. My philosophy is avoid everything. If you can't avoid it, take one thing at a time. First things first. The dead man on my doorstep was first in line.

Diamond finally stirred.

"A lousy summer," he declared.

I agreed.

"A real lousy summer," he added. "Very hot."

I concurred.

"I don't think it can get very much hotter," he said.

I provided my assent with a slight nod of my head. I like to cooperate with officers of the law, even when they're so tired they can't think straight.

"Actually," Diamond said, "I should have been in musical comedy myself. That was my big mistake—the degree in sociology. Where does it get you? You become a good listener. You clear your throat with authority. On that we agree. You know what Marie used to say. I'm a good listener. Then she left."

I never met Marie. Another one of my good fortunes. She was Diamond's first wife. Now he had a new one. He was married to murder.

"I went to the Paramount last night with Michael Moro," Diamond continued. "Moro got the tickets. Freebies. He knows I can't afford it. He took me backstage when the show was over, and as soon as Suzanne found out I was a cop, I was booked for the night, Nick. No bond. Like I say, she thinks somebody's trying to extinguish the light of her life. Three times in the past year. She says she's talked to the cops in New York and they tell her to take a hike. They're too busy cracking down on the biters. More people were bitten by other people in New York last year than were bitten by rats. Nick?"

"I'm listening. But the answer is still no. A half hour ago there was a dead man on my doorstep."

"Give her a chance. Talk to her. I'll set it up. Try to see it my way. Wait and see. It's the least you can do for a lady."

Diamond meant it. He was serious. He had never run into anyone who'd heard of Harry Warren and he wasn't about to let go. Even if she was crazy.

Diamond rubbed his face with both hands. It didn't do much good. The furrow was still there in his brow.

"You'll have to give me a break," he sighed. "Been up all night. I'm not used to it. I thought this would be a desk job, but I spend more time on the street than Sergeant Canetti. Canetti says he talked to you."

"He asked me some questions. The usual. Nothing you haven't heard before."

"Sergeant Canetti says you don't know the man who started the day off wrong on your doorstep."

"Sergeant Canetti is right. Give him a raise."

"Sergeant Canetti says you were up early and you had been looking out this window here, up toward the other end of the block, and you saw nothing."

"I was very forthright with Sergeant Canetti. I picked the wrong window."

"You never saw him before in your life?"

"No."

"I don't believe you. No identification at all, except for the wedding ring. That's what I find so damned curious. You lift it?"

His eyes narrowed.

I stood up. "Why don't you go home?" I said. "Get some sleep. Let Canetti handle it. He's good with a scrub brush, he ought to be able to clean this one up in no time. You're too old to be fooling around with hoofers."

Diamond didn't move.

"I'm just trying to think out loud," he said. I considered it an apology. "I know you didn't lift it. But why no ID? Nice suit, classy-looking guy. Money in his pocket. Somebody plugged him at close range. And it was no accident that he landed on your steps. I know you better than that. You don't like people standing on your steps. Unless they're friends. In that case, you don't like them coming in the house. He was coming to see you. A total stranger. At five o'clock in the morning."

"Let's correct one thing," I suggested. "Let's say he landed across the street in the parking lot. Or back in the alley. Anywhere but on my doorstep. You know how I feel about getting my name in the papers. I don't like it. It happened once and it was nothing but trouble."

"You know how I feel about murder," Diamond said.

"You like it."

"I *don't* like it. That's why I want you to talk to her. She's a beautiful woman and she thinks somebody's trying to bump off her old man."

He ran his bony fingers up over his face again.

"Shit," he added wearily. "Why me?"

I had my back to him. I was at the window. The street was still empty. Somebody had pulled the plug on the Pee Wee. The neon sign had stopped blinking. I didn't have an answer for him. Check that. I had an answer, but it wasn't for him. It was for me. A few minutes earlier it was sprawled head-down on my steps, with half its face blown away. What I didn't have was the question. Not yet.

I heard Sergeant Canetti trudge down the hall with the bucket. Dr. Lew Diamond was still thinking things over. Suddenly his legs folded up, the chair did likewise, and he was on his feet. I turned around.

"I'll set it up," he said abruptly.

"You'll set what up?"

"There's a performance tonight. Curtain goes up at eight. We'll catch it. I'll take you backstage and you can meet her. We'll go out to dinner or something. Fried chicken. I like fried chicken. Something very funny is going on with Bernard Rococco."

I hated to do it, but I played my trump card.

"It's out of the question," I said. "Do you know what's on 'The Late Show' tonight? *Blondie's Big Moment.* You know how I am about old movies. Penny Singleton. How many big moments do you suppose Blondie had?"

Diamond glared at me. His bloodshot eyes simmered, and he slammed his hat down on his head.

"Get yourself one of those videotape machines," he snarled.

"You won't miss a thing. I'll be here at seven-thirty. I'll hit the horn once. If you don't come out, I'll drive through your goddamned front door."

Diamond spun around on his heel and headed for the hallway. That's one of the things I like about Dr. Lew Diamond. He doesn't give up. Not even when he's lost the game.

He was on his way out the door when I stopped him.

"I don't get many phone calls," I said.

"I'm busy," he snapped.

"I got one this morning. Around five o'clock."

Dr. Lew Diamond stopped in his tracks. He didn't turn around.

"This morning?"

"Maybe ten minutes before John Doe showed up."

"Who was it?"

"An old friend. You don't know him."

"What did he want?"

"He wanted to see me. He wanted me to stay right here, so it would be convenient for him."

"Right here?"

"Right. We got cut off, Lew. A bad connection. Or he hung up on me. I don't know."

"What did you tell him?"

"How much I didn't miss him."

Diamond turned around. His head was wobbling and there was a faint smile on his face.

"I'd like to know where he was calling from," I said. "I'd like to know who his messenger boy was."

Diamond sighed.

"I'm sure Blondie had a lot of big moments," I suggested. "I could miss one."

"A lousy summer," Diamond whispered to himself.

He closed his eyes.

"Why me?" he sighed.

The smile was gone.

# 3

Murder draws flies.

Soon after Dr. Lew Diamond walked down the steps without his smile, a young woman wearing a tan trench coat and a very fancy pair of leather boots walked up the steps and rapped on the door with her microphone. I saw her coming and I knew she meant business. She didn't have a smile either.

I opened the door a crack and told her good morning. Then I told her it was going to be too hot for a trench coat. Then I shut the door.

She pounded on the door with her fist.

"You lousy sonofabitch!" I heard her declare.

Three guys in beards and blue jeans were standing down on the sidewalk. One of them was balancing a little TV camera on his right shoulder. Her support troops. They were soon joined by another young woman with stringy hair, a very expensive pair of leather boots, and a baby blue trench coat. And three more guys in beards and blue jeans. One of them had a camera, too.

I opened the door again, just a crack, and both of the women started in together about the First Amendment or the

Seventh Commandment, I don't remember which. One of them stuck her boot on the doorsill. I stepped on it. She withdrew it.

When they were finished, which they weren't, I explained that the master of the house had been unexpectedly called away by a young friend of his, who was twenty-two years old and who had posed for *Playboy*, in a trench coat of all things, and who had an itch that somehow needed to be scratched, and that he was not expected home until around the time of the evening news, which he never missed because he was deeply interested in the latest poop, especially as it concerned burning buildings, stickups, traffic jams, what the politicos were doing, the latest medical breakthroughs, and the prospect of rain on the weekend.

"You follow?" I asked.

"You lousy sonofabitch!" one said.

"Scum!" said the other.

And of course, I explained, he would require a rubdown and a tonic and absolute privacy. He would not be available for interviews until around March thirty-first.

Then I shut the door again.

They didn't buy it, but there wasn't a lot they could do about it. So while they made home movies of each other on the sidewalk in front of my house on Delgany Street, eyes narrowed to slits, jaws firmly set, I slipped out the back door.

The full flood of morning light filled the mountains. Driving back through the hogbacks, I had plenty of time to think about it.

What I thought about was, you try to get away from it but you never do. Not by a long shot. We all leave little pieces of random bone in our wake—betrayals, broken promises, dreams that burned to cinder—and call it our past. We all go a little blind into the future. And we never get far enough away from the things we leave behind, because the things we leave behind are always waiting for us around the next corner. You try to keep your distance. You never can.

Dr. Lew Diamond likes murder.

He sniffs around the edges of it, and the hair rises on the back of his neck, and his ears twitch. He happens to find a Broadway dancer a long way from Broadway. She happens to have nice legs. She happens to know about a songwriter whose real name is Guaragna. He's hooked. Not on her. He's hooked on the prospect of an old man named Bernard Rococco being set up for murder halfway across the country. Dr. Lew Diamond likes murder.

I was looking for a connection.

An intelligence officer from somewhere in Maryland, an old bear of a man with more influence than most of the directors and generals put together, happens to call me in the middle of the night. He happens to be afraid, which is unusual. He happens to want to know whether I can still use the Margolin Special, which is even more unusual. He knows about the Margolin Special. He let me keep it. The gun was designed by a blind man. All you do is squeeze. The broken promise? Forget it. Saltonstall needed something I used to have. The question was whether I still had it. The question was why Saltonstall needed it so bad that he called me.

As for the dead man on my doorstep, your guess is as good as mine. Maybe not. Maybe my guess is better. The idea is to watch their hands, not their eyes. They show you one card, they deal you another. They let you think you're home free, then they grab you by the back of the neck.

I was looking for a connection but I didn't see it. Not then.

At a little chili joint back in the mountains, a place called the Hot Tomato—you just knew they were going to franchise it and make a killing on the Coast—I checked my watch, pulled off the road, and used the pay phone. It was a decent hour in Washington, D.C.

The young man who answered was pleasant and efficient. As soon as I said hello, he put me on hold—long enough to run a tracer. It wasn't going to do him much good unless he had a taste for chili.

"I'm sorry," he lied when he finally came back on the line. "I had another call."

"Saltonstall."

There was a moment's hesitation. "Mr. Saltonstall is in the field. May I take a message for him?"

"Until when?"

"He didn't say. May I take a message?"

He may. The message was my name. It was a short conversation, not so sweet.

In the field. In Washington that means anything you want it to mean. He's on leave. He's drying out somewhere. He died last year. He's drunk and can't hold the phone. He's in the copying room getting his shoes shined by his secretary. We haven't seen him since Good Friday, which surprises us, because we thought he'd be back. Take your pick.

With Bradley Saltonstall it could mean even more. It could mean he was in the field.

There was one small problem. Bradley Saltonstall never went into the field. It was difficult for him to get around in that wheelchair of his. So far as I knew, he never left that cluttered little office they provided for him somewhere in Maryland, full of flowers I could never remember the name of. Bradley Saltonstall never went to the mountain, the mountain came to him. That's the way it worked when you didn't need a number on your door or a nameplate on your desk.

Of course, that was a long time ago. I was out of touch. Everything changes.

I stayed out of touch. I didn't want my mug splashed all over page one, thanks to a man who decided to die on my doorstep. A man I'd never even met. I killed the day doing this and that, mostly that. Hiked for a couple of hours along a ridge that was already staked for development. Took a nap in the car. Had a couple of beers in a backcountry bar where a truckdriver wanted to argue about whether white shirts were going to make a comeback. I picked up some supper on the way down. The sky had already tried out a few shades of red.

It was starting to get dark when I finally got back to Delgany Street. Dr. Lew Diamond wasn't around. He also wasn't around when I cruised across town to the Paramount Theater, parked the car, and walked up to the box office five minutes before curtain time.

The girl behind the glass found two tickets in Diamond's name. She gave me one and held the other in case he showed up.

I was escorted to my seat by a matronly woman with five or six chins. She smelled like lilies of the field—a big field, a lot of lilies. The seat on my left was empty.

When the lights went down and the curtain went up, there was still an empty seat on my left.

Dr. Lew Diamond was right about one thing. She was third from the left.

Give him credit. He was right about two things. Suzanne Leeds had very nice legs. As for the rest of it, hard to say. She was one of those women who look best from a distance. I wasn't far enough away.

It was pretty obvious that Suzanne Leeds had something on her mind besides step and kick, step and kick. Her kicks got lower with each number. Her steps got shorter and more hesitant. Something was wrong. She was just going through the motions. After the finale, with about half of the crowd on its feet cheering, Suzanne walked offstage with her face turned away from the audience, as though her face might betray something that would spoil the fun.

I was close, but not that close. If I'd been closer I probably could have seen something in her face to give me a clue.

As it was, I saw something in her face an hour later—sitting across the damask-covered table from her in the crowded La Serena Restaurant. Something was the matter with her eyes. It gave her a come-hither-and-yon look. Maybe it was the color. One was a touch lighter than the other, and it threw everything off balance. Everything about her seemed a little off balance. She bit her lower lip. She was distracted. The creamy skin was drawn so tightly across the bones of her face that she looked like she was in pain, even when she smiled.

She'd been expecting me. Diamond had telephoned her that afternoon. She'd been expecting Diamond and me, and she was a little disappointed she had only half of it.

"Where is he?"

"I wish I knew. He's a cop. Now and then he gets busy."

"You're his friend?"

"On even-numbered days."

"He had good things to say about you. He said you might be able to help me."

"I don't know," I said. "These servings are pretty big. And I never did like creamed asparagus."

She leaned toward me confidentially. "I'll tell you the truth," she whispered. "This creamed asparagus is not very good."

I got her life story between bites of sirloin. Born in Rochester, New York. Pushy mother. Started dancing when she was four. Headed for New York City straight out of high school. Studied for a year with the New York City Ballet. Married that boy dancer who turned out to like boy dancers better than girl dancers. Amicable divorce. "*I* was amicable," she confided. "*He* was really very bitchy." Finally got hired for a musical or two, nothing big, but it was her first love. Met Bernard Rococco during rehearsals for a show called *Uptown*—he was one of the angels, he swept her off her feet and they were married three weeks later. Even though Bernard Rococco was old enough to be her father. "No one ever understood that," she said, "but no one was ever married to Derek." Derek was the boy dancer. She stopped dancing for a year. But then she started again, two years ago.

"Bored?"

"No," she said quickly. "You can't be bored with Bernie around. It's just that I love to dance. I'm too old for it, I'm twenty-eight, but Bernie is very supportive. He encouraged me to get back into it. I didn't want to take *this* job. I didn't want to go on the road and leave him all alone. Not with what's been happening to him during the past year. Not with somebody trying to kill him."

She stopped abruptly. Her smile was expectant; she was trying to be cool about it, although I don't know what she expected. The skin was stretched tightly across her cheekbones. She was looking right at me. Maybe she was waiting to see whether I'd get up and run. I didn't.

"But Bernie insisted," she finally said. Her smile shattered. "He tries to laugh it off. He's a very dear man, a very brave man, and he doesn't want me to worry. But when someone tries to kill your husband three times in one year, it's no laughing matter."

Her eyes didn't leave mine. She didn't look hysterical. She looked tired. She looked worried. But they have ways of hiding it.

I reached over and refilled her wineglass from the carafe.

"The first time it happened was last summer," she said softly. "I was doing a musical in Connecticut, a real stinker called *Hi! Ho! the Dairy-O!* We closed in two weeks. But while I was there, Bernie came up to see me. Not to see the show—to see *me*. He brought roses. We spent the afternoon together. But he had to return to New York to take care of some business the same day. He left about four-thirty. On the way back to town he stopped for supper at a roadhouse. The Elms. It's a very nice place. He was probably already being followed. Okay?"

"By whom?"

"By the people who are trying to kill him," she said flatly. Her eyes carried a challenge. "He had supper by himself. He didn't see anyone he knew. He went—"

"Did he see anyone following him?" I interrupted.

"He didn't know at the time that he was being followed," Suzanne explained. "When he was done eating, he went out into the parking lot of the supper club. It was starting to get dark. He unlocked the car and got in, started the motor, put it in drive. That's when it happened." Her voice dropped to a hush. "When he stepped on the accelerator, the gas pedal went straight down to the floor. He hit the brakes. They went to the floor, too. The car had been tampered with. He had no control over it—the steering wheel didn't work, the gas pedal was jammed, no brakes! The car shot out of the parking lot and crossed a freeway. Two lanes each way. Bernie wound up in a culvert on the other side of the highway. It was really a miracle that he wasn't killed. The car was totaled, but Bernie wasn't hurt."

All's well that ends well. I looked at her carefully. "Were the police called?"

"Yes."

"What did they have to say?"

"They gave Bernie a citation," she said glumly. "For reckless driving."

I shrugged.

"And damage to state property," she added. "And driving while intoxicated."

I shrugged again.

"He was drunk?"

"He most certainly was *not* drunk, Mr. Caine. He was very sober when I picked him up at the hospital. I had to borrow a car, and I got there about an hour after it happened. He was very frightened, I can tell you that, but he'd be the last one to admit it."

"Surely the police examined the wreckage."

"Of course. We got a call from the state police investigator about a week later. The accelerator was jammed. The brake line was broken. Some kind of gear had fallen out of the steering mechanism. It's very clear that the car had been tampered with while Bernie was having supper. But the police said it happened when Bernie hit the culvert. They didn't even consider the possibility that someone was trying to kill him."

"Someone was trying to kill him," I agreed.

The idea is, agree with them. That way they won't stick a fork in your heart when you're not looking. I looked around the room for Dr. Lew Diamond. It was his baby, not mine. Steak and creamed asparagus for supper was one thing. Scrambled eggs was something else.

The other two attempts on Bernard Rococco's life, let's be charitable, weren't baked all the way through either.

The previous fall, Rococco and Suzanne Leeds were spending the weekend in their New York apartment. They got a call from the harbormaster in the little Long Island town where Bernie kept his boat, a twenty-eight-foot cabin cruiser. The harbormaster said the boat was burning, he could see it from his window, and they'd better get out there. It took them two hours. When they finally arrived, not much of the boat was left. The Coast Guard had a look, especially when the harbormaster told them he'd heard a small sound—something like an explosion—before he looked out the window and saw the smoke. All they found was a rusted gas line. They forgot to ask Suzanne Leeds about it.

"It shook Bernie up," she told me. "I could see he was upset. *He* doesn't think it had anything to do with the gas line."

"What does he think it was?"

"One of those plastic bombs. The kind terrorists use."

"He told you that?"

"Of course not. He thinks he's protecting me. But I know what he feels deep down inside. I know what he's thinking. He doesn't have to tell me."

"I see. Did he use the boat much?"

"Well . . ." She hesitated. "Actually, no. He was thinking of selling it." Her eyes widened. "But what if he'd happened to be on it when it exploded?"

"He'd have jumped off."

"If he was able," she agreed. "If he wasn't lying there dead."

I couldn't argue with it. She had a point.

The most recent episode had occurred only two weeks earlier, on the last night of rehearsals before Suzanne's road company headed west with *Kickin' Up a Storm*. Rococco had driven across town to watch the tail end of the rehearsal. He seemed preoccupied, and on the drive back to their apartment he had very little to say. He let Suzanne off at the lobby level, she went upstairs, and Bernie took the car down to the underground garage. Somebody had parked in his space, so he had to park in a small section reserved for visitors. It was a long walk across the garage to the elevators, and he was only halfway there when a black car came squealing down the ramp from the second level and nearly clipped him.

"He was shaking all over when he got upstairs," Suzanne said. Her finger traced a nervous little circle on the tablecloth. "He said he jumped three feet. I believe it. He plays handball. I've seen dancers in worse shape. It's literally all that saved him. I called the police right away. He didn't want me to, but I did. And of course the police wouldn't listen. They wanted me to come down to the station."

"Did you?"

"Of course. Bernie wouldn't come. He just brushed it off as an accident. The police were the same way. They look at me like I'm . . . hysterical or something. That's what they're saying. I see it in their eyes—another hysterical woman. How did Lew Diamond get to be a policeman, anyway? He doesn't qualify. He has a little decency. I wish he was here."

"So do I," I confessed. "Did your husband notice the license number of the car?"

"How could he? Somebody was trying to *kill* him!"

Her hand was in her purse. When it came out, it was holding a checkbook. She opened it, scribbled on it with a gold pen, ripped out the check, and pushed it across the table toward me. She spelled my name right. Two grand.

"Will that interest you? Will that cover expenses if you come to New York? There's more where that came from, Mr. Caine. Would you talk to the police? Would you talk to Bernie?

I just don't know what to do anymore. Neither does Bernie. He's tough, and I know it. But underneath? He's human. He was raised in upstate New York. Cold Lake. His family was very poor—no shoes, not enough food, hand-me-downs everywhere. He told me that when he first came to New York as a young man—this was years ago—he was scared to death. He used to ride the subway from Times Square to Brooklyn. Back and forth, back and forth. He'd ride for hours. To think. To get his courage up—for the streets above. That's what he told me. And do you know what? He's doing it again. He's riding the subway for hours, to the end of the line. He won't let me do it. He says it's too dangerous. But *he* does it. That's how I know it's getting to him, Mr. Caine."

I picked up the check and placed it gently against the stem of her wineglass. I've run into a lot of strange women, including one who collected rutabagas and carved little heads out of them, but that was after she poisoned her husband and had a lot of free time on her hands. Suzanne Leeds took the cake.

I pushed back my chair and caught the waiter's eye. He hooked on a smile and started following it between the tables toward us.

"You don't believe me," Suzanne Leeds said coldly.

I tried to be nice about it. "When there's only one explanation for something, that pretty much explains it. When there's more than one explanation, that doesn't explain anything."

I shrugged. It was the most I could do.

"I'm sorry," she said. The look that crossed her face was a combination of contempt and helplessness, a very bad combination. "I'm *really* very sorry!" she added. She didn't mean it. "I'll pay for my dinner, Mr. Caine. And I'll get a cab. Don't bother yourself. I'll—I'll—" She meant it.

I wasn't ready for it. Her face was suddenly as stiff as a porcelain mask. She didn't move. She was frozen. But tears streamed down her pretty cheeks.

I stood up.

"Suzanne," I suggested. "Perhaps someone is trying to frighten him. A business partner?"

She shook her curls. "He's in business by himself."

"Let me ask you," I said. "Who do *you* think is trying to kill Mr. Rococco?"

Her face came up. It didn't look good, not with all those tears. "I wish I could tell you," she said softly. "I really wish I could. But I don't know his name. All I know is what they call him."

"Yes?"

She dabbed at her eyes with the handkerchief.

"They call him the man of glass."

"Yes, sir? May I help you?" the waiter said.

I looked at him a moment. Then I sat back down.

# 4

"The man of glass?"

Suzanne Leeds had the list in her purse. She pushed it across the table toward me: an old sheet of paper creased and folded a thousand times, wrinkled and worn smooth by worrying fingers. Prayer beads for the morning after a very bad dream.

She didn't need it.

She had their names written in big letters on her heart—the heart of a young woman haunted by an old war that never quite came to an end.

Bernard Rococco was only one of them. There had been others: Anton Konicki, Harold Yanasek, Sty McDonald, Charlie Waller, Louis Lemaire, a crazy Finn by the name of Jan Porvi, Anthony O. Nevada, C. B. Boudreau, Ted Richter, Max Sinclair.

Some of them were lucky. They were dead. The ones who weren't still heard the groan of cannon in the night, and the sharp snap of sniper fire.

Once upon a time they had all been rough-and-tumble boys who could handle themselves in the dark—with a knife or with a lady. They had lived by the simplest of rules: one for all, all for one. It was the only way to survive. They had been recruited out of the woodlots and the lumber camps of the North Woods and the Pacific Northwest, and from the wilds of Canada. Not because they were nice, but because they weren't.

They were the North Americans, 1st Special Service Force, 4th Company, 2nd Regiment. Commandos in a dark and dirty war.

A long time ago, in the spring of 1944, they found themselves in a place none of them had ever heard of. A place of indecision, attrition, and death. A place in Italy.

Call it Anzio.

They had already gone through the worst kind of warfare in the winter mountains around Cassino—fighting an invisible enemy from ridge to ridge, starving, short of supplies, locked in battle against the wind and the land and the weather as much as against the stubborn Panzer divisions that clung to the cliffs and caves above them. The wind and the land and the weather won. Everyone else was a loser.

The enemy was still invisible. Only now he was one of them.

The men of 4 Company suffered their share of casualties. Their share of casualties turned out to be fifty percent. The ones who were left were the toughest, the shrewdest, the luckiest. Considering the way things turned out, maybe not. Life has a way of turning good fortune upside down, and showing you the white grubworms and spider's eggs you never knew were there.

In February of 1944, 4 Company was pulled out of the mountains and transported south. Anzio town was already in Allied hands. They moved onto the Beachhead Line, southeast sector, ready for anything except what they found there. What they found there was four months of endless waiting in the slit trenches and gullies along the Mussolini Canal. Boredom. Rain and mud. Bodies floating down the canal in the darkness, victims of the silent night, bloated beyond recognition. Winter was coughing up the phlegm of war while the generals paced on the beach out of range of the German shells, unsure of what to do next. Cut the Via Casalina? Put everything up against the fortress of Cassino? Break out of Anzio and march toward Rome?

Nobody bothered to ask the North Americans what to do next. Encircled by German divisions, beset by the weather, they did what they did best. Every night they blackened their young faces and loaded up with grenades and bandoliers of ammo and scrambled out of the trenches in small patrols. The Germans were doing the same.

It was a roulette with death, played out in the hostile darkness of mines and barbed wire on the other side of the Mussolini Canal. The best man did not always win. Darkness has a way of tipping the scales.

Then something happened that no one could have predicted. Lieutenant Jack Perry, commander of 4 Company, got sick to his stomach. It seemed harmless enough. Short and squat and from somewhere on the Snake River in Idaho, he was the toughest man alive. He wanted to stay on the line with his men. But by evening they had to move him back to a field station. The next morning he was no longer the toughest man alive. He was dead.

Peritonitis.

Black Jack Perry would have been disgusted with the diagnosis. It was a hell of a way for a hero to go home.

That evening a young lieutenant came down the line from Division Headquarters with orders for 4 Company. The war wasn't over. The war would go on. He knelt down on one knee in the mud, the men of 4 Company squatted sullenly around him and searched his face, and he outlined their objective: a suspected German gun position in a cluster of stone farm buildings about four thousand yards over the line.

It was back to business as usual.

They'd done it before, dozens of times. But this one was different. They had finally eaten enough mud and swallowed enough stinking brown water and seen enough ghosts in the darkness of the Pontine Flats. Four months in the slit trenches at Anzio were four months too many. What La Rementanea and Sammucro and Majo couldn't do, Black Jack Perry's bad stomach had done in spades. It had caught everyone from behind, by surprise.

On the day that Perry died, Sty McDonald got into a fistfight with Jan Porvi. Max Sinclair broke it up, but not before Porvi was facedown in the mud with McDonald's big boot grinding into the back of his neck. Someone else started needling Anton Konicki. He reached for his rifle and thought better of it. Louis Lemaire pulled a practical joke on Tony Nevada—filled his helmet with mud and planted a cross in it, made out of crude sticks. Lemaire was always playing jokes. This one didn't work. It was a ghastly reminder of what waited for them out in the darkness. Anthony Nevada blew it to bits with a burst from his submachine gun and stalked off to get another helmet. The helmet he came back with belonged to Jack Perry. Ask your neighborhood psychologist about it. By the time the young lieutenant came down the line with his orders, the men of 4 Company weren't talking to one another.

They moved out shortly before ten o'clock. The wire entanglements made it slow going. So did the rain. The rain started falling about twenty minutes after they crossed the Mussolini Canal.

It drew a shroud down around each of the soldiers. It made them seem separate rather than together, individuals rather than a unit. In a sense they welcomed it. It seemed to close them off from the war they were all part of. But it couldn't wash away the strange, sullen fear that some of them were feeling for the first time in their lives—men who had never known fear. The rules had changed. It was every man for himself.

Richter and Konicki led the patrol. They located the German outpost at the edge of some burnt woods, found the lights burning in the old farmhouse, and saw that everything was very quiet. They recognized the place. They'd been there before. But they had never seen lights burning there.

The lieutenant came up, put Konicki's glasses on the place, and gave his orders. Most of the men were to fan out in a semicircle around the farm buildings, forming a snare line between the farmhouse and the canal. Richter and Konicki were to work their way around to the back of the farmhouse with the mortars. Once in place, they were to open fire and drive the Germans into the snare.

It seemed simple. It seemed sound. But that's when things started to go from bad to worse for 4 Company.

As the men took up their positions in the dark woods, someone hit a trip flare. The low gray sky, the shimmering sheets of rain, the little cluster of farm buildings standing alone in the field—all were suddenly illuminated by the phosphorescent light. It surprised everyone but the Germans. The lights in the farmhouse went out. By the time Richter and Konicki were in place, the operation was already a failure.

They lobbed in a few mortar rounds and some blind rifle grenades. And waited. There was no answering fire. The rest was up to the young lieutenant. They fired a few more rounds. And waited some more. There was still no answering fire. The rest was still up to the lieutenant.

After twenty minutes he moved his men in. They tied a knot around the farmhouse and opened the doors with mortars.

The place was cold and dark and empty.

The Germans had been there, but they were gone. All that 4 Company had for its trouble was a handful of nothing—and a terrible surprise as they slogged their way back through the woods toward the canal. In the darkness and rain, the Germans had worked their way silently through the 4 Company perimeter and set up two ambush positions on the way back to the Beachhead Line.

The resulting firefight lasted only ten minutes. Any other night, 4 Company could have handled ten hours. But on this night, ten minutes was too much. Charlie Waller was killed outright. So was Boudreau, a Frenchie from Thief River. They had been leading the column on the way home. Anton Konicki was nearly cut in half by machine-gun fire. The lieutenant loaded him on his back, carried him out of the action, and then went back to catch a single rifle bullet in the spine. Louie Lemaire finally dragged him in—covered with mud and blood, half drowned and unconscious—after the Germans had cut and run.

Not all the Germans cut and ran. The men of 4 Company brought out one souvenir, a wounded German, and wished later that they hadn't. The German soldier had been hit in the neck and cheek. He was dying and he was scared. But before he checked out, the brass got to him and pieced together the story of how the German patrol had managed to slip through the American perimeter and set up its ambush. There had been eleven men in the farmhouse. When the flare went off, they had come out, crossed the field to a point of woods, and circled around behind the Americans. They had passed almost directly over the position of one of the men of 4 Company.

Which one? No one knew. No one volunteered. And there was no way to find out. Fear had finally caught up with one of the brave men of 4 Company. He had seen the Germans coming toward him in the darkness. He had flattened himself in the mud and stopped breathing for a while. They had marched right over his position.

You could forget about 4 Company after that. There was a snake in the garden. Two men were dead, a couple more were wounded. The dead stayed dead, the wounded recovered. But they never fought together again. No one got over the night of one man's loss of nerve.

The survivors were reassigned to other companies and fought their way out to Colle Ferro and marched on Rome two days before something big happened in Normandy. Anzio became a bad dream. The war ended for all of them.

Except one.

Suzanne Leeds brushed the hair back from her forehead. Her fingers still trembled but her tears had dried.

"It was only a small part of a big war. It's not in the history books because it was about plain, ordinary soldiers, not generals. And they don't strike medals for cowards. But the men who were there won't forget it. Bernie was there. I wasn't even born then, but I've heard the story so many times that I feel like I was there. Part of me was there. Bernie."

She tried to smile but it didn't work. She reached out her hand and touched my wrist. Her fingers were like ice.

"The man of glass. He's invisible. You can see right through him. You wouldn't even know he's there."

"Is he still alive?"

"Who's trying to kill my husband?"

I wasn't in the mood for Twenty Questions. But I gave it a try.

"Who does he suspect?"

"Everyone."

"That narrows it down. Maybe it was Waller. Or Boudreau. They're both dead."

Suzanne shook her head. "No. The man of glass is still alive. I'm sure of it. Not only that, I've met him." She gave a little involuntary shudder and looked down at her wineglass. She twirled the stem in her fingers.

"Last summer, the men of Bernie's old unit had a reunion," she said, looking up. "It was Bernie's idea. He organized it, got in touch with everyone, and it was a mistake. That's when everything started—last summer. Sinclair's wife, McDonald's farm, Anthony Nevada's mining outfit, the attempts on Bernie's life."

"Wait a minute," I suggested. "Everyone came to a reunion of 4 Company?"

"No. Not everyone. But I was surprised anyone came. They'd never kept in touch. Why should they? They had a lot to forget. It was nothing special. It wasn't an anniversary. Maybe they were curious, I don't know. Maybe they're all like Bernie. After all these years they wanted to find out who it was who betrayed them. Bernie tracked them all down. Porvi is dead. He went back to Michigan after the war and was run down by a truck. A log truck. Not very glorious. Anton Konicki's dead, too. Bernie got a letter from Konicki's wife saying that he'd died five or six years ago. No details. He just passed away. Bernie couldn't locate Louie Lemaire. Like I say, no one kept in touch. No one knows where Lemaire is, or even whether he's dead or alive. He was from Canada. Maybe he went back to the woods. Yanasek was another one. He was close to Konicki, but Konicki's dead and no one knows where Yanasek is. But the others came."

I ran my thumb over the list she had given me, smoothing it out.

"Sinclair?"

"Yes. Max Sinclair is an artist. He lives in California—Mendocino or somewhere, I'm not sure. He's a very nice man, very quiet. Sty McDonald is a pig farmer. Peace Valley, Missouri. Anthony Nevada is a mining engineer in Tucson. He *was* a mining engineer. Not anymore. Ted Richter is in television. San Diego. He's a very wealthy man. Richter and Bernie made out the best of all. Maybe they were the hungriest. Richter came from the same part of the country that Yanasek and Konicki did—Iron Range country, Michigan, Minnesota. Although he never lets on. He's very smooth. He brought a young woman to the reunion and sort of showed her off. Do you know what I mean? Never even told anyone her name. He called her Puss—"

"Five of them."

"No. Four," she said quickly. "Max Sinclair, Sty McDonald, Anthony Nevada, and Richter."

"And Bernard Rococco."

She looked at me coldly. "Yes. Counting Bernie, that's five. I was surprised. It was a nice get-together. Everyone seemed to have a good time until—well, until Bernie made his toast. Nobody expected it, but I saw it coming. They were all making toasts, crazy things, to various girls they knew, and then Bernie called for order and proposed *his* toast. To the man of glass."

Her fingers darted to her throat as she said it.

"I know what he wanted to do," she said. "He wanted to say he hadn't forgotten about the man of glass. None of them had forgotten. You can't imagine the chill that went through the room. McDonald just got up and walked out. With his wife. He just walked out and didn't say a word. The whole thing broke up. They hadn't forgotten, but they didn't want to be reminded. It was a big mistake. For all these years the man of glass had gone his own way. He knew who he was. No one else did. But now? I don't know. It's as though Bernie awakened something that had been asleep for a long time. Fear. Guilt. Whatever it is, I don't know."

She reached for my wrist again.

"That's why I want you to help me, Mr. Caine. I wanted Lew Diamond to help, but he says it's not his jurisdiction. He says that doesn't bother you, nothing bothers you. If two thousand isn't enough, tell me. Double it. I need someone's help. Bernie tries to shrug it off. He tries to be brave about it. But I know he's afraid. You know what he did last week? Rode the subway for hours. At night. Just like the old days. He has reason to be afraid. Last summer, after the reunion, Max Sinclair's wife was struck and killed by a hit-and-run driver. She was bicycling, a girl my age. It was his second wife. Bernie said she was all Sinclair lived for. Sty McDonald lost his whole operation last spring. A crop duster came over, with some kind of chemical. He lost all his stock. Thousands of hogs. Now he has nothing. The police said it was an accident, but Bernie says they never found the plane. Don't you see? The same thing happened to Anthony Nevada. His business just blew away. Some kind of rumors were spread, his suppliers stopped working with him, he started drinking. He's ruined. It's all happened since the reunion. One way or another, he's going to get to them. Each of them. The man of glass is going to destroy them one by one."

Her face made a little patchwork of pain. Tears started to well up in her eyes.

"Now it's going to start all over," she said. "It's going to be even worse." She dabbed lightly at her eyes. "The second reunion is next week. Here. At the Arnold Hotel. Bernie had me make the arrangements. I didn't want to, but I did. He wants it here. He wants to be near me. He needs me. And they're all coming, Mr. Caine. Even the man of glass! Unless you can do something—"

I could hear the people behind me shift uncomfortably in their chairs. They weren't used to tears, except on television in the afternoons.

Suzanne Leeds pried the handkerchief out of her fist and used it on her eyes again.

"We forgot someone," I said. "The lieutenant."

Her face went white, and she shook her head violently.

"The lieutenant is dead!" she sobbed. *"Why do they want to kill Bernie?"*

She had something to cry about, and she did.

# 5

"Well?" he demanded. "Is she or isn't she?"

"Yes and no."

"I'll be honest with you," Dr. Lew Diamond said wearily. "I figured she was crazy. I would have bet on it. It's the damnedest thing I ever heard of. A man of glass. An invisible man. A war so long ago no one remembers it except for three drunks in an American Legion hall somewhere in Florida. That stuff about her old man is so much crap. You know what it is? It's a goddamn fairy tale."

"A fairy tale for tough guys."

"I figured she was crazy, but I didn't want to take a chance. Not with the circus coming here. Hell, this *is* my jurisdiction. I don't want trouble. That's why I wanted you to talk to her. I'll tell you something. It's reassuring to know that she is and she isn't. Now I can relax."

Dr. Lew Diamond pushed the recliner back, his head flopped back so that he was staring at the ceiling, and one of his shoes dropped off. Loafers. Argyle socks.

It was very late.

Back at La Serena, Suzanne Leeds had finally regained control of herself. Even if it was a fairy tale for tough guys, you could see that she believed in the big bad wolf. So did I. It wasn't a fairy princess with a magic wand who put a dead man on my doorstep that morning, it was somebody else with a .45. Suzanne kept her mouth shut in the car on the way back to her hotel. Once in a while the little pink handkerchief fluttered up to her face, but she had no more to say. Not after I stuck the check for two grand in my shirt pocket, stood up, took her by the arm, and steered her toward the door.

I had watched her walk across the deserted hotel lobby with her chin up, a Broadway dancer a long way from Broadway, a young woman with very nice legs and very bad dreams. She never looked back. Maybe she figured it was over for her. Maybe not.

I was a block away from the hotel when the unmarked police car pulled up alongside me, the driver tapped his horn twice, and I pulled over to the curb. Dr. Lew Diamond unfolded himself from the rider's side, said something through the open window to the driver, and the car sped away.

"Your place is as good as any," he said as he opened the door to my car and collapsed on the seat next to me. My place was better than any. Quiet, out of the way, very secure. Nobody ever bothers you on Delgany Street.

I fixed Diamond a drink and looked him over. His eyes were bloodshot. His skin was pale. He'd been awake for thirty-six hours, maybe more, and he wasn't used to it. His mouth hung open.

He blinked at the ceiling and spoke very slowly:

"Of course, I didn't get to the theater. But I checked the box office. One of the tickets was gone. So I knew you made it. But I didn't know where you took her. Canetti and I hit all the doughnut shops in town. Finally I figured, what the hell. Gas is expensive. I had him drive me over to the hotel, we parked at the cab stand, and we waited."

He still wasn't looking at me. He looked at the ceiling, as though he could see right through it.

"I'm so tired I'm seeing visions," he announced. "Looks

like some kind of stain there on your ceiling. A face or something. You ever notice that? It's a man with a beard, with his arms outstretched...."

"The roof leaks. But only when it rains. It hasn't rained since April, don't worry about it."

Diamond's hand came up to massage his face. When it came down, he noticed his drink for the first time. He killed it with one gulp. I watched him carefully. I wanted to catch the precise moment that he passed out. But he didn't. He was too tired. It had only one effect. He stopped blinking.

"We had this one by the ass, Nick, and it got away. The dead man is Roger Penrod. You never saw him before in your life? I'm inclined to believe you. He kept to himself."

"It got away?"

"Right. A nice young man. He worked in the district Internal Revenue Service office here. Twenty-four years old, very bright, no enemies except you and me. Taxpayers. He transferred in from Washington about five months ago. The neighbors considered him cheerful, kind, obedient, thrifty, brave, reverent, and so forth. Why not? They hardly ever saw him. I could use another drink. His profile was so low he didn't have a profile. Maybe it's like that in all the subdivisions, I don't know. He leaves a wife in Cedar Crest, one kid, and a rather large balance due on his bank card. He had two cards, actually. One for the family, one for himself. Why not? It's the age of indulgence. The balance due was on the card reserved for his family. He didn't make a lot of money. But he ran up a lot of big numbers on the other card, Nick, sometimes more than his take-home pay. And they were always paid off promptly. Porno movies, on video cassettes. He collected the damn things. Had over two hundred in the closet. Now we know where our taxes go. His wife knew about it, by the way. I'll tell you something. A very hard woman, very uncooperative. I talked to her myself. Says she watched the stuff with him after the kid was tucked in bed. Twenty-four years old, you wouldn't think they'd need it. These kids don't feel anything on their own. I'll have another drink. They're like diesel engines or water pumps. They have to be primed."

I got up and went into the kitchen to make him another double. "Easier than I thought, Nick," he called out. "We made his prints just like that." I heard him trying to snap his fingers. He wasn't very good at it.

"Of course, we had a little help," he said glumly when I handed him the drink.

"Drink it slowly."

One swallow, it was gone.

There was a touch of anguish in his voice. "It's not my case anymore, Nick. I can't touch it. We'll never clear it." He slammed the empty glass down on the table a little harder than he expected.

"You've been taken off the case?"

"The chief came into my office this afternoon and told me I have other things to do. Meaning somebody got to him. It was my baby and they took it. What can I do? I'm only a cop."

Diamond wiped his chin carelessly with his palm. He was staring at the ceiling again.

"The feds," he muttered. "They broke it, they got it. I hate dealing with those bastards. I'm out of it. I have better things to do than solve a murder, right? When I left here this morning I went down to the morgue. They had nothing—nothing but a stiff with half his face blown off. I went back to my office to think. I shut the door and I tried to think. You know what I thought? I figured he was a friend of yours. Or an enemy. Either way, you knew him. Now I'm not so sure. I was still sitting there an hour later when one of the FBI locals showed up with Penrod's prints. Fast work? You said it. We hadn't even sent them the prints to be identified. They had their own. They were tipped off. Who even knew the guy was laying there on your doorstep? Who even knew he was dead? You'd think he'd be home in bed, trying position number one hundred thirty-seven."

Diamond's hands were clenched into fists. I'd seen him that

way once before—when the state's attorney had the chief's son-in-law in the cooler and reduced a Murder One to involuntary manslaughter.

"It stinks, Nick. I almost made a mess on my desk. Two hours after Penrod is killed, the FBI shows up with his prints. At that point we don't even know who he is. We don't have a goddamned thing from the morgue. They hadn't touched him. They were changing shifts. They were saving him for dayside. But when we finally did get prints from downstairs, they matched. You bet they did. They matched what the feds brought in. The feds had it nailed. Christ, they're wonderful. They have all this terrific training, they wear nice suits, they have great posture. I love 'em. Not only that, they talk directly to God. I'll tell you something. They have God on a retainer. When things get tough, they just pick up the phone. Who do we have? Ribs Malone. The Snake. Tiny Coppoletto. It's no contest."

The lines around his eyes crinkled. His jaw was trembling. It took me a moment but I finally got it. Dr. Lew Diamond was laughing silently to himself.

"Why you?"

"Me?"

"Yes. You hard of hearing? Why you, Caine? Why Delgany Street? Why your particular doorstep?" He didn't wait for an answer. "I'll tell you why. Because you're right down the street from the Pee Wee, and that's where he called you from."

"The Pee Wee?"

Dr. Lew Diamond shook his head sadly. He tried to smile.

"You're a very wise son of a bitch, Caine. Pardon me. I suppose you want to see the printout from the phone company? Forget it. But you can take my word for it. I'd like to know who you were calling in Argentina, but that's your business. My business is murder. At least it was, until the chief came in and told me I've got better things to do. We have the calls coming in and the calls going out. I checked your sheet and I checked the Pee Wee. The call shows up precisely at four minutes to five o'clock this morning."

Diamond tried to lean forward in the recliner, but he couldn't get the chair to fold up. He stared at me intently. "We took a picture of Penrod over there before lunch and made a few people sick. He wasn't pretty. But they remembered him. Him and the cripple. The guy in the wheelchair. You said you got a call from an old friend. You said you never saw Penrod before in your life. That narrows it down. Who was he? Who was the joker in the wheelchair?"

For the hottest day of the year, the room was suddenly pretty chilly. Diamond must have felt a draft. He was having a coughing fit. He wiped his chin with his hand again. His words were slurred:

"Forget it," he said softly. "Forget the whole damn thing. It's not my problem. Not anymore. They showed up at the Pee Wee just before five. That's the way those bastards work—the feds. It's five o'clock or nothing. They like to get you when you're heavy with sleep. And the wives like the overtime. Christ, am I ever tired. Two witnesses. Both Mexicans. Don't worry. I'm not prejudiced. They saw Penrod and the cripple in the hallway by the pay phone. Went out the door together. The guy in the wheelchair came right back in. He was in a hurry. You never saw a guy in a hurry until you see a guy in a wheelchair in a hurry. Went through the bar, into the kitchen, out the back. Disappeared. But don't try to kid me. What the hell time is it? I know the guy in the wheelchair didn't chase Penrod down the street and put a slug in his head, because the way I figure it, Penrod was on the top step when he caught it and that's three steps up from the sidewalk which is three steps too many if you're confined to a wheelchair. I don't know if I'm making any sense. You know what I'm thinking? I'm thinking, what if you could get out of your wheelchair anytime you wanted to?"

Diamond thought about it a moment, his head resting back on the chair, his eyes fixed blindly on the ceiling. He was going under. He waved a paw in front of his face but he didn't blink.

"We had this one, Nick. A fairy tale for tough guys. You're right. I had a man checking the taxi companies when the chief came in and blew the whistle. What the hell, I'm only a cop. A good one. I take orders. I'd just come back from the Arnold. I was checking out what she said, Nick. About that old gang of her husband's. She was right. He's registered. Roger Penrod is also registered at the Arnold Hotel for three days next week, and the poor bastard is just not going to make it. . . ."

Dr. Lew Diamond's eyes slowly closed. His mouth fell all the way open.

He was out like a light.

# 6

Morning came too early. Dr. Lew Diamond woke up sometime during the night, figured how the chair worked, got himself out of it, and left the house. He locked the door behind him. When I came downstairs the place was empty. And hot. There was something close in the air, something closing in. I opened the windows but it didn't help.

I found a jar of black olives in the refrigerator and called it breakfast. Then I left the house, too. I left the phone book open, with Roger Penrod's name and address circled in black ink.

It was going to be another slammer.

The morning sun had softened the strips of tar on Delgany Street. All across town the traffic signals were stuck on yellow. Caution. People were standing at the bus stops like cigar-store Indians—mobs of them. Their faces were blank. They didn't move. They were already sweating and they were trying not to breathe.

The Cedar Creek subdivision sprawled off onto the prairies southeast of town. A straggling line of railroad tracks and shacks made from corrugated tin separated it from the rest of the civilized world. The place was dead or dying. All the trees were four feet high—withered sticks held in place with thin wires. The houses were all the same. Bicycles lay overturned on brown lawns. The streets were deserted.

Penrod lived on Prairie Lane.

Prairie Lane looked like Evans Drive. Evans Drive looked like Colorado Trace. Colorado Trace looked like Mountain Way. Mountain Way looked like Prairie Lane. You get the idea. It didn't look promising. The house was white frame, blue shutters. Someone had forgotten to plant enough grass.

I went up the front steps and knocked on the door and waited. No answer. I knocked again. The answer was the same. I looked over my shoulder. Nothing moved. No one was in sight. The sky was like sour milk.

I walked around to the back of the house and my luck improved. I didn't even have to knock. I caught a glimpse of her through the double sliding glass doors that opened onto a small stone patio.

It was pretty obvious she was on her way out. It wasn't only the bags under her eyes, it was the bags in the hallway behind her. And the cardboard boxes stacked against the kitchen wall.

She came to the door, the door slid open about six inches, she took one look at me and she said: "You want to read the meter?"

"Thanks. My name's Caine. I just flew in from Washington this morning. Saltonstall wanted me to—"

The door slid shut.

I rapped on the glass. She didn't want any. She walked back to the kitchen table and sat down. She glared directly at me. She had her hand wrapped around a mug of coffee. She didn't move. She was a good-looking woman—brown corduroy jeans, a lavender top, green eyes, a body that was much too nice to belong to a widow.

I raised my arms so she could see I didn't have any dangerous weapons. She wasn't impressed. Her eyes were like cold green stones. She was plenty mad. So I took matters into my own hands. I opened the door, and stepped inside. Everything should be so easy.

Her head turned slowly toward me.

"On second thought," she snapped, "you can tell Saltonstall to go fuck himself."

She looked back at the sliding glass doors. The backyard wasn't much to look at, but she was looking at it. I walked over to the table, kicked a chair out with my foot, and sat down. It didn't seem to bother her, having company.

"Saltonstall didn't have the decency to call. No one did."

"It's like that."

"I know it's like that. Roger said it would be like that. It doesn't make it any easier."

"I'm sorry."

"I'm sorry, too. That makes two of us. We're both sorry."

She turned toward me and her face softened.

"I know it's not your fault," she said. "I'm sorry."

"That's established."

"You're from Washington?"

"Yes," I lied.

"Is it this hot there?"

"Worse."

Her eyes were hard and dry. I could see what Diamond meant. Roger Penrod's widow didn't look like she could be pushed very far without pushing back. She got up from the table, refilled the mug, poured me a cup of coffee without asking, and sat back down. The walls of the kitchen were bare and discolored. She'd already cleared them off. Pots and pans were piled on the countertops. She was on her way out, as stated. Right away wouldn't be soon enough for her.

"I was against it from the very beginning," she said. "He was an area specialist. A nice quiet job. It suited him. He was a scholar, a damn good one. He wasn't a thug. He wasn't a gangster."

"What area?"

"Mideast," she said curtly.

"A long way from home."

"Yes."

I tried the coffee. It was good.

"Saltonstall came in yesterday?"

"The day before. Honest to God, do me a big favor. Tell him that Janet Penrod tells him to go fuck himself. I mean it." The line of her jaw was set hard. She meant it.

"Your husband must have felt differently."

"Roger worshipped him. Roger thought he was some kind of goddamned hero. I know the type. They play it for all it's worth. Roger was being used. I told him so. It didn't make any difference."

"That's the trouble with heroes."

"Tell him to go fuck himself."

"Thanks. I have the message."

"I'm sorry."

She wasn't. She was bitter. She was bitter like all the wives of all the men who work in the dark and keep part of themselves beyond reach. Men who keep secrets they share with no one.

"It must have been a big operation."

"Pornography. Something personal."

"Personal with you?"

She shot a sharp glance my way. "Personal with Saltonstall. The big hero. That's the thing. It wasn't even government business. Roger was technically on leave. Saltonstall pulled him off the Mideast desk a couple times before. Little things. Nothing like this. Roger was hooked, you know? He thought it was a heck of a lot more fun than keeping track of oil production in some godforsaken emirate."

"He didn't know what fun was."

"Not fun. Dangerous," she corrected herself. "He was *magna cum laude* from Princeton. A little danger goes a long way."

She looked back to the window and ran her fingers nervously through her hair. "I'm going back to Ohio," she said, almost to herself. "That's where the funeral will be. He's already gone. He's gone ahead of me."

"You were here a long time. Five months."

"Yes. Just uproot yourself and go where they tell you to go. Forget about the rest of your life. You know, I covered for him yesterday. With the local police. Some detective—"

"Lew Diamond."

"Yes. A real creep. He kept looking at my legs. I told him we were in it together, all those pornographic videotapes. It was our thing—nobody else's business. Anything to forestall questions. Then I thought, what the hell am I doing? Why keep up the masquerade? I never looked at the damn things. I'm not a middle-class white male with dreams of glory. It doesn't do a thing for me. It didn't do anything for Roger either, except it got him killed. So what do I owe those bastards? Nothing."

She thought about it a moment and added: "I owe Billy."

"Billy?"

"Our son. He's down the block. A neighbor's watching him while I pack. The *one* neighbor we were able to make friends with in five months in this wasteland. I owe Billy. I owe him the chance not to go to Princeton and not to go to work for the government and not to think there's something exciting about infiltrating yourself into a gang of gangsters and pornographers and crooks. Especially not to have heroes."

"It was a good cover."

"The IRS. Hell, yes. They sucked right up to him, once he started ordering those tapes. They figured they bought him outright."

"But things went bad."

She shrugged. "I don't know. Roger never talked about it. He had to keep his mouth shut and he did. Even with me. Especially with me, I suppose. It's a big business. Four billion a year. With a big market—everyone who has a video recorder sitting on top of his TV set. That's why the crooks want a piece of the action. It's a nasty business. He didn't like it any better than I did, but he did what he had to do because it was his job."

"Things must have gone bad if Saltonstall himself came out here. He lives in a cave. Never comes out."

Janet Penrod winced. "He's sick. He's a sick man. I mean it. I don't even know why you're here. It had nothing to do with government. It was strictly a personal thing with Saltonstall. That's what Roger told me."

"Saltonstall was involved in it?"

She laughed despite herself.

"A cripple? I don't know. Maybe he was. It wouldn't surprise me. Roger said the demand for fat women is incredible. Maybe there's a market for big shots in wheelchairs."

"Where are the tapes?"

"I boxed them. Put them out in the garbage this morning. They're gone. Some white middle-class American garbage man is on his way to the appliance store right now, to buy a videotape player."

"I know it's not pleasant, Janet. They want me to find out what happened. Why everything fell apart."

"Tell them to ask Saltonstall."

I tried to look uncomfortable. "Here's the thing," I said softly. "The old man's under investigation himself."

"Christ! I knew it!" she snapped. Her green eyes flashed. "The sonofabitch!" She shoved her chair back suddenly and stood up. She walked over to the glass doors. "Look at this! We lived in Alexandria. Look at this!" I looked. What grass there was in the backyard was still brown. It wasn't much of a view. Brown grass and a chain-link fence and more brown grass and the back of somebody else's house.

"I'll tell you what happened," she said, turning toward me. "He showed up the day before yesterday around five o'clock. Arrived in a taxi, I assume straight from the airport. Roger wanted a fancy dinner and I made one. But he wouldn't eat. Said he wasn't hungry after the flight. He sat at the table with us and watched us eat. It was the first time I'd actually met him. I'd heard a lot about him. You better believe it. But it was the first time I laid eyes on him. There was something—I don't know—did you ever meet someone and know right away you were going to hate him? He was like that. There was something about him. Calculating. Cold. Something intolerant. He had the strangest eyes. He tried to be casual, but I could see he was very—I don't know, disconcerted. At dinner they talked about the weather. Of all things. It was *very* stimulating. After dinner they went into the living room and I went out on the patio with Billy to watch TV. I got the idea I was not expected to join them, so I didn't. I left them alone. Roger came out about ten o'clock. It was dark, of course. Said they were going out, not to wait up. You know how that is—"

She looked sharply at me again. "Maybe you don't," she added. "I went to bed about one. He hadn't come back. I woke up again at three. He still wasn't here. I had a hard time getting back to sleep. It was almost eleven in the morning when that detective, Diamond, came by." Her voice dropped. "He told me that Roger had been shot. That he was dead."

"You never saw Saltonstall again?"

"No. I didn't tell the police about him either. I was a good soldier, right?"

She gnawed at her lower lip.

"A couple of those lousy cassettes were sitting on the arm of the sofa. I don't know how they got there; Roger must have taken them out to show Saltonstall. I don't know. The policeman started wandering around, opening doors. He didn't even have a warrant! I didn't think to stop him. I couldn't. I was in shock. We kept the tapes in a closet, the hallway closet, and he found them. Two hundred and thirty-five of them. I'm sure he figured—I don't know what he figured. So I lied again. One lie after another. I was covering. I don't know why, but I was. Good breeding, I guess. I have good breeding."

She stood with her arms crossed, her body arched slightly backward, as though she were daring someone to contradict her.

"That's as much as I know," she said firmly. "We'd talked about it in a general way. But believe me, Roger was not about to deal in specifics. He was too good for that. So that's all I know. It was a job. It was *his* job, and I'm sure he did it well.

He had to ingratiate himself with gangsters, and he'd never met a gangster before in his life."

"Did he mention their names?"

"Don't be ridiculous!"

Her green eyes narrowed and her finger came up to her lips. "Mr. Ice," she added.

"Mr. Ice?"

"Yes. One night I heard Roger saying that over and over in his sleep. 'Ice . . Ice.. . . Ice.' He was very restless. I asked him about it in the morning and he just laughed. 'Mr. Ice?' he said. 'A man of glass.' "

Janet Penrod tried to smile.

"I'm the very last person you should ask. I was only his wife. Now if you'll excuse me, I have to finish packing. I have to go to the airport. My brother-in-law's coming in from Ohio. We're leaving tonight. I have a funeral to attend. I'm sorry What did you say your name was?"

"Caine."

"Good. Will you do me a favor, Caine?"

"Yes. What is it?"

"Nail Saltonstall's hide to the wall."

# 7

His office was across town on a side street off Colfax. I stopped for a moment to check out the reflections in the window of a seedy-looking store that bought and sold gold coins, candelabra, and high school class rings. Then I opened the street door, went up the stairs to the second floor, took a right at the landing, and noticed that his office door was closed. The fresh black lettering on the frosted glass said: "Mouthpiece Inc."

He must have heard me coming. His voice boomed out from behind the door:

"The door's closed! Watch out! Come on in!"

I did.

Michael Moro was sitting at a secondhand desk with his feet up and one of those cheap cigars stuck in the corner of his mouth. There were ashes on his shirt. The shirt was pink. So were his pants. He knew how to dress.

"Hey! Caine!" He was surprised to see me. He jerked the cigar out of his mouth. More ashes fell on his shirt. "Shut the door! Come on in!"

" 'The door's closed? Watch out? Come on in?' " I asked.

"Right," he said, waving the hand with the cigar in it. He looked at his watch. "I'm expecting this client, a magician who plays in the horn family. Does tricks with a trumpet. Unfortunately he's a blind man. Like Stevie Wonder, you know? I don't want him getting hurt, walking into the door, something like that. And I gotta keep the door shut on account of the heat. Business is tough. Know what I mean? You gotta look out for the clientele." He glanced around the office. "I don't know what I'm gonna do with the dog. If he's got a dog. He didn't tell me if he's got a dog."

He looked worried about it.

The office was nothing to worry about. There was the old wooden desk, with nothing on it except a used Princess phone and Michael Moro's own size-sevens. He has very small feet for a press agent who dresses in pink. There was an old wooden chair, same vintage as everything else. The walls were bare and dirty. The window hadn't been washed since April, when the rain did it and left streaks.

Michael Moro used to run Facettes, which used to be a disco, which used to be on Delgany Street. Not anymore. He had boogied on to better things. He still smoked those bad cigars, which he still claimed were Cuban. He still touted every two-bit magic show, wrestling championship, and extravaganza that passed through town on its way to the big time in Walla Walla and Spokane, because he was still the press agent supreme. But now he had a new feather in his cap: Wells Mouthpiece Inc. A one-man public-relations firm specializing in something called "personal imagery."

Michael Moro was the one man. It simplified bookkeeping. He calls himself a consultant, which makes his price schedule very flexible, and he coaches people who want to be on TV. The trumpet player with the seeing-eye dog, if he had a dog, meant that business was booming. The only other client I knew about was a 290-pound football player from Grambling College who was scheduled to be one of the guest hosts on a three-day telethon opposed to diabetes. He'd wanted to make a good impression, so he'd come to Michael Moro.

The client was a hit. Michael Moro put him in a big orange

hat with a floppy brim that came out to his shoulders, and a blue cowboy shirt opened to his breastbone, and tight powder-blue pants tucked into his size-fifteen oxblood boots. He pasted a gold star on the guy's front tooth. Not that the football player couldn't have dressed himself; he could have, but it's nice to be told you're on the right track. Moro's job, he told me, was to "emphasize the natural aspects of the client's personality after doing a lot of research." I don't know what research he did. Maybe he checked out some books from the library. The client, at any rate, made a terrific impression. During the one hour he was on camera, they had more than fifty dollars in pledges. I watched the show out of loyalty to Michael Moro.

"Where'd you get that name? 'Wells Mouthpiece Inc.'?" I asked him once.

"H. G. Wells," he answered proudly.

Sometimes he surprises me.

But he didn't surprise me this time. He removed his feet from the desk and placed them on the floor. He walked behind me and shut the door. With his pink shirt and pink pants, he looked like something that was migrating through on its way to Florida. His feet went back up on the desk.

"What happened to H. G. Wells?" I asked. "Your sign just says 'Mouthpiece Inc.'"

Michael Moro winced. Some ashes fell on his shirt.

"I had to cancel him. People kept asking. They never heard of him. I dropped him like a hot squash. Cost me four bucks to get it scratched off the door, but the guy did a nice job."

He squinted at me.

"What do you want?"

"You know a lot of people, Michael. Including one or two I never heard of."

"Start anywhere."

"Pig farmers."

"Let me consider it. Pig farmers."

He shifted his cigar from one corner of his mouth to the

other without touching it. His hands went up behind his head and locked. He was getting comfortable. It helped in the thinking process.

"We'll come back to that one. Pig farmers."

"Forget it," I suggested. "Artists."

"Do I know any artists?" he snapped. "Picasso was an artist. One of the best. What do I win?"

"Finger paints. Tell me what futures are."

"Sure. Buy short, sell long. Buy long, sell short. Everybody knows that. It has to do with soybeans. I'm not into finance, Nick. You know that. I still owe rent from last month. You know what the overhead is here?"

"Try television."

Michael Moro's voice beamed. "Show biz," he said. "You came to the right place, Nick. I know everybody who's anybody." He rolled the cigar around in his mouth. "Name one," he demanded.

"Ted Richter."

"Never heard of him. Name somebody else."

I knew I'd come to the right place. Michael Moro did know a lot of people; some were worth knowing, some weren't. Best of all, he knew people who knew the people he didn't know. I put a city on the end of Ted Richter's name, San Diego, and Michael Moro reached for his phone. "San Diego. No wonder," he muttered to himself. He thought for a moment and then dialed. "This is Mouthpiece Inc.," he said when the call went through. "Michael Moro speaking, and I want to be put in connection with Joseph Salerno. Lady? This is a long distance so shake your leg, okay?"

He clamped his hand over the telephone mouthpiece—suddenly it dawned on me where he got the name—and he smiled confidently. Some more ashes fell on his pink shirt.

I got up from the chair and walked over to the grimy window. Moro was babbling into the telephone behind me. He kept saying: "That's interesting. That's interesting. Now that's interesting. How's the wife? Sorry to hear that. That's interesting. Now that's really interesting."

I didn't know whether it was or not, I couldn't hear the other end of the conversation. I was looking out of Michael Moro's window at the street below. A blue van was parked at the curb directly behind my car. Not three spaces back. Not a block away. Not across the street. The driver's arm rested on the door, which was partially opened. I couldn't see his face but that didn't matter. It was still interesting. I'd seen the van before.

When I left Janet Penrod, the same van had been parked down the street from her house, at the corner, facing the other way. When I drove past, the van started up and followed me for about a block. Then it turned off to the left, down one of the spaghetti streets of the Cedar Crest subdivision. I didn't think any more about it until I finally found my way out of the place and was crossing the tracks. That's when I spotted it again—this time off to the right, cruising very slowly down an access road along the railroad tracks. I thought some more about it.

If he was tailing me, he was pretty good at it. I never did pick him up on the way across town to Michael Moro's office. But now he was giving me another chance. Nice of him. Maybe he was the feds. Maybe he wasn't. But it was pretty clear he'd been keeping an eye on the house of Roger Penrod. He'd followed me out of the subdivision. And now he wanted to make sure I knew it.

Michael Moro said, "You hard of hearing?"

"What?"

"I said," he said, "Salerno's a wonderful singer."

I pulled myself away from the window, walked around Moro's desk, and sat down.

"He does the fights, baseball, weddings, stuff like that. His 'Star Spangled Banner' is tops. So's his 'Ave Maria.' " Moro waved his hand in the air. The cigar was wedged between his fingers. "That's right." There was a self-satisfied smirk on his face. "I did a favor for him once, the favor was about five-five with a very nice figure, a brownette if I recall. We struck oil on the first hole. He knows this guy, Nick."

"Salerno?"

"No. Salerno knows Richter. Both in the same business, TV sales, San Diego. Different stations. They keep an eye on one another, you know how it is. You want Richter's number? You can call him yourself. On your nickel."

He gave me the number. Then he added:

"It won't do you any good."

"It won't?"

"Richter's not home. Flew the coop two days ago."

"Where'd he go?"

Moro waved his hand toward the window. "You're looking at it. According to Salerno, he came to Denver."

"Can you find him?"

"It's a big town, Nick."

"It's a small world."

"You're right." Michael Moro looked at his watch again. Then he looked at me. "That horn player was supposed to be here half an hour ago. He must have gotten lost." He shrugged his shoulders. "Sure. I can find him, Nick."

He looked like he meant it.

I praised his genius. I commended his taste in apparel and cigars. Then I gave him a few more names: Sty McDonald, Max Sinclair, Anthony Nevada, Bernard Rococco. I wasn't counting on much, especially with the pig farmer, but you never know with Michael Moro.

"How's his wife?" I said.

"Hey! You heard of Salerno?"

"Who hasn't?"

Moro's face fell.

"Sorry to say, she left him."

As I closed the door behind me, Michael Moro was already dialing the phone. His cigar had gone out.


I went down the stairs, opened the door to the street, and the afternoon wrapped itself around me like a hot towel in a Turkish bath. The sidewalk was empty, but the blue van wasn't. The driver was still sunning his left arm, with the van door partially opened.

I walked over and slammed the door shut so he wouldn't fall out and get hurt. It didn't seem to bother him. He was a young man with sharp features and blond hair that was going dark. He had a smile that someone had put on upside down. It turned down at the corners. He was wearing aviator sunglasses that didn't want to let you see his eyes.

"If you get caught at a light, I'll wait for you," I said.

His expression didn't change.

I got in the car and pulled away from the curb, and he pulled out after me. There was nothing deceptive about it. It wasn't necessary. We went through town like the Bobbsey Twins, but when I turned abruptly into the parking lot at police headquarters, the van kept going. All he left me with was his license number.

Dr. Lew Diamond was alone in his office. Sheets of notepaper covered his desk.

"I'm busy. What do you want? Go away."

"Mr. Ice."

Diamond looked up.

"Ring a bell?"

"No," he said. "As you can see, I'm busy. I'm writing a speech. I have to give a speech to a Moose lodge. The chief set it up. I told you. I'm off the case."

"Mr. Ice rings no bell?"

"This isn't New York. This isn't Chicago. This isn't Vegas. I told you, I never heard of him." He put his head back down and scratched something on his notepaper. When he looked up, he said: "How does this sound? 'The sociological basis of crime must be carefully examined for the kind of oppressive conditions that foreclose the options of the poor. Among these elements are—' "

"I also have a license number here," I stated. "I need to know whether a name goes with it."

Diamond wrote the number down on a sheet of paper. He looked at it for a long time. Finally he said:

"Well, I'll be goddamned."

I waited.

"Where did you get this?" he asked.

"From a license plate."

"When?"

"Today."

"In the rearview mirror?"

"You're very perceptive."

"I'll be damned."

Lew Diamond reached down to the bottom drawer of his desk, opened it, pulled out a mimeographed sheet, and handed it to me.

"This came through last night," Diamond said. "I didn't see it until this morning. As you can see, it's a complaint written up by an Officer Sullivan. Airport detail. What was the license plate attached to?"

"A blue van."

"Who was driving?"

"A young man accustomed to abuse."

"Could you pick him out of a lineup?"

"Of course."

"Could you identify his photograph?"

"Of course."

Diamond looked sharply at me. He shook his head.

"I'm sorry. I'm off the case," he said. "I don't know this Sullivan at all. He says he was approached in the parking lot at the airport yesterday by a male citizen who said that his van had been commandeered by a man with a gun. A man in a wheelchair. Two blocks from the Pee Wee. Yesterday morning. Not long after Penrod caught it. He was forced to drive to the airport and he was aggravated. As you can plainly see, Sullivan took down all the details. Complainant's name, his address, the license number of the Dodge van. Canetti checked it out. The name is phony. There's no such address. The license number looks familiar."

"It's the same."

Diamond stuck the end of his pencil in his mouth and started chewing.

"It certainly is," he said. "But don't ask me. I'm off the case. My job is to write speeches. Sullivan looked through the airport. He didn't see anyone in a wheelchair. Of course, I don't know how long he waited until he started to look. I don't know Sullivan. The subject could have boarded before Sullivan finished his coffee. I have nothing to do with it. It's out of my hands."

"He could have asked the flight attendants. Or the boarding clerks. They go out of their way for people in wheelchairs."

"Nobody's perfect."

"Did Canetti check the license number?"

"Sullivan did. Canetti rechecked. Same name, same address. Both phony. That's why it's funny. He picked up Penrod's sidekick, took him to the airport, then tried to finger him. And he's still cruising around town." Diamond wagged his head again. "It's not my baby. How's this? 'The parameters of urban crime can be defined by any number of sociological and psychological categories, not excluding the areas of education, job opportunity, previous dependence upon welfare, the pressures of—' "

"I think it stinks."

Diamond was massaging his face.

"So do I," he mumbled. "I think the whole thing stinks. But don't worry. The feds will have it cracked before long. They're wonderful. Very wonderful."

He swiveled his chair around so he was facing away from me. I took the hint.

I got home a half hour later. I left police headquarters by a different door than the one I'd entered through; my car stayed in the lot, it was in good hands, and I caught a bus back to Delgany Street. The house was stifling.

Answers? I had plenty of answers. I had a few questions, too, and there was only one place to try them out. It took a while for the call to go through.

"Yes?"

"My name is Caine. I want to talk to Saltonstall. I called yesterday. Wait a minute. Don't put me on—"

"One moment, please."

He put me on hold. What the hell, it was cocktail hour in Washington. Maybe he had an interesting conversation going, about the weather or something, and didn't want to stop. But when he came back on the line it wasn't with small talk.

"Mr. Caine? I'm sorry."

"I've heard that one before."

"You're a friend of Mr. Saltonstall?"

"I was."

He paused for a moment. It wasn't what he expected. Or maybe it was.

"I understand, sir. You may have heard. It's very distressing. Brad was involved in a serious accident yesterday afternoon out on the Bay. With his wife. They were boating—"

He paused again, waiting for something. He didn't get it.

"An explosion. The boat blew up." His voice was strangely weary. I realized he'd been telling people the same thing on the phone all day. "Mrs. Saltonstall received a broken arm. Exposure, of course. They say she'll be okay. The Coast Guard picked her up. They're still looking for Brad."

"He hasn't been found."

"We're confident the body will be found, sir."

He didn't sound confident. I didn't feel confident. I still had plenty of answers and a few questions. But I had no one to try them out on. Not anymore.

# PART TWO

# 8

The best way to describe it is Punk Harmonica. Really punk. After you said he was loud, there wasn't much more you could say about him.

Except that he was wearing a pale yellow suit with red velvet lapels and little red velvet cuffs on his sleeves and trousers. His hat was square and blue, with gold piping. He looked like one of Michael Moro's clients but he wasn't. His Louis Armstrong eyes popped with strain as he huffed and puffed on his Hohner Marine Band. He stood at least four feet ten inches tall, and that included his high-heel shoes. Take those away and you didn't have much. It made it hard for him to reach the high notes.

His name was Johnny C. Low and he was the house "entertainment" at a little Georgetown bar not far from Wisconsin Avenue. He had a certain style, no doubt about it. Baroque. But he lacked the essentials of greatness.

The young woman down at the other end of the bar, however, had all the essentials.

She was on the up side of twenty-one, which meant she could do whatever she wanted to do, which she did. She was wearing a tattered blue sweatshirt with somebody's picture printed on the front of it, Robert E. Lee or George Sand, I couldn't tell which. Every time the bartender turned his back on the railbirds, she swiveled around on her barstool, lifted the sweatshirt high above her breasts, and flashed the crowd.

They appreciated it.

Johnny C. Low was blowing harder and harder, but his harmonica was strictly second fiddle to the brunette down at the other end of the bar. I wagged a finger at the empty stein in front of me, the bartender made a hasty swipe at it, and I grabbed his wrist.

"In addition," I counseled him, "pour one for the wallflower down at the end of the bar. Whatever she's drinking. Kerosene? Gasoline? Gasohol?"

"Tania?"

"For sure," I said. I wanted to fit right in. "Excellent," I added.

The bartender peered up at me through bushy eyebrows of black and white. His tanned, round face was sweating profusely. He needed a shave. He sniffed as he turned his back on me and the crowd.

The crowd roared behind me.

A few minutes later the girl who called herself Tania worked her way up the bar toward me. The crowd watched her every move. From where I sat, it looked as though she just might have every move. Her voice was soft and husky, obviously she'd worked on it a long time, and she put it very close to my ear.

"Thanks for the Stinger. You come here to watch Johnny C. Low?"

"He's very terrific," I agreed.

"I play the mouth organ better than he does."

"That I believe. You've got quite an act."

"I do encores."

"I should think so."

"I don't mean almost anything. I mean anything."

Her hand was holding tightly to my arm. She was a little

drunk but not a lot. She'd have to do in a pinch, and I was in a pinch.

"Anything?" I suggested.

"For sure," she said. You see what I mean about fitting in.

"Excellent," I said. "I was counting on it."

I stood up suddenly, her hand stayed glued to my arm, and I steered her through the crowd toward the door. The crowd groaned. They were disappointed. Why not? Who wants to watch a professional harmonica player when the professional amateurs are twice the fun?

The sidewalk outside was empty. Some kind of flying insects were holding a convention around one of the street lights. Otherwise there was no one around.

"Who's the picture of?" I asked. I pointed to her chest.

"Gertrude Stein. That's not *all* you want."

She was right.

I told her what else I wanted. She took the twenty and looked it over carefully. She squinted up at me, trying to figure it out. "You don't have a purse," I suggested. "Slip it in your bra."

"I don't have a—"

She started to laugh. She had a wide face, a trace of freckles, and eyes that had grown dim around the edges. She may have been fresh and pretty and innocent once, around the age of ten.

"The price is right," she finally said with a shrug. She was a philosopher. She slipped the bill down inside the front of her jeans. That made it a deal. She was still laughing softly to herself as she disappeared up the block into the darkness, beyond the reach of the glaring orange street lights.

I disappeared back into the bar.

The bartender's eyebrows did a high gainer when he slapped another beer down in front of me, but he didn't speak unless spoken to. He wasn't spoken to.

I'd been right. The weather in Washington was worse. Everything seemed to be wilting. It was perfect weather for anything that didn't take a lot of energy, such as a funeral. In that kind of weather you get it over and done with, you don't stand around wringing your hands and talking about how good he used to look, because it doesn't take very long for him to not look very good.

My plane had arrived earlier that morning at Dulles. I rented a car at the airport, but turned it back in because the oil light kept making dire predictions; no one had checked it. They gave me another one, and then I found a motel room in Silver Spring for only seventy-eight dollars a night. Don't worry, I got my money's worth. The room had its own TV.

After I unpacked, I hiked down the highway to a greasy spoon. I forked over fifty cents for a cup of coffee and five times that for an egg and a muffin. Then I settled down with the morning paper.

There was good news and bad news. The problem was, you couldn't tell which was which.

Bradley Saltonstall had finally been found by the Coast Guard shortly before dark the evening before. He'd been burned over ninety percent of his body, they didn't say which ninety percent, and when they pulled him out of the waters of Chesapeake Bay, they noticed that something very bad had happened to his face—apparently from having tangled with the propeller of the cruiser after the boat blew up. The teeth were intact. They matched perfectly the set of dental charts in Saltonstall's medical file. You see what I mean about good news.

It convinced everyone except the newspapers.

The newspapers were already having a go at it, wondering in print whether the dental charts in Saltonstall's medical file actually belonged to Bradley Saltonstall. And if not, whose were they? And who put them there? And why? You get the idea. It's called freedom of the press, and it sure beats having to run another story about some society dame's hot-tub party or the pandas in the National Zoo.

Let them eat guesses, was the way they put it at an official level.

"We are convinced beyond the shadow of a doubt that the body recovered yesterday evening from Chesapeake Bay was that of Bradley Saltonstall III," an official spokesperson said. I know it was a spokesperson because I saw it on the noon news. It wore a gray skirt with little red threads running through it. "Mr. Saltonstall held a minor and nonsensitive position within the clerical branch of the Central Intelligence Agency. His access to classified documents and information was restricted. Although the investigation is still under way, there has been no indication that Mr. Saltonstall had at any time been in contact with agents of any foreign government. Speculation to this effect in this morning's newspapers is unfounded and irresponsible. During the day yesterday, naval marine experts from Annapolis examined the remains of the small boat on which Mr. Saltonstall was a passenger. They have tentatively concluded that the explosion and resulting fire on the vessel was caused by the faulty connection of a fuel line adjacent to the engine housing. This resulted in a leakage of fuel. There is absolutely no indication that an explosive device had been planted on the boat, as has been suggested in this morning's papers. I would like to emphasize that. There is no evidence that an explosive device had been planted on the Saltonstall boat. There is no evidence at this time to suggest that this was anything other than a very tragic and unfortunate incident, claiming the life of a man who has served his country well and with honor in war and in peace."

And so on. And so forth. Etcetera.

I spent a few minutes trying to figure out just how much shadow a doubt casts—a big shadow or a little one, a long one or a short one—and just how far away from a doubt you had to get before you were out from under its shadow. Then I got in the rented car and headed east. I didn't take any answers with me. I wasn't anxious to do what I'd come all the way across the country to do: walk back into a lot of bad memories with the Margolin Special still at home under the pillow.

By midafternoon I called it quits and wound up at a little town called Havensville, on the Bay. What I found was a lot of water, some gulls, and an oyster-shell sky that promised rain. Not to speak of the old codger I cornered at the end of the marina after I'd eaten lunch.

He was sitting in a cane-back chair tipped back against the shaky railing. His cheek was stuffed with tobacco. He was at least ninety years old, and his watery eyes were fixed blankly on three boys playing down near the other end of the marina.

"Any rumors of bluefish?"

"You're kidding."

"You a sailor?"

"Used to be."

"Have your own boat?"

"Yep. Used to."

"What kind?"

"Sloop."

He turned his head to watch the three boys at play. Maybe he wasn't watching the boys. Maybe he was watching what lay beyond the boys. The flat gray face of the Bay turned toward the open sky. The faint ruffle of whitecaps out on the water. The wind, rising.

"*Sweet Marie*," he finally said, as though he'd had a hard time pulling her name through the shoals and fogbanks of his memory. "Went down in forty-three. September the second. Off Hatteras."

"Blow up?"

"You sonofabitch," he laughed. His lips were cracked. He had only two or three teeth left, and they were covered with brown tobacco juice.

"Ain't no boat o' mine ever blow up," he muttered to himself.

One of the boys looked over in our direction.

"Doan talk to him, mister," he said. "He crazy."

We had a nice talk, Charlie Vee and me, that was his name, and I never did find out what the Vee stood for. He wanted to talk about politicians, Social Security, inflation, and the *Sweet Marie*. He was an authority on all four subjects. I wanted to talk about how a cabin cruiser could blow itself out of the water on a nice summer day in Chesapeake Bay. It took him a while, but he finally got around to an answer:

"Never trust a politician."

"I don't think he was a politician."

"Had a boat, didn't he?"

Charlie turned toward me, his face split ear to ear by that macabre smile.

"Stole somebody's money or he stole somebody's wife. Shit, boy."

That ended it.

Charlie Vee was crazy, all right. He'd worked twenty years to buy the *Sweet Marie*, that was twenty hard years a long time ago, and he didn't have much to call his own since the day she went down off Hatteras. He'd sailed all over the world, he'd been carried by the winds from the past into the future, and now that he was here, all he had was dog food for dinner and a cane-back chair next to the water. The winds had carried him too far.

When I left him he was still looking out over the gray water, seeing things that no one else could see because no one else had been where he'd been. His face was very calm. His eyes were closed.

It was nearly dark when I got back to town. The future didn't bother me. The past did. The past that lay curled and burned and brittle in a funeral parlor just down the street from the little bar in Georgetown.

I was waiting until it was late.

I was waiting until it was so late that nobody would be there except Salty and me, and all those answers and all those questions. Penrod. Who shot Roger Penrod? Someone Saltonstall was after? Or someone who was after Saltonstall? Maybe someone who was after Penrod. And what was Salty after?

I'd gone over it a hundred times. Something big, to have Penrod spend months away from Washington. Something big, to spring Saltonstall from his cage. And something personal. He'd come out to Denver, tried to see me, and instead he'd seen something he didn't like on the street outside of the Pee Wee. Something that made him turn and run, a signal of danger. He was picked up two blocks away by a man in a blue van. Convenient. Too convenient. He was picked up by the man who killed Roger Penrod.

I tried to imagine what was going on in Saltonstall's head. All I knew was what I'd heard in his voice. Fear. He must have put through a phone call from the airport, telling the feds where to find Roger Penrod. And then he was gone before the man in the blue van could interest the airport cop. Gone back home, to die in Chesapeake Bay.

The timetable was perfect. Too perfect. It left no margin for error. It left me the one answer for which I still didn't have a question:

The man of glass.

I was halfway through another beer when the crowd erupted in a cheer behind me. It wasn't Johnny C. Low, hitting a high note. He was in the men's room, washing his mouth out.

It was Tania.

She was standing in the doorway to the bar with her tattered blue sweatshirt pulled up high over her face, and she was looking the crowd over.

# 9

"You were right," she whispered.

"Sorry to hear that."

"But you were wrong."

"Wrong?"

"Not one, honey. Two. There were two of them."

I swept the loose change off the bar and dropped it into my pocket. Then I dug it out again and left it on the bar. The crowd had broken into rhythmic clapping behind us. They wanted a rally from the home team. They wanted more of Tania than the back of her old blue sweatshirt.

She edged closer to me.

"Where are they?"

"But you were right," she added.

I was right. She even talked like a philosopher.

"Right?" I asked.

"Yes. They're both in the same car."

"Where?"

"Two guys."

"Where's the car?"

"A black Buick. I couldn't tell what year. I'm not into cars."

"Where is it?"

"It's on the other side of the funeral home, pointed this way."

"Which side of the street?"

"This side. Six or seven spaces back from the front entrance. They're the only ones, honey. I looked. All the other cars are empty."

She searched my face, hungry for approval. I pulled another twenty out of my pocket and gave it to her. She'd make a great lapdog.

"Thanks," I said. "I appreciate it."

She wasn't listening. "I didn't think it was a camera at first. But you were right. You—how did you know?"

"A hunch. I read my horoscope this morning."

"You're funny. I mean, you're really funny. I made sure."

"Sure of what?"

"I made sure it was a camera. I flashed them! The guy on the passenger side pointed it at me!"

"He got an eyeful. Did you spot anyone else?"

"Hell, it sure didn't look like a camera. It was—you know—bigger."

"There was no one else around?"

"No."

"You went around the block?"

"You told me to."

"Did you?"

She pouted. "Yes."

"You didn't see anybody in back?"

She shook her head.

"There's a driveway along the side of the funeral home. Nobody there?"

"I don't *think* so."

Her face flattened out into a blank.

"There *is* a driveway," she said. "But I don't think . . . I was looking for a cat in a car, like you said. But I don't think . . . now I'm not sure." She looked confused—confused and disappointed. "You want your money back?"

I looked down at her jeans. "You owe me."

"I owe *you*?" she laughed. "Oh! God! I've heard *that* one before, honey! I *owe* you!"

I'd heard that one before, too. The one about the guy sitting outside in his car, pointing his little infrared camera this way and that, keeping track of who comes and goes. Now he'd have something good to show the boss. Tania. What I didn't want him to have was me.

I pinched Tania on the cheek, went out the door, took a right, and walked around to the other side of the block. The funeral home was visible through the dark shapes of the trees and houses. A nice white stucco building, Colonial modern, with brown trim. It was discreetly lighted. I could see the small parking lot in back. Two cars were parked there. They looked empty, but I couldn't be sure. If the front of the joint was being covered by recording angels, the back might be covered as well. The side entrance was the big question mark.

At least it lowered the odds.

I cut down a dark passageway next to a large brick house and worked my way cautiously through a couple of postage-stamp-sized backyards. Somewhere in the night a dog started to bark. I was on his turf and he didn't like it.

A line of tall shrubbery stayed between me and the parking lot. The same line of shrubs marked the driveway. I walked along it, found an opening, and crossed the driveway quickly to the side door.

It was unlocked. They were still open for business. I pulled the door open and went up the carpeted stairs to the lobby.

Ornate archways led toward rooms in every direction. The double doors were closed on all but one of them. Inside I could see the subdued yellow lighting, standing sprays of flowers, and a big bronze casket with the lid on. A bunch of blue flowers rested on top. They looked familiar, but I couldn't place them.

To my right was a small business office. A young man with white hair shuffled out to greet me. He looked like being very helpful was his business. I didn't need any help. With all the rooms closed off except one, I'd already narrowed down the possibilities.

I started to move but he stopped me.

"Sir? We'll be closing in five minutes."

"How long has he been here?"

"This morning."

"And the funeral's tomorrow?"

"Yes, sir."

"Pretty quick."

He put on a sad face. "The family has made all the arrangements. Sir? I don't mean to rush you—"

"Okay," I agreed. Obviously he had a hot date.

The place was empty except for the flowers, the big bronze casket, two long maroon sofas, some folding chairs, a couple of silk screen room dividers with Japanese doodads printed on them, three or four floor lamps, and a very comforting arrangement with a soft spotlight mounted on the ceiling and sending a weak ray of sunshine down to the closed casket. Add one thing to that, I almost missed it. A middle-aged man in a gray suit who sat alone in the corner of one of the sofas, off to the side of the room. He was as far from the casket as he could get. His giant hands dangled lifelessly from his knees.

He didn't look up.

The guest register was open on an oak stand near the doorway. I picked up a fancy pen and signed it. I wasn't the first, that was for sure. A lot of people had come to pay their final respects to Bradley Saltonstall, the low-level official who never had access to any classified information. Eleven pages of them. And he'd only been in residence one day.

I flipped back through the heavy cream-colored pages of the guest register and found what I was looking for. Everything should be so easy.

They'd been there:

Anthony O. Nevada.

Louis Lemaire.

Bernard Rococco.
Clayton McDonald.
Ted Richter.

It was interesting news. They'd dug up Louis Lemaire somewhere—he was a no-show at the reunion—and they'd all come together. One for all and all for one. Their names followed one another on page three, but it was impossible to say precisely when they'd signed in. Maybe that morning. Maybe that afternoon, while Charlie Vee was telling me about the rise and fall of the *Sweet Marie*. Either way, you had to hand it to them. They moved quickly. Word got around.

It dawned on me that if Ted Richter had been in Denver, we may have flown into Washington on the same plane. It dawned on me that I should have given Michael Moro two more names to track down—Louis Lemaire and Yanasek. Bernard Rococco had told his pretty wife that he couldn't locate either of them. And yet—here one of them was. Dr. Lew Diamond was right. Nobody's perfect.

As I approached the casket, the man in the gray suit forced himself reluctantly to his feet. His eyebrows matched his suit. Gray. So did his skin. His hand was on automatic. It reached out to take a cold grip on mine.

His gray eyes scanned my face. "You knew him," he said. He didn't put a question mark at the end of it, he assumed it.

"We were out of touch."

"I'm Bill," the man said suddenly. "Brad's son."

It was news to me. I didn't know Saltonstall had a son. He never talked about his family.

I looked the guy over good. He was not only in his late thirties, he was in his late everything. He didn't have any of the old man's drive, that was for sure. Whatever he did for a living, it didn't require him to get out of bed in the mornings. His dull gray eyes were washed with a faint trace of blue. His broad shoulders were curled forward in a perpetual slouch. Like a leaf that had fallen from a tree and had dried up and was getting ready to blow away.

We stood there for a moment in an uneasy silence. He didn't know what to say. Neither did I. So I said it:

"Closed coffin."

"Yes."

"Did you see him?"

"No," he answered softly. "I'll leave you alone with him."

How do you know it's him? I thought. There was no hint of grief or any other emotion in his voice, unless you call weariness and lack of interest emotions. He backed up about three steps, as though he were leaving the throne of a powerful king. He turned in slow motion and went back to his little hiding place on the sofa at the other end of the room.

He was only there a moment. Out of the corner of my eye I saw the funeral director walking gingerly across the room to join him, then leaning over to whisper something. Such as how late it was getting to be.

Bill Saltonstall forced himself to his feet again and shuffled toward me.

"I'm very sorry," he said.

"I am too."

He looked at me very carefully.

"My mother would like to meet you."

"Your mother?"

"Your name is Mr. Caine?"

I glanced back toward the guest register. The mortician was standing there, head down, hands folded in front of him, rocking gently back and forth on his feet. He seemed to be keeping an eye on his wristwatch.

"Yes," I said.

Bill Saltonstall tried a weak smile. It didn't look good on him.

"So many people have come," he apologized. "Friends of my father. I don't know any of them. My mother was here earlier. All afternoon and most of the evening. There were many people that even she didn't know. My father knew a great many people."

He looked down at his shoes. He wasn't accustomed to looking anyone in the eye for more than a few seconds at a time.

"My mother asked me—when she left—she asked me to be on the lookout for a man named Caine. Nick Caine," he said softly. His eyes rose unsteadily to mine. "That's you."

"It is."

"I've been—you know—on the lookout."

"I don't believe I know your mother."

"No. That's what she said. She said—she didn't know what you looked like. Or anything. But I believe she's especially anxious to—I know she wants to see you, if you can spare the time, because she specifically asked me to—you know—"

"Be on the lookout."

"Yes, sir."

"It's late."

The faint smile trickled back onto his lips.

"No. You don't know Mother. She's not a sleeper."

# 10

I went out the way I'd come in. It wasn't glamorous but it was efficient. It kept me in the shadows—through the bushes, across the backyards a step ahead of the sound of the barking dog, down the dark walkway of somebody's house to the adjoining street, and back around the block past the little bar where a girl named Tania was tickling everyone's fancy.

The night was close. There was a scent of something overly sweet in the air. Death.

I found the rented car where I'd parked it, about three blocks away. By the time I'd driven back around several blocks to the front of the funeral parlor, Bill Saltonstall was sitting at the wheel of his big brown Oldsmobile in the middle of the narrow street, engine running, gray exhaust curling upward from the twin pipes. His was one of the cars that had been parked in the small lot in back.

The two birds in the Buick were gone. I made a point of noticing that. The joint was closing down for the night, the impatient young man with white hair was turning everything over to the dead for a few hours, and the two peepers were in a big hurry to get back to the lab and see whether their pictures turned out.

It meant they hadn't picked me up, or they would have put

in for overtime. It also meant that someone was very interested in learning who might come out of the thick Georgetown night to pay his last respects to Bradley Saltonstall.

Someone very official.

Bill Saltonstall stuck a big limp paw out of the driver's window and waved me up behind him. His car started to move slowly down the street. He made a halfhearted attempt to honor the stop sign down at the end of the block. Then he peeled out into the main drag. The car seemed to change color under the orange street lights, like a chameleon. He was off to the races. A strange man.

I followed him—turning left, turning right, following a dark side street for a few blocks and then doubling back to the main drag. Strange didn't cover it. He was a middle-aged man who still played games. A spy's kid who never got over it. Or lived up to it. The closer I stayed to him, the wilder he drove. He finally gave it up and settled down to a slow but steady speed, without the fancy frills.

It gave me time to think. Saltonstall's widow? All I knew about her was that she had survived. Widows usually do.

The mourners? They were survivors, too. Five of them. Rococco, Nevada, Lemaire, McDonald, Richter. I knew as much about them as I knew about Saltonstall's widow. Not very much. They had gotten together in a war a long time ago to do something good. Now when they got together, there was nothing good about it. Yanasek was still among the missing—maybe dead, maybe not. One of them had failed to show, an artist who called himself Max Sinclair. I didn't know much about any of them, but I knew even less about one of them—the one you could look straight at and see right through, as though he weren't even there. The man of glass. The man I figured Saltonstall was about to nail before Roger Penrod started the day off wrong on my front doorstep. Before Saltonstall himself went for a cruise and didn't come back.

The man of glass had kept it inside himself for a long time. It's like looking in a mirror and seeing something that no one else can see—something in your eyes, the way the skin

**85**

stretches and sinks over your bones, secrets that you don't want to try to explain. The man of glass looked in the mirror and he didn't like the looks of it, even though he was the only one who saw it. He was the only one who knew that he'd given in to the worm of fear on a battlefield far away. You'd think he'd try to forget about it. You'd think he'd get an old house somewhere out of the way, and watch a lot of old movies on TV, and try to get back in the mountains once in a while to fish. Try to get away from it all. Try to stay out of it. You'd think he'd want to put all the bad things that had ever happened to him down in the dusty subbasement of his mind, and slam the door, and throw the bolt.

But he couldn't. Not anymore. Not after Bernard Rococco made the mistake of reminding everyone that he hadn't forgotten what happened on that dark and rainy night in the no-man's land across the Mussolini Canal.

For the man of glass, guilt was like a death beetle trapped inside his tired flesh all these years. He was a time bomb. And now it was working its way out.

There was only one problem with it. I didn't buy it. On that restless morning when Saltonstall called me from the Pee Wee Lounge, frightened for the first time in his life but still playing the same old game—give me the answer, let me try to find the question—he hadn't given me just one answer. He'd given me two.

The man of glass was one. But there was something else that meant it didn't matter.

It took about twenty minutes before Bill Saltonstall pulled slowly into the gravel driveway of what looked like it used to be a château. Three stories of red bricks and rusted black ironwork and a sharply slanting green tile roof. There was a musty air of disrepair about the place, as though it had gone to seed a long time ago and would never bloom again. A single yellow bug light illuminated the wooden porch. The lattices were tilted at an odd angle. The lawn was scratched down to dirt.

Somebody didn't live there anymore.

I watched the red taillights of the Oldsmobile bounce down the drive toward the back of the house. Its headlights caught a sad garage of peeling boards, and then went out. I parked on the street and waited for Bill Saltonstall to find his way back to me in the dark. He finally did, nearly tripping over the downspout runner that stretched across what used to be a lawn.

We went up the sagging front steps together, without speaking, and entered the house.

"Lydia?" he said, when we got into the huge parlor. She looked up, startled. "This is Mr. Caine. He came tonight to visit Father."

Mrs. Lydia Saltonstall removed herself from a very dainty little chair next to a writing table in the far corner of the room. She was as faded as the house, a relic of another age, an elegant over-the-hill woman. But she obviously knew how to take whatever life dished out to her. Her bearing was erect. Her dress was immaculately black. Her left arm was in a white silk sling. Her step was steady. Her makeup was a little excessive, but maybe she had a lot to hide. Such as her heart.

She stopped a few feet from me and looked at me. She didn't offer to shake hands. Bill Saltonstall was gone. He had been sent to his room by some unspoken signal I wasn't in on.

"You all look the same," she said finally. "A face easily forgotten. Difficult to remember. No past, no future, just a point in time. I don't believe we've ever met."

There was a slight disdainful twist to her crimson mouth. The white skin that surrounded her lips was deeply lined, etched with something more than age. Her eyes were crystal clear. She didn't know me. I didn't know her. All her life she'd been on the outside looking in. It couldn't have been easy.

"You must have been one of Bradley's friends, Mr. Caine." Her voice was cold.

"It seems like a long time ago. We'd been out of touch." I watched her eyes narrow. "I admired him."

She didn't answer.

She turned her back on me and walked over to the little writing table in the corner. She sat carefully in the chair, picked up the cut-glass tumbler that was on the desk, and emptied the contents into her mouth.

"Scotch and codeine," she said abruptly. "It cures your cough. Few did. Few people admired him. Even fewer could get close enough to know him."

She looked at me sharply. Her eye was like a trapped bird. It suddenly struck me that she had spent her life caged by circumstance, and now that she was free to fly she preferred the corners of old rooms to the open sky.

"Did you work for Bradley?"

"No."

"Well, you must have been a very good friend. He left you something."

Her expression didn't change. But she wrapped the silence around her like a comforter on a cold night. Deep inside, perhaps, she had begun to thaw. She picked up the empty glass, looked at it, and placed it gently back on the little table.

"He called me a couple of days ago," I offered. "Very early in the morning. We hadn't talked for a long time, and we didn't talk long then. He seemed a little—"

"Preoccupied," she said. Her voice was dry and bitter.

"I was going to say he seemed a little frightened. In fact, he seemed very frightened."

The spark of something ignited in her eye. Her voice softened.

"Mr. Caine," she smiled. "You *did* know Bradley. Preoccupied was part of the arrangement, being married to Bradley. So was being alone. Love, honor, and spend a great deal of time alone. You won't find it in the Book of Common Prayer. Being preoccupied was a natural part of Bradley's life. Fear was not. You're very right, sir. He was afraid. May I fix you a drink?"

She started to get up but I stopped her.

Her eyes seemed to flood with light. From inside. She was a mannequin coming slowly to life. The reserve was melting out of her. In the slant of her mouth, in the tensed yet perfectly natural way she held herself in the chair, you could see the underpinnings of toughness that had made her a match for Bradley Saltonstall. Her legs were crossed at the knees. She paid no attention to the arm that hung lifelessly in the sling in front of her body.

"The most curious thing is, Bradley was deathly afraid of boats."

"Boats?"

"Because of his condition. Don't you see? That's what makes it so highly unusual. He hadn't been on a boat in years. Not since the war. He refused to set foot on a boat, Mr. Caine. The boat was mine. I grew up on boats. I crewed for my father when I was in pigtails. Ronald Patton. Perhaps you've heard of him?"

"Yes," I lied.

"He won the America's Cup. Twice. In the late twenties. That was far before your time, I'm afraid, but his name is still legendary among sailors."

"I wasn't suggesting—"

"I understand you perfectly, Mr. Caine. Bradley had been out of town for two or three days. When he returned the other morning, I didn't see him. He returned to the office, not to his home. They told me that he checked in shortly after eleven o'clock A.M. He stayed only briefly. You're right. Bradley was very preoccupied. Bradley has been preoccupied for thirty-seven years. But it strikes me that he was somewhat more preoccupied during the past several months. In fact, it struck me more than once that he was more than preoccupied. That he was—afraid."

"Not of boats."

"No, sir. Not of boats."

Her hands fluttered around the silver buckle on her dress. I noticed for the first time that she was holding a lace handkerchief wadded up in her fist.

"Yet that's what makes it so curious," she added. "That he was afraid of boats. And that he came out with me." Her voice drifted off. Her eyes closed. They hid for a moment behind the lace handkerchief.

"What was bothering him? You knew him. You lived with him. Did he give you any indication?"

The corners of her mouth flickered helplessly.

"I've learned a few things in thirty-seven years. One of the things I've learned is not to ask why, Mr. Caine." She stiffened a little in her chair. "I take the boat out alone every Tuesday. It's not much of a boat, but it's adequate. Bradley bought it for me many years ago. I keep it at Oxford, in the Tred Avon. That's on the Eastern Shore. I certainly didn't expect to see Bradley at the marina. I just happened to glance back that morning—I was bringing her around the breakwater—and I saw him there at the mooring, watching me. He looked so—forlorn. Like a big sad dog, sitting there in his wheelchair at the edge of the water. I came back for him, of course."

"But he'd never gone out with you previously?"

"Of course not. I go alone every Tuesday. Everyone knows it. Everything ceases on Tuesdays, Mr. Caine. I'm afraid it's my one indulgence. It compensates for many things."

She pursed her lips, asking me not to ask.

"It's true he had never been out with me on the boat," she said. "On the other hand, I am his wife. He had been in the field for several days. There is the remote possibility that he sought my companionship." If she smiled, it was deep inside; it didn't make its way to the surface. "But let's be honest. He didn't. He was not very communicative that morning. He never was. He was tired, I could see that. He looked as though he had been under a great deal of strain. He did not leave his office very often. He said only that he needed to get away. Out of reach of the powers of earth, is the way he put it. He asked if he could accompany me. Requested my permission! I granted his request. I did not seek its reason, Mr. Caine. I'm housebroken. After thirty-seven years I am housebroken. I've learned not to interfere in affairs of state and high office."

She nodded slightly, acknowledging something. A fact of life, perhaps. Her face was as calm as porcelain but she couldn't hide the cracks of contempt that had grown over the years for a man who was always somewhere else, even when he was with her. It made an odd combination—contempt and a kind of honor, a grudging appreciation of having been very close to power and of having paid the price for it.

"I assisted him up to the front deck and stowed the chair behind," she was saying. "He asked for a life jacket. I gave him one, buckled it on him. That's why they were eventually able to find his body, of course. Dead, in a life jacket." She thought about it a second and then went on: "The cruiser ran beautifully, as it always has done. It's a passable vessel, not the best in the world, but I keep it well maintained. We nosed around in the Little Choptank for a while. Perhaps an hour. It occurred to me to ask Bradley if he wanted any lunch. I had no idea whether he'd eaten. But he didn't answer me. He just sat there on the front deck with his eyes fixed on the horizon. And the wind in his face. As though he were trying to wash something from his mind. He was escaping from the powers of earth, you see."

Her hand went up to her face again and then dropped back into her lap.

"I headed into the Bay. We had just passed the Turtle Islands when the bomb was detonated."

"The bomb?"

"Of course, Mr. Caine. They killed him. There was no warning whatsoever. I'm told that I blacked out, and that it's just as well. But the doctors are quite incorrect on that point. I did not black out. I was fully conscious the entire time. The bomb must have been attached to the hull, below the waterline, and was detonated by radio. It had no connection with the engine whatsoever. The fireball moved from the front of the boat to the back—toward me. The force of it threw me clear of the boat. I may have leaped. It happened very quickly. I may have struck my arm on something. I don't recall. Perhaps the doctors are right. Yet after the first few moments—the sight of that orange and black ball of flame suddenly appearing before my eyes—I thought, Oh, God! Oppenheimer! Oppenheimer! I thought of Robert Oppenheimer!—after that—after that moment, I recall everything with clarity.

"I found myself in the water, several yards from the boat. The flames subsided very quickly. If you will have a look at it, I believe you'll see that the engine compartment was not even damaged. Of course, she was taking water. I kicked my way over to the boat—my arm was quite impossible—and by then I'm sure that Bradley was gone."

She screwed her eyes shut for a moment, pale little bird's eyes that tried to blink away the memory of those last moments with Bradley Saltonstall.

"I know he was gone," she said flatly. "He was very badly burned. He floated directly beneath me, facedown in the water, just under the surface. I reached for him, but it was impossible. My arm was broken in three places. It was not a pretty picture. His life jacket was all but torn away. He was very badly burned. I lost track of him. I don't know where—well, they found him a half-mile away."

"How long were you in the water?"

"Twenty minutes, I suppose. A runner from the Coast Guard station at Taylors Island picked me up. By then the boat was almost down, but they were able to save it."

"Were there no other boats around?"

A faint smile came back up to her lips.

"I thought of that myself, sir. Yes. There were a dozen or more vessels in the Choptank. But there was only one—another small cruiser—when we came out into the Bay. He stood down from us about half a mile. I can't imagine how he could have failed to see or hear the explosion, but the fact is—he did not come to our assistance. When the runner arrived, the captain commented on the fact that the Bay was empty. Of course, by then twenty minutes had passed, or thirty."

"You told the authorities about the other boat? Your suspicion that the explosion had nothing to do with the engine?"

"It's not a suspicion. It's a fact," she said sharply. "I am an expert boatsman. Yes, I told the authorities. They took it all down. If you have seen the newspapers, you're aware that they place a different interpretation on my husband's death."

"It's in their interest."

"Yes. The nice thing is, one is never quite sure what their interest is."

"I want to ask you a difficult question."

"All questions are difficult. It's the answers that are easy."

She looked directly at me. Call it osmosis. She couldn't have lived thirty-seven years with Bradley Saltonstall without some of it rubbing off. I'd heard that one before—questions and answers.

"Question," I said. "Did you see his body after it was recovered?"

"No. I understand your question, sir. Yes. It's Bradley's body. I'm quite convinced of that. There is no way he could have survived that explosion. He was badly burned. He couldn't swim. He didn't have the use of his legs. I can't imagine how—"

"Did you know Roger Penrod?"

She looked up quickly. I thought I saw the same startled flash of lightning break in her eyes that I'd seen when I first walked in the room. Distrust and suspicion.

"Mr. Penrod?"

"Yes," I said. "Roger Penrod."

"No." Her hand darted toward her face, but stopped halfway there. She smiled. "You see? The answers are easy."

"He worked for Bradley."

She shook her head. "No. I don't want to go into it. Bradley had many friends with whom I was never acquainted. And many people who worked for him. Apparently you are one of them."

Lydia Saltonstall opened the drawer to the writing table and removed a thin manila envelope. It was taped shut. But my name had been scrawled on the outside with a thick felt-tip marker.

"Yesterday afternoon, while I was going through some of Bradley's things, I found this in his bureau. Atop the socks, as though he'd placed it there for me to find. I'm sure that he left it there before he went out of town, as a—precaution. He was a very cautious man, Mr. Caine. Your name is on the envelope, as you can see. I'm sure he would wish for you to have it."

She handed the envelope to me.

"No, I haven't opened it," she said. "Because I'm sure he would wish for me not to. This is my role—the role he assigned to me in his caution before they killed him. To find you and make sure you received this. You've saved me some trouble by coming. I appreciate it. The investigators arrived an hour or so after I found this in Bradley's drawer. They had the run of the house, but they did not have the run of me. I didn't tell them about this. I had no idea who you were, Mr. Caine, or whether you had heard of the accident, or whether you even knew Bradley was gone. I had no idea whether you would come. I'm glad you did. It's important to Bradley. Perhaps—I'm sure—this may be the last thing I can do for him—"

Her jaw stiffened, and I could see the muscles working hard along the sides of her face. Her eyes were suddenly very soft.

"You're doing very well," I said quickly. I didn't want tears. "I wish you well."

She managed a crooked smile.

"This is not my first role, Mr. Caine. I've been on the stage. I used to be an actress. Strictly an amateur, of course. But with great range, so it was said."

We were near the door to the parlor when I noticed a small cream-colored vase of pale blue flowers sitting on top of the corner mantelpiece. She noticed me notice them.

"Do you enjoy flowers, Mr. Caine?"

"Yes. Those. I never could remember their name."

"Sky blue, with a yellow eye," she said softly. "They were Bradley's favorites. Forget-me-nots."

It was long past midnight when I finally opened the envelope. There was no hurry. I figured I was way ahead of him.

We were at thirty thousand feet, deep in the night over America and heading even deeper into the darkness. The three stewardesses were sitting together in the front row of the half-filled plane, heads resting back on the seats, talking quietly to one another.

Inside the envelope was a brittle sheet of parchment, a memento from a war that had started all over again. It was nicely calligraphed by someone with a deferment and plenty of time on his hands, and it awarded Lieutenant Bradley Saltonstall some sort of medal for exceptional bravery in combat with the 1st U.S.–Canadian Special Service Force, the North Americans, during the Italian campaign. It was dated June 1944.

The medal was gone. But that didn't matter. What counted was the message.

At the bottom of the envelope, pressed and faded and starting to disintegrate into a million pieces, were the remains of a small sprig of flowers.

Sky blue, with a yellow eye.

# 11

I looked at the face in the mirror. His eyes were blue-gray, mostly gray. The skin was still tight over his cheekbones. The little quarter-inch welt that came down at an odd angle from his lower lip was still there. It wouldn't go away, even though the man who put it there is dead. Lydia Saltonstall was right. It was just a point in time, with no past and no future. It told you nothing, unless it happened to be your own face, and then it told you something you couldn't tell anyone. Not anymore.

"He knew," I said.

The face in the mirror said nothing.

"He knew they were going to try to kill her and he knew he couldn't do anything about it. Not from a wheelchair. So he went with her."

The house was very quiet. The face in the mirror said nothing.

"He went with her so that when they got her, he'd go too. And for me he left forget-me-nots."

The silence was like a noose around my neck.

The face in the mirror looked at me: calm blue-gray eyes. It was the face of a man who could kill without blinking. It was the face of a man who had betrayed something. Himself.

I smiled at him. He looked at me, without blinking. And said nothing.

The day had started out wrong. Again. A telephone call. The voice at the other end of the line was very cold and controlled. I squinted at the clock: 11:00 A.M.

"This is Lydia Saltonstall, Mr. Caine. I'm very sorry to be a bother."

"No bother at all."

"We buried Bradley this morning."

Cold doesn't cover it. Her voice was like dry ice.

"Yes," I said.

"I find it necessary to call you, sir."

"Yes," I said.

I didn't know whether I was glad or not. But I wanted to give her a chance. Her words came slowly:

"You were the only one who mentioned the flowers," she said.

"Yes," I said.

"Perhaps you knew things about him that no one else knew."

"Perhaps."

"Not even his wife."

"Perhaps."

"There is no perhaps about it, Mr. Caine." A blade of sarcasm cut through her voice. "Bradley received a package in the mail this morning."

"Bradley did?"

"Yes," she said. "I opened it."

I nodded, but she didn't catch it. She was too far away.

"Mr. Caine, are you with me?"

"Yes," I said.

"The package contained some video cassettes," she said. "Three of them. Perhaps you will recognize them. One of them is called . . . 'Bum Rap.' I'm holding it right here in my hand, Mr. Caine. There's a sticker pasted on to it. It shows a young woman facedown on a brass bed. Her hands and feet are bound to the posts at the corners, sir. She's quite without a stitch of anything on—"

"She is?"

"She certainly is, Mr. Caine. The other two are mercifully untitled, but I imagine they are of the same high quality. One has a picture of a young lady mounted on a very large—"

"I get the picture. Where were these tapes mailed from?"

"A very large horse, Mr. Caine," she said icily. "In the manner of Lady Godiva. I'm terrible with postmarks, Mr. Caine. The package appears to have been placed in the mail a day or two before Bradley died."

"Where was it sent from?"

"I thought you might tell *me*, Mr. Caine."

"I'm not in the mood to guess."

"*Your* name and *your* address are listed here on the return portion of the shipping label," she said. "And *your* telephone number."

"My number?"

"How else could I call you, Mr. Caine? Directory assistance has no listing for you."

I was waking up fast.

"I didn't send that package, Mrs. Saltonstall. Brad sent it. He must have sent it to himself. He was a very careful and thorough man. Wrap those cassettes up. Send them to me."

She was silent a long time. When she spoke again, the ice had melted from her voice and what was left was something close to despair.

"No, sir. I am going to destroy them. They have served their purpose. I know *you* didn't send this package, Mr. Caine. After thirty-seven years of marriage I believe I can recognize my own husband's handwriting."

I don't know whether she was hurt or not. I think she was. Her voice said she was. On the other hand, she was doing what Salty wanted. He had left a calling card with my name on it, and she was calling. As usual, he had covered all the bases. All but one.

With Bradley Saltonstall, you expected the unexpected. In

98

this case the unexpected was pretty simple. He was dead. He had been scared and now he was dead. No matter how I added it up, I got the same answer. Forget-me-not. And now this garish little reminder of his adventure with Roger Penrod. It was a personal matter, a private operation, and somewhere along the line Saltonstall had realized that the odds were against him. He was an old man who had come to the end of the road, and he knew it, and he faced it on the deck of his wife's cruiser with the wind and sunlight of Chesapeake Bay in his face. He knew where I was. He kept his promise of silence until he couldn't keep it anymore. And then he did the only thing that was left for him to do. He left me an invitation to the darkness. Forget-me-nots.

I reached for the towel, wiped the rest of the soap off my face, and put the shaving gear away.

The Margolin Special was where I'd left it, the gun designed by a blind man. I felt like a blind man myself. Salty didn't leave me much, but he left me enough to let me know I was going to need the Margolin Special. It was one of his questions. Do you still have that little number designed by a blind man? Someday I was going to have to drop it off a bridge, or carry it back into the mountains and leave it, or set it out at the curb with the rest of the garbage. But not now. Not yet. I stuffed it in a lead-lined film bag and jammed it in the leather duffel. It was going with me—the gun and the invitation to the world of darkness, where good and evil grow from the same root and can't be told apart. You don't get away from it.

I carried the duffel downstairs and left it in the hallway by the front door. I used the phone and called Dr. Lew Diamond. He was free for dinner. He was free for anything. He sounded as though a weight had been lifted from his shoulders. I didn't hang around to ask him about it. I didn't have much time.

I went out the door into the blinding afternoon light. Twenty minutes later I was climbing the creaky steps to Michael Moro's office.

Moro was sharing his desk with a ham and cheese. He had

his back to the door. His feet were resting on the sill of the window. He was fanning himself with the daily *Racing Form*.

"Don't worry," Moro said. "The guy didn't have a dog."

I walked around the desk so I could look him in the eye. Sweat was pouring off his round face. We got right down to business.

"You don't want much," Moro grumped.

"All I want is a handle on it."

"That's what I mean. You don't want the world and the moon and the stars. All you want is the moon and the stars." Moro clasped his hands behind his head, the *Racing Form* fluttered to the desk behind him, and he looked out the window at the yellow sky. "It so happens that I know this guy in Sausalito and it so happens that his name is Frank Moon. Frank Moon and me, we used to be in the same business. It was a war. Korea. I went back to New York, he went back to California. He has gotten to be very successful in the line of imports. He knows the whole scene—arts, crafts, rugs. I asked him if he ever heard of this guy Max Sinclair. The artist."

"What did he say?"

"He heard of him."

"What did he hear?"

Moro stuck out his fist. His thumb was pointed straight down, toward his sandwich.

"No good, Nick. He's down the tube. He has the reputation of being a very good artist, maybe five years ago, ten years ago. But he don't show anymore. Once you don't show, you're dead. Maybe he don't even paint anymore."

"Tell me something new."

"You knew that?"

"Try the pig farmer. Sty McDonald."

"You don't ask much. It so happens that I know this guy in St. Louis. He worked in the front office of the St. Louis Cardinals baseball team. Fowler, that was his name. I called, but it so happens he was let go last year on account of his drinking problem." Moro shrugged. "I don't follow the standings, so I don't know why Fowler was drinking again. I struck out, I'm sorry to say. They don't know where Fowler went. It so happens that I'm not real big on Missouri, Nick. This guy Fowler is the only guy I know who actually lived there. So the pig farmer has to remain a real big question mark. And while I'm at it—"

"Nobody's perfect."

"Thanks. I knew you'd understand. Missouri is the pits. While I'm at it, I gotta tell you something else. Ted Richter? The TV hotshot from San Diego? No such personage. I checked every hotel in town. I checked all the motels, including that one up north with that waterbed and that love nest, as they call it. No luck. He ain't here. I went to considerable expense, which I won't give you the details of, including I took out to lunch Mary Catherine Mahoney, the press lady at Channel Three, who as you know I promised to punch in the nose the next time I saw. Don't worry, that's water over the bridge. She don't know nothing, but she promised to check with the sales people here and guess what? They don't know nothing either. I even called Salerno back in San Diego, another expense, but this guy Richter is not at home."

"Now," Moro added, stretching his legs. There was the gleam of something in his eye. I'd seen it there before and I knew what it meant.

"You're saving the best for last," I said.

"Now," Moro said. "It so happens that I know this guy in Tucson, Arizona, by the name of S. Marsden Patch. You're right. He parts his name in the middle. He used to work in New York but his health got the better of him and he moved to the Southwest. As a matter of fact he used to be with the Port Authority in the capacity of public relations. He's into sundials now. Got a franchise."

"A sundial franchise?"

"Yah. You guessed it. Says he's doing real good. We had a nice long talk. I'll find out how nice when the phone bill comes." Michael Moro reached around and picked up his *Rac-*

*ing Form.* I noticed that he had scribbled all over it. "Anthony Nevada is the guy you're looking for. Sam looked into it. We call him Sam because we could never bring ourselves to call him S. Marsden. I dunno. Maybe the 'S' stands for Sam."

"What did he learn about Anthony Nevada?" It was hard to keep Michael Moro on track. Business was lousy, he was lonely, and he liked to hear himself talk. It reminded him of home.

"It so happens that Sam knows a lot of people down there, including a couple of cops. Anthony Nevada is in the tough cookie line, Nick. Drunk driving. Assaults and batteries. Nothing serious, but he's in a mess. He used to have a lot of dough. He used to know a lot of judges, bought tickets to all the dinners, that's how he beats the rap. But he's down and out. Unreliable. He had a big consulting outfit—he would consult about your gas or your coal, that sort of stuff—from which the bottom dropped out when the word got around about his drinking and his being unreliable, according to Sam. He lives on the desert now. A town called El Gato. In Spanish, that means 'moon.' I think."

"You're saving the best for last, Michael."

"You know me like a book that really fits, Caine. I'm gonna have to bill you for expensives on this one. Lotta phone work. You're right, boss. I'm saving the best for last."

Michael Moro pulled in his feet and put them on the floor.

"It so happens that I know this guy in New York, whose name is Tony DaVinci. He used to work for *Variety* but now he works for everyone. He's what they call a stringer, like one of them pappaloozis, but without the camera. His line is items. Who was seen where with what. Get me?"

"Like Gallagher."

Gallagher was a mutual friend. Harry Gallagher, a real prince among paupers. Harry was the main columnist on the *Evening Standard,* or at least he used to be until he started serving a twelve-month term at Grayville correctional facility twenty miles south of town for contempt of court. Harry had refused to disclose his source for an item he ran about a Circuit Court judge and a sixteen-year-old ballet student. Four months had gone by and Harry still wasn't corrected. He was still upholding the Constitution, and working on a book about prisons.

"You're right again," Michael Moro agreed. "Like Gallagher. Only Tony DaVinci is big time." Moro had a long cigar in his mouth, one of those jobs he claims is from Cuba, and he was lighting it. "Tony is well aware of this guy Bernard Rococco. He knows him. Not to talk to, but he sees him around now and then. Rococco. A very wealthy man. He plays the market. Got a nose for Broadway. You know what I mean? He hangs around the shows, that sort of stuff. He loves New York. The word is, he backed a couple of bombs, but he can afford it. There's only one rap on him, otherwise he's a good time. You ever hear of a gentleman named Dominick Iceone?"

Michael Moro put his head back and puffed. A cloud of blue smoke hovered over his head like a halo.

"Iceone?"

"Yah."

"Mr. Ice?"

"You heard of him, huh? He's an untouchable. You know what that means? The cops can't touch him. Pretty slick character. Rackets, juice loans, stuff like that." Moro waved the smoke away. "The word on the street is, this Bernard Rococco and Dominick Iceone are going steady."

"Going steady?"

"More than that. They're sleeping together, according to Tony DaVinci."

"He's seen them together?"

"Nah," Moro said. "All I'm reporting is what the word on the street is, according to Tony. They're sleeping together. Nobody in their right mind would be seen with Iceone. Not if they're smart. I assume this Bernard Rococco is in his right mind and he's smart. Like I say, Tony don't know him to talk to him. Only to see him around. He seen him last week on Forty-second Street with a dancer by the name of Honey Mellon."

Moro started to cackle. He jerked the cigar out of his mouth.

"Wait a minute," I said. "Rococco was seen on Forty-second Street last week with a dancer by the name of Honey Mellon? He's sure of that?"

Michael Moro slapped his hand down on the desk. He was still cackling.

"I love New York myself," he sputtered.

Dr. Lew Diamond was a half hour late, as usual.

"I have good news and I have better news," he said as he sat down at the little table in La Serena and blew out the red candle. "I hate candles. It reminds me of my Catholic boyhood. Ever get beat up by a nun?"

He was in a good mood. I wasn't.

"I need good news," I said. "All I've had today is bad news."

"Bad news? Let's hear it."

Diamond's mouth opened in anticipation. His eyes glistened. He *liked* bad news. Bad news was his business.

"Bernard Rococco," I explained.

"Yeah? I agree. Bad news. He doesn't deserve her."

"He's two-timing her. The cat's away, the mouse will play. She's on the road and he's scooting around New York with someone who calls herself a dancer. Honey Mellon."

"That's her name?"

"Honey Mellon."

Diamond reached inside his coat, pulled out a notebook, opened it up, and wrote something in it. I looked at him.

"Honey Mellon isn't enough for him," I added. "He's also hanging around with a mobster by the name of Dominick Iceone. Let's just call him Mr. Ice."

It was Diamond's turn to look at me. He stared at me for a long time. Then he wrote something else in his little notebook.

"I can't believe it," he said when he looked up. "She's nuts about him."

"She's just plain nuts," I corrected him. "I thought you were off the case."

Diamond glanced down at his notebook.

"The good news is, they found the van," he said quietly.

"The blue van? The one that tailed you?"

"Where?"

"North of town. It was burned out. Not a print or a mark on it, I'm afraid, except for the serial number on the engine block. I had it traced. It was stolen three weeks ago from a used-car lot outside of Boulder."

"You consider that good news," I stated.

"It means they know we're onto them. We've got them thinking, and once they start thinking, they're in trouble. They're going to make a mistake."

"Who's going to make a mistake?"

"That's the problem," Diamond said. "We don't know yet. But we will."

He closed his notebook, slipped it back inside his jacket, and then pulled it out again. He slapped it on the table.

"That's the good news," he said. "There's better news. I bombed."

"You bombed?"

He beamed. "I bombed with the Moose. They didn't understand a word I was saying about the sociological roots of criminality. Christ, I was terrible! I almost put myself to sleep! As a matter of fact, they didn't even let me finish the goddamn speech. They started singing—one guy started, the rest followed. 'Home on the Range.' What could I do? Hell, *I* know the words to 'Home on the Range.' I joined in. Then I got 'em going on 'Clementine.' Pretty soon everyone was on their feet, they had their arms linked, sort of like a human chain, a couple of tables in the back fell over and the creamed tuna went on the floor. We had a hell of a time! The head Moose complained to the chief, and the chief came down this morning and complained to me. I'm under orders, Nick. No more speeches. It's bad for the department. He told me to stick to murder."

He flipped open his notebook.

"I'm sticking to murder," he said. His face was suddenly very serious. "A man by the name of Roger Penrod was murdered on your front steps. And his wife has already blown town, I can't find her. And somebody was tailing you in a blue van, which is later found burned out and abandoned. And you pop into my office when I'm busy and ask me if I know a character named Mr. Ice, and because I don't read the comic books I never heard of him. But now you say Dominick Iceone. I'll find out. I've got contacts. I'm a cop."

He tapped his forehead with a long, bony finger.

"I went over to the feds this afternoon and I told them I want a piece of it," Diamond said. "It's my jurisdiction. Delgany Street. You know what they said? Half of nothing is still nothing. There's nothing to have a piece of. They had word from Washington to lay off, leave it alone, forget it. They're smart enough to follow advice from Washington. I'm not. I'm only a cop."

"You know what?"

"I give up."

"I think they're right."

"Washington?"

"Half of nothing is still nothing. I get the feeling this is not a matter for the police."

Diamond screwed a frown onto his face.

"Murder is always a matter for the police," he said flatly.

"Do I get an opinion?"

"Yes."

"My opinion is, this is not a matter for the police."

"Do I get a question?"

"Yes."

"Why not?"

"That one's easy, Lew. You've got to follow rules. This one's going somewhere where there are no rules. This one's going down into the mud and the darkness and the slime. If you follow rules there, you're a goner."

"I'll get back to you tomorrow," Dr. Lew Diamond said grimly. "I'll have a sheet on Iceone. I'll have a sheet on Honey Mellon. I'll have a sheet on that lousy sonofabitch Bernard Rococco—"

"Lew."

"What?"

"I have a feeling that they're all the same. They're all heroes who have gone bad. Rococco's no worse than the others."

"What about the man of glass?" he said softly.

I stood up, glanced at my watch, and reached for the check.

"I won't be here tomorrow," I said to Diamond. "Save the stuff for me. My plane leaves in ninety minutes, and I've still got to get home and pick up my bag."

"Where are you going?"

"I want to see the man who wasn't there," I said.

# 12

The plane touched down in San Francisco at an ungodly hour. I knew it was an ungodly hour because there were no Hare Krishnas at the airport. I rented a car from a sleepy-eyed brunette. Maybe she tried harder, maybe not. I didn't hang around to find out. I found an empty freeway and headed north.

Morning caught up with me in what seemed like another country.

The air was cool and heavy. Cranberry light spilled over the hills from the east. It collected in pools of glazed purple on the hypnotic highway ahead. Dairies and body shops and chrome-plated shopping centers drifted past me in the thick morning light. A peaceable kingdom. Lotus-land.

I wasn't ready for it. Not for California.

I left the highway at Santa Rosa and located a little motel just off the main drag, next to something called the "Ma & Pa Reptile Zoo." A huge painting of a snake covered the front of the building, with two red doors located just beneath the painted fangs where the snake's mouth should have been. I told you I wasn't ready for it.

Ma & Pa were still asleep, but the little motel next door was open for business. It was done up in Mexican style, with a narrow tube of green neon framing the window of each room. A scrawny, middle-aged woman came through the curtains at the back of the office when the buzzer went off.

"A night flyer," she said flatly.

"Right. The wind blew me ashore. I need a room and I'm afraid of snakes."

"Ten dollars."

I paid my money and took the key. The room was last in line. It was filled with milky light and the sharp scent of disinfectant. The air was clammy, the sheets on the bed were cold and stiff. I didn't bother to close the drapes. A different kind of darkness slammed my head down into the straw pillow and left me for dead.

Dead doesn't cover it.

The heat of the summer, all the sad motions of pretending to stay out of harm's way, had left me dry and empty. They set you up and give you a place to sleep and feed, let's say Delgany Street, and they give you a couple of bank accounts to tide you over, let's say in Switzerland and Italy, and they call it a quiet life out of harm's way. After that it's up to you. No more back alleys. No more dark streets. No more dead hours in high places. What they don't tell you is that it's a long dry season living on the jagged edge between darkness and light and not belonging to either one. What they don't tell you is that you can hide from everyone except yourself. Your heart's like a spinning arrow on a chancy gameboard, and somewhere along the line it comes to rest and points you in a direction you don't want to go.

It was pointing me back into the dark alleys of the human heart, where fear and a greed for life stalk each other. Where every motive wears a mask.

At the end of the alley stood Max Sinclair, the one member of the old gang who hadn't bothered to show up in Georgetown to pay his last respects to Bradley Saltonstall. If what Michael Moro had found out was halfway close to home, Sinclair was a man whose life had been etched away by something. By what? The acid of circumstance? He'd made a grab at life with a younger woman, and wound up with a fistful of dead flowers over her grave.

Maybe there was more to it than that. Maybe Max Sinclair was hale and hearty, and hadn't got the word about Bradley Saltonstall. Maybe he got the word before everybody else did.

Either way, I wanted to find out where he hung his beret. And why he kept it on a hook instead of on his head.

For five months Bradley Saltonstall had been wrapped up in a hunt for a ghost from his own past, a man you could see right through: the man of glass. Now Saltonstall was dead. Even if he wasn't, they were going to bury him anyway. I didn't like the choices. They cut me off from everything that had gone on before and left me with a man who had his own sense of time, his own ticking clock. He'd waited more than thirty years to start it.

I didn't like the dream either, but I didn't have a choice.

Another nightmare, somewhere out in the desert, with huge concrete tunnels running through the base of the mountains and opening into the blinding sun. I was running through one of the tunnels. The man in the wheelchair was coming after me. It was too dark to see his face. But I could hear the high-pitched whine of his wheels behind me, and the rasping, metallic echo of his breath.

I beat him to the mouth of the tunnel, I always do, and I ran out into the heat and blinding light without even thinking—as though I would be safest where I was most obvious. When I turned to look back I saw that the man in the wheelchair hadn't followed me. He sat at the very edge of the tunnel, on a curving lip of concrete. The sunlight hit his face, darkness loomed up behind him. What I saw scared the hell out of me, because I hadn't thought about it for a long time. Gleaming steel teeth, black sunken eyes, the high tanned cheekbones where someone had practiced with the tip of a leather whip—carving the leathery skin into permanent sutures of pain. He looked like he had been dead a hundred years. A man it had once been my misfortune to know, long before I ever met Bradley Saltonstall. A man who had come out of the mountains on horseback in another part of the world and who took so much pain that he became an expert at inflicting it on others.

He was laughing, and it looked as though he'd caught the desert sun in his teeth, and when I reached for the Margolin Special it wasn't there.

It never is.

You get used to it—bad dreams and a bright sun. Someone had turned the sun all the way up. It was shining directly in my eyes. I reached under the pillow and touched the barrel of the gun. Then I moved my head and squinted at the window. The thin green drapes were drawn back. The sky was a bright and blinding blue. Empty.

It took me some time before I realized that it was the middle of the afternoon. I was as safe as I could be, out of harm's way.

It was the first time I'd missed her in more than a year—the girl who could read dreams. She had brown laughing eyes, and she sat crosslegged in the blue mountain shadows, and she cast her yarrow stalks on the Indian blanket in front of her. Looking up at me with tears in her eyes, letting her lips slowly make the silent words:

> *If the superior man persists*
> *Misfortune comes.*

We carry it with us, little scars that no one sees, little knots of failure and betrayal in the blood. They crowded me in that Santa Rosa motel room. They followed me out of town: the shreds of a bad dream that doesn't want to go away, the haunted look of a hoofer with her heart in her mouth, an old man in a young man's game, suddenly frightened and helpless and dead.

The road through the mountains took me through groves of

redwoods where the light seemed to rise white and ghostly from the understory of the forest. It twisted down past hidden farms and communes, experiments in futility, and spilled me out like a single ivory die on the coastal highway.

Suzanne Leeds had narrowed it down to "Mendocino or somewhere." That was close enough. North of Fort Bragg I found a little restaurant and pulled over to see if a five-dollar hamburger and a glass of beer were worth it. They weren't. The joint was called the Three Chimneys, for obvious reasons. It was real cute. Not only was it real cute, every seat had a view. My view was of a back counter, two stainless steel coffeepots, a pile of dishes, a case of Twinkies, and a grimy white door opening into the kitchen.

"I ran away from home," the waitress said. Her name was Lena.

"That makes two of us."

"I'm not going back."

"Me either."

I knew I was in California. She sat down.

"It's sure slow. You know? Where you headed?"

I explained, "Going to visit an old friend I never met. His name is Max Sinclair. A painter. You know?"

Her eyes brightened.

"Wow! I'm into art myself. I do constructions. Never heard of him. What does he do? Houses?"

"Pretty good," I conceded. "What's a nice girl like you doing in a dump like this?"

"It supports all my bad habits."

But she was a bighearted girl. She watched me eat the hamburger, passed the napkins, fetched another beer on the house, and asked around the restaurant to see whether anyone had heard of an artist named Max Sinclair. Unfortunately the clientele was limited to me and a young man sitting in a booth by the front window—all alone except for the big folding camera sitting on the table next to his half-finished salad. Fortunately he had heard of Max Sinclair.

"About four miles up the highway," Lena said when she returned. "He keeps to himself, I guess. It's a big white house up on the slope, overlooking the ocean. You can't miss it. Look for the 'For Sale' sign down by the highway. You know?"

I glanced behind her to see a broad Mexican face peering at me from the kitchen. On the way out, I nodded to the young man with the camera. He had a full black beard and dark eyes that acknowledged nothing. He turned his head toward the window, measuring the light.

I almost missed the sign, catching it only out of the corner of my eye as I was going past it, and had to turn around and go back. The highway was empty. So was the ocean below it. The sun was starting to bleed all over the sky to the west. I left the car unlocked at a little gravel turnout, crossed the highway, and started up the steps. They were worn and crumbling, and I counted them. Eighty-seven, with two landings on the way up.

The house was located at the top of the ridge. A wide glass-enclosed porch ran along the front of the house, reflecting the sun—a single bloodshot eye gazing out into the Pacific distances behind me. I followed the path past the porch door and around to the back. The place seemed deserted—not only of people, but of hope. A mariposa tree stood guard behind the house. The yard was filled with junk. Beyond it, on the crest of the ridge, were deep woods.

It was an old frame house put together by someone with obvious psychological problems. Maybe an artist. It bulged and heaved in six different directions at once. It was a collection of afterthoughts, right down to the heavy back door that was lying facedown in the scraggly grass behind the house. It had been replaced by an aluminum screen door without a screen.

I looked through the door and saw a young woman sitting at an oval table with her back to me. Her legs were crossed, I caught the back of one calf and a smooth white thigh, and the kitchen chair kept me guessing about the rest. She hadn't heard me. She was bent over the table, writing. Her long brown hair fell carelessly over her shoulders.

I tapped very lightly on the aluminum door frame, and she stiffened.

"Is your husband home?" I said.

She relaxed, and turned slowly in her chair. Whatever she was afraid of, it wasn't strangers.

"I don't have one of those," she said. "Am I missing something?"

I looked her over. She wasn't missing a thing. She had high cheekbones, sleepy violet eyes, and everything it took to fill out the white cotton blouse and shorts.

She shrugged. "The door's not locked."

It was open house at Max Sinclair's. The sink was full of pots and pans and dishes. Three or four of the cabinet doors were open. If she was the housekeeper, she wasn't very good at it. On the other hand, whoever had landscaped the grounds may have done the inside of the house. They went together. A strange, asymmetrical archway let me look into the living room. Hand-me-down furniture, bare wood floors, stacks of books leaning wedged against the long sofa, and at the far end of the room a set of double doors leading out onto the front porch.

"Father should be up soon," the girl said. "Unless you're here to see the house?"

She brushed the hair away from her face and looked at me quizzically. I shook my head. It dawned on me that she was a stranger there herself.

"Are you a friend of Father's?"

"A friend of a friend," I said. "My name is Caine."

She put out a hand.

"Caine, I'm able." She laughed aloud, and her eyes sparkled. "I'm sorry," she added immediately. "I couldn't resist. I'm Barbara. Max's daughter."

"Where can I find him?"

She moved around me and went through the archway

toward the front of the house. I followed her. The light from the porch windows changed the color of her eyes. Far below us I could see the stepped pathway going down to the empty highway, my car parked off the road, and then the precipitous tumble of rocks that led down to the beach.

A thin figure in a bright red running suit was jogging along the surf.

"Back and forth. Forth and back," Barbara Sinclair said softly. "It's all he does." There was something sad in her voice.

As she spoke, the figure cut a wide curve away from the water and headed for the rocks. He came up through them slowly, legs still churning. I lost sight of him for a moment. Then he reappeared at the highway. He paused a moment at the car, put his head down, crossed the highway without looking, and started up the steps.

Barbara and I were back in the kitchen when Max Sinclair pulled open the empty screen door and stepped inside, gasping for breath. He was too thin for his own good. His cheeks were sunken, his lower jaw hung open, and his large eyes seemed to pulsate. His face was beet red, shading to gray where it hit his hair. The veins on his temple were doing a crazy little dance.

"This is a friend of a friend, Daddy," Barbara said.

"Yours or mine?" he rasped.

His mouth didn't move. He forced the words out from his heaving gut and looked at me. The sweat was pouring from his face.

"Brad Saltonstall's," I said.

Max Sinclair's face drained entirely to gray. His eyes rolled back, as though he were searching the inside of his head for something that was no longer there. All I saw were the red rims turning inward, and the gray face slid past me on its way to the kitchen floor.

# 13

Barbara Sinclair was on her hands and knees on the kitchen floor, bending over her father.

"It's okay, it's okay," she said rapidly. She was saying it to herself. She turned her father over onto his back and tried to unzip his running jacket. The zipper was stuck. She put her face close to his. Her fingers gently massaged the side of his neck.

Max Sinclair wasn't buying it. He didn't move.

I went through the cabinets, looking for something that would encourage an ex-hero to get off the floor. I finally found Sinclair's stash in the cabinet over the stove. It was all the same brand. Cheap. I pulled down a nearly empty bottle; the label said bourbon but your guess is as good as mine, and it did the trick.

Most of it went down Sinclair's throat. The rest trickled down the side of his gaunt, gray-stubbled jaw and collected in a little pool on the dirty linoleum.

Sinclair's eyelids fluttered. It was a good sign. It meant he was still alive.

I put my hand on Barbara's waist and pushed her away. "He's okay, he's okay," she kept saying. "It's happened before." She was soft and compliant. The old man wasn't. He was a stiff, knotted rope of bone and gristle.

I bent over him. "Sinclair."

He looked at me.

"I'm going to move you to the other room. You'll be more comfortable. Linoleum's hard on the back."

He gurgled.

When I lifted him from the floor he felt like a bird with hollow bones. I carried him into the living room and put him down on the sofa. His eyes opened and closed. Barbara appeared behind me with a blanket. She threw it over him and drew it up under his chin. She shoved a pillow under his head and his face slid sideways. His mouth was still slack. An elastic cord of spittle dangled from the corner of his chin.

Except for the rasping gasp of Max Sinclair's breath, the house was very quiet.

"I don't drink," Barbara said. "Not much. But I think I could use a drink right now."

She was standing alone, arms folded protectively around herself. Her eyes were calm, she was looking at her father, but her lips betrayed her. She bit them nervously.

I followed her into the kitchen. "Look above the stove," I advised. "It's generic, but it'll do."

"I'm sorry. He's been like this for months. Pushing himself. It's almost as if he's trying to—"

She stopped in midsentence, pulled a full bottle of something down from the cabinet, I couldn't see the label, and put two plastic tumblers on the countertop. She turned to look at me. I didn't raise any objections. Then I thought better of it.

"Put a little water in mine. About half a glass."

By the time she brought the plastic tumblers over to the kitchen table, whatever it was that had made her lips so nervous had worked its way up to her beautiful eyes. I glanced into the other room. Sinclair wasn't moving.

"It's almost as if he's trying to kill himself," Barbara said softly. "Push himself over the edge." She took a sip of bad whisky. It didn't agree with her.

"This has happened before?"

"Yes. A couple of times. He hyperventilates or something, I don't know. He comes out of it. But he's not young anymore, and he's pushing himself. It's not like the old days. He used to push himself all the time. Never like this. It wasn't the same." She shook her head. "Where did you say you're from? It's terrible you should walk into this."

"Denver."

She frowned.

"May I ask what you wanted to see him about?"

"That's between us."

"Oh! Business," she said. "You may have come a long way for nothing. He sold out last week."

"He did?"

She nodded. "Yes. But what good will it do him? He's been sick. He doesn't work. He doesn't paint. He just—nothing's been the same since his wife died. Last September, a hit-and-run." She grimaced. "Look at this place. It's a mess. I used to come down once a week and clean up for him, but I gave it up. What's the use? He would have torn things apart before I left. It makes you wonder."

I agreed.

"It makes you wonder who the victim is," she added.

Barbara Sinclair shifted uncomfortably in her chair. Behind her, the living room was filled with a soft golden light from the front porch. Either she felt sorry for herself or she felt sorry for me. Maybe both. She got up from the table, refilled, and came back with her life story. Her words were tinged with a loneliness that I suspected was self-imposed. But I had to hand it to her. She had more going for her than those big violet eyes. She'd seen a lot of old movies on television.

"You've heard of the dutiful daughter?" she asked. "Here's looking at her, kid." She lifted the tumbler of bad whisky into the air and brought it down to her lips.

It turned out that Barbara Sinclair belonged to that helter-skelter house as much as Max did, even though she lived thirty miles away in a little town called Cedars. She worked as a records keeper in the hospital there, keeping track of who died and who didn't, and it was easy for her to say why she liked it. Nobody bothered to bother her. It kept her out of harm's way.

I'd heard that one before.

Barbara's mother had died when Barbara was about eight years old. They'd lived down south in Los Angeles then, and Max was studying hard to be an artist. He worked in a bookstore. He worked for a florist. He scrubbed the hulls of other people's yachts. At night, he painted. Barbara grew up fast. She learned how to open a can of Spam and she learned how to kick things under the bed so the place looked cleaned up. She had an aunt who wanted to take her in, but she stayed with Max. He wouldn't let her go. Nothing personal, of course. She reminded him of her mother. They were pals. They were a team. And by the time Barbara was ready for high school, Max had given up bookstores and florists and other people's yachts. He had made a name for himself as a painter of "purism, simplicity, and force." I don't know what it means either. He was picked up by an out-of-the-way gallery in Glendale, and he covered all the bases by hitting the arts-and-crafts show circuit in the summers. He had purism, simplicity, and force, but he still lacked one thing: a view of the ocean. So he sold the house in L.A. and moved north, with his dutiful daughter in tow.

"It was really very nice, once upon a time," she said. "We even kept a couple of horses. Of course, the barn's gone. The fence is down. Things change, don't they? I was in high school when we moved. Never had much to do with boys. I was too busy. I went to college down in San Francisco." She smiled. "I was an art major." She smiled more broadly. "I learned more up here on my breaks and during the summer than I ever did at school. Father had people up all the time—photographers, painters, potters. He knew everybody. And everybody loved him. He was such a—he was a good time, you know? He loved showing off. He'd do the most incredible things. Daredevil things. I used to think he was the bravest man in the whole world. Even when he met Georgia. He took up skydiving—at *his* age! It opened my eyes. I'm older and wiser. Older, anyway. I used to be impressed, but now I can see he was just trying to prove something. I don't know. It was *more* than fooling around or showing off—"

"Georgia's the woman who died," I said.

"Yes. Last September, two days before their anniversary. She was my age. A very attractive girl, really. He met her in Fresno at an art show. And I guess he fell in love." She shrugged her shoulders.

"He was trying to prove something to himself."

"Thanks. Then I *am* older and wiser."

"You moved out when she moved in?"

Barbara nodded. "After all!" she said. "I wasn't down much, not until she was killed. I could see he needed me. He needed *someone*, and I was the only one around. People get over it, right? Well, he didn't. The worst thing is, he's stopped painting. After Georgia died, he burned all the things he had here. I mean everything. All his work. She must have meant— she meant more to him than anything, I guess. He hasn't touched a brush or a palette in months. He just runs. And works out. He won't see a doctor. He won't see anyone."

"Maybe he'll see me."

She twisted around in her chair and looked into the living room. Max Sinclair hadn't moved, but one arm had fallen to the floor by the side of the couch.

"Yes, maybe," Barbara said softly.

She looked at me and her voice dropped even lower.

"This same thing happened to him last week, when he brought the check back from San Francisco. This is my vacation, if you can believe it. He left the day after I came down. That night he came back, changed clothes, and went down to the beach. It was like he had to work something out of his system. Or he couldn't miss a day. I don't know. He was down there for about an hour and a half in the dark—running. He literally crawled in here on his hands and knees, and passed out on the floor. The same thing happened a couple of weeks before that, although I wasn't here. He told me about it. He was running on the highway, up the road, and he suddenly realized he was at the spot where—where Georgia was killed. She'd been bicycling, and was hit by a car. He said he felt dizzy, and stopped, and the next thing he knew it was dark—"

Barbara Sinclair bit her lip and looked at the empty tumbler in her hands.

"I'd be interested in knowing who my competition is," I said.

She looked up suddenly. "Your competition?"

"You said he sold out."

She slapped the side of her face lightly. "Yes. I'm sorry. Mr. Peter DeHooch. Father said he's an accountant."

"Never heard of him."

"He signed the check. I know because I put it in the bank the next day."

"What kind of business was it?"

She looked at me for a long time before she answered. Her eyes narrowed. They looked pretty good that way, too.

*"You don't know?"*

I tried to look innocent. It was easy.

"I forgot," I said.

"You're a funny guy, Caine." She laughed. "You drop in here out of nowhere—I don't even think you're from Denver—do you know where Denver is?—and you want to talk to Max about business. And you don't even know what kind of business he does!"

"I play dumb," I said. "Keeps me out of trouble."

She laughed again. "The funny thing is, we're even. I don't know either, and I'm his daughter. He never talked about it. He *wouldn't* talk about it. It was something he had going with his old Army buddies, an investment fund or something. He got into it three or four years ago. He said everyone kicked in what he could. His share was ten thousand, and that was about all he had. His savings. But he never would talk about it."

"I hope he made a profit."

"Yes. A large profit, as a matter of fact. Fifty thousand dollars. But tell me something, Caine. What good is it?"

She waved her hand carelessly in the air, but it wasn't the kitchen she was pointing to. It was the soul of a painter who didn't paint anymore. It was the soul of a man in whom something had snapped in half. Barbara Sinclair looked down at the table and shook her head.

"I just don't know what I can do about it."

When she looked up again, there were tears in her eyes.

She had most of my attention, but not all of it. The rest belonged to Max Sinclair. He suddenly appeared in the doorway behind her, blocking the blood-red light from the porch.

"What you can do is move out of the way," he croaked.

Max Sinclair's thin arms were shaking badly. He braced himself against the door frame with one hand. His head seemed abnormally large for his wiry body. His bug eyes wobbled around in their sockets and tried to stay focused on mine. It was a struggle, but he managed. They were haunted eyes, veined with fright. I knew the feeling. Everything about him said he was a man on the way down for the count, but it was hard to say what frightened him.

It couldn't have been me. The Margolin Special was still in the holster under my coat.

It couldn't have been the girl with tears in her eyes. She was only the artist's daughter, a work of art, and she'd jumped up and moved out of the way as soon as she heard her father's voice behind her.

Maybe it was something else. Maybe it was the snub-nosed .38-caliber revolver he held in his shaking hand, pointed straight at my heart.

"Daddy!" she cried. "What are you doing!"

"Who are you?"

"You're not going to need the gun, Max."

"His name is Caine," Barbara said. "Daddy! Put the gun down!"

"Who are you?" Sinclair croaked. "Cops?"

"No, Max. Why don't you put the gun down?"

I could see the blood rushing to his face. The gun was doing a little dance in his hand.

"I'm out," he snapped. His lips peeled back from his teeth.

"You're out?"

"I'm out," he repeated. "I'm out. You can tell Saltonstall that. *I'm out!*"

"Saltonstall's dead."

It straightened him up. I could see that he hadn't known about Bradley Saltonstall. His lips stayed peeled back and I suddenly realized why. Max Sinclair had started to laugh. I'd never heard a laugh like that. A high-pitched squeal, like something was being pinched inside.

"He's dead!" he squealed. I could barely make out his words. I noticed that Barbara had backed off into the corner. She had her hands over her face.

Sinclair shivered. I stood up slowly, keeping my hands on the Formica tabletop. The gun in Max Sinclair's hand hadn't lost its sense of direction.

He looked right at me.

"I'm going to give you three to get out of here."

"Max," I said.

"The first number is one."

"Max," I said. "I heard you're a good shot. I'm going."

"The second number is two."

I could see he knew his numbers.

I took one slow step backwards, spun around, and dove through the open screen door. I rolled over and picked myself up just as a slug crashed out of Sinclair's revolver and smashed the doorjamb into fragments. Forget the steps. I was already zigzagging my way down the steep hill toward the highway. The gun and Barbara's scream had gone off at the same time. Behind me I could hear that high-pitched whine that came from somewhere deep down in what was left of Max Sinclair's guts.

The air outside was heavy and red. It was cold. Somebody's thumb was on the sun, squeezing it down into the gray waters of the ocean. I ran toward it. I didn't hear any more shots.

When I got down to the car I looked back up at the house. It was bathed in blood-red light. It was a ruined outpost from a war that would never be over and would never be won. It had been overrun by the enemy.

I don't like to take "no" for an answer. In this case, "no" was the only answer left. I sat there for a few minutes in the car, with the Margolin Special for company, thinking about how easy it would be to work my way up through the wooded hillside on either side of Max Sinclair's property, and how easy it would be to take him. And what it would get me.

It would get me what was left, and there was nothing left. Suzanne Leeds was right. They were flies at the point of a pin. Someone was toying with them until all the life and hope and reason for living had been bled out of them.

It was a lousy summer, a dry time. Everywhere.

I was only a couple hundred yards down the highway when I saw her moving like a ghost through the trees on the hill to my left.

I pulled off the road and backed up.

She came out of the woods and crossed the highway without looking and came up to the car. She was breathing hard. Her face was pale and I could see that her legs had been cut by the fallen branches in the woods.

She put her hands on the sill of the car window to steady herself. Her eyes looked into mine, and then down at the gun on the seat beside me. She didn't understand.

"I'm sorry," she said.

"We're even," I reminded her.

"He wouldn't have shot you."

"Right. His hand was shaking. Not a chance."

She bit her lip. "Caine, he's sick. He's an old man."

I slid the gun over and patted the seat next to me. "There's plenty of room."

Her eyes didn't leave mine. I'd seen that look before. Her eyes were telling me one thing, but her mouth said no.

"I can't leave him. Not now. He needs help. I'm all he's got." She stood erect suddenly and pulled her hands back from the car. "I don't know what you came here for," she said, "but I hope you got it."

"I did."

"It wasn't business, then, was it?"

"No."

She shrugged and kicked the gravel along the highway with her foot. "You wouldn't have a card or something, would you?" she asked softly. "I mean, in case—if something should—"

I didn't have a card but I did have something. I scribbled my address and phone number on a scrap of paper and handed it to her. She took it, and her hand fell limply to her side.

"I apologize for him," she said.

"You don't have to. He laughs a lot. Takes the sting out."

"Caine?"

"Yes?"

"To laugh is no proof of being happy."

I left her there by the side of the highway, a lovely Florence Nightingale in the fading California sunlight. I liked her. Her mother must have been quite a woman.

# 14

It was a tough way to eliminate a killer. Max Sinclair hadn't left California—not for Saltonstall's funeral, not for Saltonstall's death. He didn't even know about the boating accident in Chesapeake Bay. That answered one question but it raised some others. Sinclair had seemed relieved when I'd told him Saltonstall was dead. Why? And who was Peter DeHooch? And what kind of racket were these ex-heroes running? Suzanne Leeds hadn't mentioned Peter DeHooch. The only business arrangement she'd mentioned was the one that was putting people out of business. People like Max Sinclair.

I got back to Delgany Street in midmorning. The house was hot and drowsy. I opened a couple of windows, headed for the refrigerator, and found the old jar of black olives. This time I called it lunch. It went real well with what the airline had called breakfast. I'd caught forty winks in the airport at San Francisco, waiting for the first flight out. I caught another forty winks on the plane. When I got home I realized there was only one thing I needed: a total of about 120 winks.

I'd just settled down in the recliner when the phone rang. I ignored it. But then it rang again. It was Lew Diamond.

"You're home," he observed.

"You'll have fifteen seconds to give your message when you hear the tone. I'll get back to you when I return—"

"I'll be there in twenty minutes. Don't go away," he snapped.

He was there in twenty minutes, standing on my front porch. He was wearing a yellow windbreaker. Sergeant Canetti was at the curb in the black car, and the engine was running.

"No," Diamond said. "I can't come in. I'm already late. Today's the department's annual golf outing. A holiday from murder. I was supposed to be out at Loch Lommond at eight o'clock but it's been a lousy morning. At seven o'clock one of our undercover narcotics guys was found unconscious in an alley behind Sterno's Tavern."

"Mugged?"

"No. He OD'd. Turned out he was a user."

Canetti's round face suddenly appeared in the passenger window of the car parked at the curb.

"You're already late. Sir," he growled.

"Canetti's a lousy golfer. Worse than me," Diamond said quickly. "He's running me out there but I'm sending him back. I can't stand to be out of touch. I checked out both of them with the NYPD, just like I said I would. Honey Mellon is a lousy dancer. She's a fringe player. But for the rest of it, she's SRO. She's got a vice sheet as long as your arm. I hope Suzy doesn't find out about it. It would break her heart. The other guy, Dominick Iceone, doesn't have a sheet at all, unless you count traffic arrests. He's an ex-advertising man who gave it all up to live high on the hog with no visible means of support. They've tried to nail him on drugs, stolen goods, juice, a few other things. Nothing sticks. He associates with criminals, but that's not a crime. I do it myself. Now," he added. "What have you found out?"

"Black olives and hash browns don't go."

Diamond stared at me.

"I see. Have the feds talked to you about Roger Penrod?"

"No."

"I see. You were out of town."

"Yes."

"I see. I'm only chief of homicide. Keep it to yourself."

"California," I said. "One of the boys on Suzanne's Christmas list. His name is Max Sinclair, he's alive and well, but he finds things a little hard to handle."

Dr. Lew Diamond scratched his head. "He's the one whose wife was killed."

"I talked to the deputy sheriff on the way out. He handled the case himself. Sinclair's wife was clipped from behind at high speed. They figure she flew eighty or ninety feet through the air before she landed. She was dead before she hit the highway."

"It could have been an accident."

I shrugged. "They don't know. They never found the car that hit her. The sheriff has a theory, though. Fifteen points if you get close enough to scare them and make them fall. Twenty-five points if you nick them on the back of the bike and tip them over. A hundred big ones if you kill them outright—just run right over them. That highway's full of people on bicycles. Whoever clipped Georgia Sinclair got a hundred big ones."

"I see."

Canetti hit the horn. He tried to be discreet about it, but it was a loud horn.

"I've got to go," he said. "But she was right."

"Suzanne?"

"Yes. This man of glass—he's pretty smooth. He makes everything look like an accident. But you know something? I don't believe in accidents."

"We're even. But I'm not sure I believe her either. I want to talk to her again."

"Tonight," Diamond said. "She's got a matinee, and a performance at eight. Maybe we can set up dinner. I'll give her a call. Maybe we can— Listen. This won't take long. To hell with dinner. We don't have that much time. I've only got to play nine holes. You know, for appearances. Show 'em I'm one of the boys. I'll call her from out there and pick you up on the way back in."

"You're right about not having much time. The reunion starts in a couple of days. Some of those birds may already be in town, Lew. Early birds."

"I've been thinking about that."

"Right in your own backyard."

"I've been thinking about that, too."

"A bunch of ex-heroes with fresh blood on their hands."

Dr. Lew Diamond spun around and went down the steps just as Canetti hit the horn again. I didn't bother to tell him about Bradley Saltonstall III. Not just yet. I didn't want to ruin his concentration.

My concentration was still pretty good, despite the black olives. What I was concentrating on was Barbara Sinclair's question: Who was the real victim?

Georgia Sinclair was gone for good, but Max Sinclair was still the victim. If you wanted to make him suffer, that was one way to do it. Eliminate the one thing that meant the most to him. When his young wife said good-bye on the Coast Highway, everything fell apart for Max Sinclair. He became a haunted man, killing himself by inches down on the beach while the surf reached for him with its ghastly white fingers.

Max Sinclair showed me something about the man of glass. He showed me how smart he was. Barbara Sinclair told me something, too. It made me put a maybe on the whole thing.

I made a list and stared at it.

Sty McDonald, a pig farmer who lived in a place called Peace Valley. Lost his farm. Anthony O. Nevada, a mining engineer tasting life as a desert rat. Lost his business. What else had they lost? At the worst they'd be like Sinclair. Shell-shocked. Broke. Broken. But I knew they wouldn't be. There was something different about them. They'd gone to a funeral in Georgetown. Lemaire was still a blank. He'd been a no-show at the first reunion, but the others had dug him up somewhere and he'd gone to Georgetown with them. If Louie Lemaire was in trouble he hadn't told me about it. Yanasek? Nobody knew whether he was alive or dead. My money was on dead. I backed it up with a line through his name. Bernard Rococco? According to Suzanne Leeds, it was a miracle he was still alive. He was almost a victim but not quite. There'd been three bungled attempts on his life and each one had ended with the same little question. Why? There were better ways to make a man suffer than by killing him. It didn't fit the pattern. Neither did Saltonstall, but there was a reason for that and I'd already figured it out. So had Saltonstall. He knew who the man of glass was. He knew what had been going on since that first reunion of 4 Company when Bernie Rococco had made the mistake of proposing a toast to the wrong man. That left Ted Richter at the bottom of my list. Maybe he belonged at the top. A television executive whose moneybags were as heavy as Bernard Rococco's, and who liked to drop out of sight now and then.

A bunch of over-the-hill heroes.

I went through the list twice, starting at the top and then starting at the bottom. It didn't matter. I still stopped at the same place.

Saltonstall.

He was a very careful man. He did everything in duplicate. His life was in danger and he still did it in duplicate. He sent me two messages after Roger Penrod picked my doorstep to die on. One was a bunch of forget-me-nots, and his service papers from 4 Company. The other he sent to himself, knowing I'd get it. A package of pornographic video cassettes.

Penrod would have been enough. I'm easy to impress.

The dirt road going into Grayville Prison hadn't been watered down. A lip of yellow dust curled behind the car. I parked in the lot at the side of the Administration Building, got my bearings, and headed inside. It was twenty minutes before the officer came back and patted me down. Then he ushered me down a long grim hallway and showed me into a small room.

Harry Gallagher jumped to his feet.

"You bring me a cake?"

"You look pretty good in gray, Harry."

He pumped my hand and squeezed my arm, and vice versa. It's something he picked up by watching a lot of old movies. If I'd been wearing a tie he would have grabbed it and pretended to blow his nose in it—it's one of his fashionable tricks—but I wasn't.

"No cake, no hacksaw," I announced. "This is strictly a social visit. How's the book coming?"

"You know how hard it is to write when you're surrounded by criminals? They're after me all the time for cigarettes. Listen—Nick?"

"Yes."

"Got a cigarette?"

His dark eyes gleamed. I handed it to him. Harry hadn't lost his touch, not even after all those months in the pen doing time as a martyr to the First Amendment. Harry Gallagher was the best newspaper columnist I ever never bothered to read. In person, though, he was even better. And he knew people Michael Moro had never heard of.

Gallagher lit the cigarette. A wreath of blue smoke surrounded his birdlike face. "I'm becoming an expert at bank heists and basketball," he declared. "Shot fourteen free throws in a row yesterday afternoon and had a couple of the brothers calling me 'Dr. G.' You don't fool me. There's nothing social about it. If this is a social visit, we stop the presses."

"The Arnold Hotel."

"Oh! It's like a game, huh?" He peered up at the ceiling. "I've spent the night in worse places. You ever hear of Guam? Or Naples, Florida? Don't distract me. You want information." He pursed his lips. "The Arnold Hotel," he stated. "Not bad, if you can afford it. I'd say a hundred rooms. They have

131

rugs on the floor, bellboys, the works. What do you want to know?"

"I want to know who you know at the Arnold Hotel."

"Who I know," he repeated. He thought about it a moment. Then he scratched his head. "Nobody. Why don't you try Michael Moro? He knows people I never heard of."

"Are there any bars at the Arnold? Restaurants?"

"There's a bar. Wicker's. Just off the lobby."

Gallagher's face fell. There was a touch of confusion around his dark eyes. "I'm sorry," he said softly. "I've been away a long time."

"You know anyone at Wicker's?"

"Yeah. Joe Scruffiato. If he's still tending bar. I'm sorry. We don't have bars here, you know. Not that kind."

"I'll look him up. One other thing, Harry. I want to hire a photographer. Tonight."

"I've got one for you," Gallagher snapped. His eyes brightened again. "And he really knows his beans."

"His onions."

"He knows his onions, too. What do you want him for?"

"What's his name?"

"Harold Square. He's in the Yellow Pages. He's an old-timer, used to work for the *Gazette*. Tell him I sent you. Nick? Where you going?"

I paused at the door.

"You need anything, Harry?"

He rubbed his face. "Naw. It's a charmed life."

The officer escorted me back down the hall. Another officer escorted Harry Gallagher the other way. Behind me, I could hear the inmates shouting out to him: "Harry! Hey, Harry! Hey! Harry!"

I didn't turn around to look, but I knew he was waving to them.

The house on Delgany Street was still hot. Opening the windows hadn't done a thing. I found Harold Square in the Yellow Pages, dialed his number, and got an earful:

"Is this a wedding?" he demanded before I even had a chance to identify myself. "I don't do weddings. I'll do a funeral before I'll do a wedding. I do portraits. I do publicity. I don't do weddings. If you got a wedding, you'll have to find someone else."

He was Gallagher's kind of guy.

I explained to him what I wanted; it wasn't a wedding, it was more like a funeral, and he agreed. Five bucks a print. Plus expenses. Plus a slight surcharge because it was a rush job. When we had it all settled, I gave him Gallagher's regards and hung up.

Then I disassembled the Margolin Special, cleaned it, put it back together again, and placed it carefully in the center of the kitchen table while I changed clothes. When I came back downstairs I was even wearing a tie. When Lew Diamond called, I wanted to be ready. I had plenty of questions for Suzanne Leeds, and I figured Wicker's bar in the Arnold Hotel was a good place to ask them.

Diamond called about twenty minutes later. And I wasn't ready.

"Copper Peak Road," he said tersely. His voice was tinny and cold. In other words, all business. I shifted the phone to the other hand and reached for a pencil. He wasn't calling about a birdie.

"Seven or eight miles past the turnoff," Diamond snapped. "You know where that is? Wait a minute. What? Make it eight. There's a quarry on the left about a mile back. Wait a minute, Nick. What? A gravel pit. I'm sorry. Good Christ—"

Dr. Lew Diamond was carrying on two conversations at once. Only one of them was with me.

"She was right, Nick," Diamond said. "But she was wrong. It wasn't her husband they were after. It was her. You wanted to see her one more time? This is your chance. Wait a minute—"

His throat was full of dust. I could hear him shouting hoarsely to someone in the background. He was calling from his command car and the connection was not good.

"They're both dead, Nick," he said quickly. "We don't know who the guy is. Not yet. Nick? Wait a minute—they're bringing her up right now. I've got to run. You got it? Copper Peak Road, seven or eight miles past the turnoff—"

"I've got it."

"The bastards aren't going to get their hands on this one," Diamond declared. "It's mine. Not only that, I've got a witness."

He slammed down the phone.

I did likewise. I still had some questions for Suzanne Leeds, but I was going to have to come up with the answers myself. When I left the house, the kitchen table was empty. My tie was tossed over the back of the chair.

# PART THREE

# 15

"I remember you from somewhere," Dr. Lew Diamond said softly. That was strictly between him and her, and I didn't ask. Diamond was leaning over my shoulder, looking down at her. He was grief on stilts. Sergeant Canetti lifted the blanket a little higher. The late-afternoon sun fell on her face.

"She must have been a beautiful baby," Canetti said, "but, baby, look at her now."

Canetti had a way of saying the wrong thing at the right time. I felt Diamond's fingers grip my shoulder, like talons. He wanted to reach out and touch something that was alive, not dead. Except for the ugly greenish-blue bruise that covered her forehead and spread out across her cheek like a grotesque pirate's mask, Suzanne Leeds was just as beautiful as ever. There was a trace of blood on her lips. Her mouth was twisted open in a little cry of surprise.

The young man who shared the blanket with her on the shoulder of the road wasn't in much better shape.

He was in his mid-twenties, his long black hair was still curled and wet with sweat, his face was unmarked. There were plenty of muscles under his faded blue T-shirt, and you could tell by the expression on his face that he knew it. There was a smug, defiant turn to his lips. It wasn't going to make any difference. His chest was crushed in as though he'd run into a wrecking ball or a steering wheel when he least expected it.

He was just as dead as Suzanne Leeds.

Diamond straightened up. He'd seen enough. More than enough. His shadow fell across the face of Suzanne Leeds like a cold blue warning.

"Where the hell is the ambulance?" he snapped impatiently.

He was upset.

Canetti dropped the blanket.

Two county police officers in business suits were leaning against the fender of a squad car parked sideways on the gravel road a few yards away.

One of them drawled, "Ten minutes, Lew. There's no hurry."

"Oh! Shit!" Canetti moaned. "Look at those flies!"

He was right. As soon as he dropped the blanket over the bodies, it was covered by about a million and a half black flies, give or take a dozen.

"Another accident?" I asked.

Diamond didn't answer. He winced and looked past me down the road into the distance. The air was full of fine particles of dust. They floated in the sunlight. Lew Diamond still didn't answer. He turned on his heel and stalked up the road toward the command car. Canetti took four or five quick strides, got ahead of us, opened the door for Diamond, and closed it gently after him. I did my own door work on the passenger side.

Copper Peak Road snaked back into the desolate brown hills, with no particular purpose in mind. On the way up from the interstate I'd kept my eye on the billowing cloud of yellow dust in the rearview mirror. It obscured everything behind me, which was nice. But it was following me, which wasn't. The wrecker was on its way down, being chased by its own blossoming cloud of yellow dust, and I pulled off to the edge of the road to let it pass. A white Camaro staggered behind the wrecker on a hook. Its front end was crunched together like an accordion that hadn't been played for a long time. The hood and top of the car had been crushed into a dangerous combination of jagged glass and metal. There was a gaping hole where the boys in the wrecker had used their acetylene torches to cut open the driver's door and reach inside. The back of the front seat had been removed, too. It wasn't needed anymore. The dashboard and steering column had been pushed back so far that it looked as though you could drive very easily from the back seat.

Diamond's hands gripped the steering wheel of the command car. His knuckles were slowly turning white.

"Canetti knows something," he whispered.

"Canetti?"

I glanced behind us. Canetti had walked back down the road to the blankets and was taking another look.

"He sees something I don't see," Diamond said. "I don't know what it is. But I know Canetti. He's waiting."

Diamond didn't turn his head.

I looked back at Canetti again. He was waving the flies away from in front of his face.

"How do you know?"

Dr. Lew Diamond looked straight ahead.

"He's waiting for the county cops to go home. He knows how bad I want this one."

He suddenly shoved open the car door and stood up. "You guys can take off!" he shouted to the two plainclothesmen. Their answer came drifting up the hill: "We'll wait, Lew."

Diamond collapsed back into his seat. This time when his hands went up to the steering wheel, his fingers hung down limply. He was forcing himself to let go.

"It's really their baby. I'm out of my jurisdiction again," he said vacantly. "But I want it."

"Who's the guy with her?"

Diamond turned toward me. His face was pinched and drawn.

"Don't have the slightest idea. Just a cocky guy who likes to drive around these godforsaken hills with $750 in cash in his left front pocket and no billfold. No ID of any kind. Did you see the expression on his face?"

Diamond's eyebrows did a little leap upward.

"I'll say one thing for him," he said. "He had good reflexes. It looks to me like he killed the ignition before the Camaro hit bottom. Then he got the wind knocked out of him for good. You saw what happened to her. Hit her head. At least it was quick. That's a real consolation."

"I thought she had a matinee this afternoon."

"She ducked it," Diamond said sourly. "Obviously. I'm going to have to check it out."

His head went slowly back against the headrest. His eyes stared at the sun visor. "Goddamn ambulance," he said to himself. "Bastards stopped for a hamburger. All the same to them."

I left him alone with it for a minute.

I'd already been down the road with him to the point where the Camaro had gone over the edge, coming out of a tight curve, and he'd filled me in on the details. The drop was about two hundred feet down from the shoulder. No guardrail. There were a few fresh scrapes and gouges in the baked earth down where the Camaro had hit and up a little higher where the wrecker had dug in to bring it up. The boys in the wrecker had left a few pieces of scrap metal down on the flat. Otherwise, nothing. The first rain would wash it all out. Then everything would be just the same as it had been before. Except for a few metal bones as a memorial to a hoofer who'd done her last one-two.

Suzanne Leeds and her muscle-bound driver had gone off the gravel road at high speed, like a rock out of a slingshot. And the way Lew Diamond put it together from his witness, there was nothing accidental about it. They'd had a little help.

If you followed the twisting road back into the hills some ten or twelve miles, you'd eventually find yourself back on the interstate—on the far side of Copper Peak. In between were a couple of lodges that tried to live off the slim pickings of the seasons. Cross-country skiing in winter, hunting and horseback riding and loafing around the rest of the year. It was back in at one of these lodges that Lew Diamond's witness had been applying for part-time work. A college boy.

The kid was on his way back down Copper Peak Road when he was passed by a Berlinetta in a hurry. He never did see the Camaro, it was ahead of him, and he didn't get much of a look at the Berlinetta—except for its color: steel gray. It came out of the yellow dustcloud behind him with its horn going full blast, swerved around him, and kicked a little sand in his face. The Berlinetta was really moving. The kid had to slam on the brakes, of course. He could hardly see because of the swirling dust. When he started up again, he took it very easy. He never saw the Berlinetta again. But he spotted the Camaro about a half-mile down the road. It was lying upside down on the flat. The front wheels were still spinning.

The steel-gray Berlinetta had overtaken the Camaro, come in tight on the curve, and given it a little hip check right over the edge. That was Lew Diamond's diagnosis, at any rate, and you could read the same story in the gravel.

The college boy was good enough to stop and offer assistance, but Suzanne Leeds and her driver were beyond the need of assistance. The driver was nailed back in his seat by the steering wheel. Suzanne had been whipped all the way around on her side of the car. She was lodged backwards in the front seat, staring out the shattered rear window. They were both very dead, and it didn't take a college education to figure it out.

The witness picked up Suzanne's purse, which was lying in the alkali dirt by the side of the smashed car. Then he scrambled back up to the road, got in his own car, turned it around, drove back up to the lodge where he'd applied for work, and used their telephone to tell the county police they could put away the pinochle deck and get back to work. Canetti had been hanging around the radio room at headquarters down in town, practicing with his putter on the rug, when he heard the call go through on the county radio channel. When he heard the name Suzanne Leeds, he knew what it meant. It meant get Lew Diamond off the golf course.

Sergeant Canetti's head appeared in the car window, next to Diamond's arm.

"They're coming, sir."

We didn't need to be told. We'd been watching the plume of yellow dust roll toward us, right on the tail of a beige ambulance. "I don't want to look," Diamond said under his breath. He didn't.

The ambulance boys did their job, turned around on the narrow road, and drove on down the road past us. Dust filled the command car. The county cops started to follow but their car stopped when it was even with Diamond's. The driver looked past me.

"You've got the kid's address, Lew. If you can go over it with him again, it might help. License number, any marks on the car. Anything. Steel-gray Berlinetta sticks out like a sore thumb. Especially if you're right, and the left side's carrying some damage. We'll find it."

"Sure," Diamond said. He was looking straight ahead, following the winding progress of the ambulance as it moved down toward the interstate.

"We'll get the coroner's report down to you," the county cop said. "And the guy's prints. We'll make 'em."

"Sure."

"You sure, Lew?"

"Sure."

"You still want to take the rest of it? Her husband?"

Diamond turned to look at him.

"I'll take care of that," he said slowly.

"I'll come back up and check out the lodges. Hard to say where they came from—the girl and the guy, or the Berlinetta. But I'll check it out. How does that sound?"

"Yeah."

The county cop looked at Lew Diamond for quite a while. He was trying to be helpful and he wasn't getting very far very fast. Lew Diamond was somewhere else.

"Okay, Lew," the cop said. He meant it. He pulled away, and the silence of the barren hills came after him like a shroud of yellow dust.

"I know you want this one, boss."

Canetti's round face had suddenly appeared in Diamond's window again. The sergeant was flushed red, but it wasn't from the heat.

"I recognize the guy. I don't know his name or nothing, but I seen him before."

Diamond turned to face him.

Canetti's hands were making nervous little circles in the air, like birds that were shivering in the cold.

"I didn't want to blow it with those other guys around, boss," Canetti said quickly. He gritted his teeth. "I have this friend, works for the city, he's into video. You know what I mean? That's the way he calls it, 'into video.' Videotapes and stuff. You know where I'm driving?" Canetti tried to grin. It looked more like a grimace. "I knew I seen that guy before. That's where. He's a movie star or something. The one I saw him in was called *Swinging in the Rain*."

Diamond stared at him.

"I don't know his name," Canetti said meekly. He was looking at his shoes. "I never saw him with his pants on before."

"Pornography?" Diamond asked gently.

"Yes, sir," Canetti gulped. "And very good pornography at that, sir."

# 16

Dr. Lew Diamond's command car disappeared down an exit ramp before we got downtown. I followed him off the interstate. It didn't take long to figure out where he was headed. At the end of the street I could see the gawdy orange and blue sign of a Bar None Beefburger joint. One of his weaknesses.

Canetti wheeled the limo into the lot and parked under the canopy of corrugated plastic. I did likewise. When Canetti got out of the car and headed for the service window, I moved over to the back seat of Diamond's car. It gave me a nice view of the back of his head.

"You want anything to eat?" he asked without turning around. His voice was as brittle as a dead leaf. I know Lew Diamond. He was holding it in, but he was ready to blow away. "No, thanks."

"I have to eat," he explained. "If I don't eat, I'll be sick."

He still didn't turn around.

"Lew. It was fast. The rest of us die by inches."

"Yeah." His voice was flat and empty. He shook his head. "I've been thinking about it. I've been on the radio and I've been thinking about it like a cop and I could kick myself. What the hell, I *am* a cop. But that's no excuse. They give us a badge—you know what the real badge is, Nick? Words. We hide behind 'em. The subject proceeded south on Copper Peak Road. The subject was dead at the scene. Death was caused by a blow to the head. Doctors and cops, we're the same. We hide everything behind words. Your chest hurts? Bullshit. It's only a myocardial infarction. Arise and walk. Nick? Death was caused because I listened to her, but I didn't listen to her hard enough."

"It's not your fault."

"Death was caused because I liked her, I admit it, but I didn't like her enough. I didn't do anything, that's the problem. I didn't do anything. Where's Canetti? I'm going to be sick if he doesn't get back here."

"Nobody did anything. It's not your fault."

"The hell it's not. Nobody's clean, Nick. Not me, not you. You think your business is your business, not anybody else's. Well, you're wrong. I think—I think you helped get her killed, Nick. So did I. It's a lousy summer. Nobody cares. Nobody's clean. Nobody's in the clear. It's slow motion. It's like a dream. Everybody's dancing but nobody's touching. What the hell was she doing up on Copper Peak, Nick? She's supposed to be dancin'. What the hell am I going to tell that two-timing sonofabitch Bernard Rococco? Let's assume Canetti's right. I mean, just for the sake of argument. Canetti's got a good memory for faces. I assume Canetti's right."

Diamond let the thought trail off as Sergeant Canetti's round face appeared in the driver's window. He passed a tray of burgers through and wedged it between the windshield and the dashboard. Then he glanced back at me.

"You want anything?"

"Coffee."

"You would."

Canetti turned around and went back inside the burger joint. He took his place at the end of the line.

"I assume Canetti's right," Diamond continued, "and that makes me dead wrong. When Roger Penrod was murdered on

145

your front steps, and I showed up to tell you about Suzanne Leeds, that off-the-wall story about a man of glass—hell, I figured I was killing two birds with one stone. I was wrong. It was the same bird. Penrod was involved in the same racket as that muscle-bound stiff up there in the hills. The X-business. I want to know who he is. We'll get an ID on him before the county even gets around to taking prints. I want him, Nick. I want to know what that sonofabitch was doing with Suzy. I want to know what they were doing up on Copper Peak."

The brittleness in Diamond's voice finally cracked. It was replaced by anger.

"Four billion bucks a year," he snapped. "More than records and movies put together. The X-business. It's a snake pit. It's full of pirates and entrepreneurs and guys with M.B.A.'s and home cooking. And the mob. You bet. It's bathtub gin, but nobody bothered to scrub out the tub. You know how I feel?"

Diamond swiveled around in the front seat and stared at me. His face was sunburned.

"Helpless," he answered. "I'm supposed to be chief of homicide. They put the cuffs on me anyway. They wouldn't let me touch the Penrod case, would they? Hell, no. Now there's nothing left to touch. And Suzy?" He started to choke up again but caught himself. "Let's face it, Nick. She picked the wrong place to go over the edge. The next county. Out of my jurisdiction. All I get out of it is a bunch of old croaks kicking up their heels in the Arnold Hotel for auld lang syne."

"Here's your coffee," Canetti said sullenly.

He'd appeared out of nowhere, I hadn't been watching him, and he thrust the open cup of steaming black coffee over the seat toward me. His voice was sullen.

"I don't mean to complain, officer, but I wanted cream."

Canetti stuck his head in the window and scowled at me and looked over at Dr. Lew Diamond. His expression changed. He was suddenly enlightened.

"I get it," Canetti said. "You don't have to hit me over the head with it." He reached his arm inside and grabbed a couple of the Bar None Beefburgers from the orange tray on the dashboard. "I'll eat these inside," he announced. "They like me in there. They're getting to know me." Then he stalked off.

"You liked her, I didn't," I said to Diamond. "That's okay. But don't blame yourself. I don't know what kind of promises you made—to her or to yourself. But I told her I'd look into it. I told her I'd try to find out if there was anything to this business that somebody was trying to bump off Bernie. I did and I didn't, Lew. I was busy with something else, an old friend of mine who promised he'd never get in touch with me again and broke his promise. Maybe it's the same thing. Different sides of the same mountain. But don't put the blame on yourself. Spread it around a little. This is a democracy."

Diamond was silent a moment. Then he said softly, "I've been holding out on you. Dominick Iceone? The sheet on him was a little longer than I suggested. It's true he's a refugee from Madison Avenue. It's true New York has tried to get the goods on him for the past five or six years without much luck. Drugs, stolen goods, juice. Like I said. He's also up to his hips in pornvid. He's on the merry-go-round. He used to run an outfit in Westchester County, Body & Soul, distributed the stuff. Video cassettes, skinbooks, peep shows. He folded it about three years ago and New York thinks he's gone into production. On a big scale. If you're going to distribute the stuff, why not produce your own? New York doesn't know where. They can't put their finger on it. Ever try to catch a snake with your bare hands? Maybe I should have told you. But I'm a cop. We have rules."

"There are no rules on this one."

"I'm beginning to see that," Diamond said. "What am I going to tell that sonofabitch?"

"Which one?"

"Rococco. On the way down, I had headquarters patch me through to the Arnold Hotel. He's not registered. He's probably still in New York. But two of them are here already. One is Ted Richter. The guy from Los Angeles. He checked in at ten A.M. The other one is named Sinclair. He's the artist. He checked in at noon. The damn reunion is still two days away.

But they're here early. I'm going to have to talk to them, too. See what kind of cars they rented. Maybe a Berlinetta. I'm sorry, I'm thinking out loud."

Diamond twisted around in his seat and looked at me.

"You're not holding out on *me*, are you?" I'll give him credit. He tried to look innocent.

"Let's go over it," I suggested. We did. I told him about Bradley Saltonstall, from the beginning. That Roger Penrod worked for him. That I was sure Salty knew who the man of glass was, that he had it all figured out, that they were on their way to Delgany Street to rope me into it when Penrod made the mistake of saying good morning to murder. I wound up with the way Salty died, and the funeral in Georgetown, and who was there and who wasn't. I included the forget-me-nots, the service record from Anzio, and the package in a plain brown wrapper that Saltonstall had mailed to himself before he died, knowing that it would get back to me. I even told him what I wanted to see Suzanne about earlier that day. When we met at La Serena and she spun out that fairy tale for tough guys for the first time, she ran through the entire roster of 4 Company except for one man: the young lieutenant who'd come down the line in darkness and led 4 Company out on its last fatal patrol. I asked her about it and her answer was simple. Too simple. She'd said, "The lieutenant is dead! *Why do they want to kill Bernie?*" As it turned out, she was right. The lieutenant *was* dead. At that very moment, Bradley Saltonstall was still floating serenely beneath the waters of Chesapeake Bay, and I wanted to know how Suzanne Leeds found out about it. It was a question that was too late for both of us.

I was very honest and forthright with Dr. Lew Diamond. I neglected to mention only one thing. There was another name in the game—someone named Peter DeHooch, who'd bought out Max Sinclair's interest in the little "investment fund" of 4 Company veterans.

But I've said it before. Nobody's perfect.

# 17

Lights were going on all over the city, even though it was only six o'clock. Nobody wanted to be caught alone when the sun went down and it got dark.

Dr. Lew Diamond crumpled up the wrappings from his beefburgers, dropped them absentmindedly on the floor, and kicked them back under the front seat of the command car. Then he reached over and tapped lightly on the horn.

I watched Canetti through the plate-glass windows. He stood up and headed briskly for the door of the burger joint, a look of annoyance fixed on his face. By then I was on my way out of the parking lot. It took me twenty minutes to work my way across town to the Drovers Hotel, where the cast of *Kickin' Up a Storm* was staying during its road tour.

The Drovers is an old hotel, set off in the shadows of a side street about a block and a half from the Paramount Theater. There's a brand-new hitching post out in front to remind people just how old it is. Cowboys used to hang their hats there, but cowboys aren't allowed anymore unless they wear ties. Not since a committee of old ladies came in, rubbed all the crud from the brass fittings, and declared the Drovers a civic treasure.

I crossed the tiny lobby, smiled at the deskperson, I couldn't tell if it was a man or a woman, and headed for the narrow, carpeted stairway around the corner. I was going to ruin someone's supper and I knew it. She didn't. Her name was Pepper Jones, her room number was 333, and her roomie used to be a hoofer by the name of Suzanne Leeds. Diamond had filled me in on the details.

The door was partly ajar. I knocked anyway.

"Door's open! Come on in!" she called out. She sounded like someone was strangling her.

I pushed the door open the rest of the way and walked in. It was a small room, big enough for one cowboy or two dancers, or one cowboy and two dancers, depending on how well they knew each other. It was done up distinctively in authentic old hotel: bare radiator, flaking paint and plaster in the corners and under the window, heavy mauve drapes. The light in the corner was on. The TV was off. Pepper Jones sat Indian-style on the double bed, facing herself in the mirror of the dresser across the room. I knew the type. She was the kind of woman who used to be attractive and was still trying to figure out where it went.

She was wearing a black top and red shorts that showed off her monumental thighs. They looked like they could strangle a calf. Her mouth was full.

I noticed the orange wrapper on her lap and the mess it contained.

"What is it?" I asked.

She chewed deliberately, and swallowed.

"One of those Bar None Beefburgers, honey."

She took another bite.

"Is it any good?"

"Depends on what you had for lunch," she said. She shoved her mouthful from one cheek to the other, and chewed. She swallowed hard. "What can I do for you?"

I walked around to the foot of the bed and put myself between Pepper Jones and the mirror. I wanted her attention.

"I have bad news."

"I'm used to it."

"Suzanne Leeds," I said.

"What about her?" Her eyes narrowed.

"She had an accident."

Her hand flew to her mouth, and she stifled a little involuntary gasp of surprise. The only problem was, she didn't sound surprised. She'd been waiting for it. Her legs snapped out from beneath her. She twisted around on the bed and put her bare feet on the floor. She sat facing away from me, looking out the window at the dying day.

"How bad?" Her voice was very small.

I didn't answer. I let her figure it out for herself. She did. Her body stiffened, and she said:

"Real bad, right? She's dead."

Her voice trailed off. The room was silent. Pepper Jones sat very still on the edge of the bed, hiding her face from me. She was whispering something to herself. It took me a moment but I finally got it. "I'm used to it," she was saying softly. "I'm used to it."

Eventually her head turned and she looked back at me. Her eyes were still glazed.

"You're with the police?"

"You could say that."

She could and she had. She twisted around and put one dancer's leg back up on the bed.

"Suzy Leeds. I knew she was in trouble. I knew something was very wrong," she said. Her voice was husky. "What happened to her?"

I told her. A simple accident. I didn't bother to mention the steel-gray Berlinetta. But I did mention the young man with $750 in cash in his left front pocket and no billfold and no identification.

Pepper Jones thought about it for a minute.

Then she nodded toward the door. "Do they know about it?" she asked. She meant the rest of the cast.

I shook my head. "But you were her roommate. You might know something about it, such as why she was up on Copper Peak when she should have been in the kick line at the Paramount."

Pepper stood up abruptly, straightened the legs of her shorts, and walked between me and the bed. "Excuse me," she said hoarsely. She disappeared into the bathroom. I heard the water running. It was several minutes before she returned, but when she did her eyes were dry. She was wearing jeans. And there was a faint scent of bad whisky as she brushed past me.

She put herself in the chair in the corner, next to the window, and lit a cigarette. I could see that she had her act together. She'd only let it get through her defenses for a moment. Bad news. I gave her the benefit of the doubt. She was used to bad news.

"Sit down," she said. "Suzy was a good kid, a hard worker. A little mixed up, but a good kid. She loved to dance. Oh! How she loved to dance! What can I tell you?"

I walked over and shut the door to the room. Then I came back and sat on the foot of the bed.

"She missed the matinee," I observed.

"Yes. Foxie filled in. Carole Fox. Another dancer."

"She didn't care?"

"Of course she cared! She never missed a performance. I mean—this was the first time. She even danced hurt. She was a pro."

"Then this was a special case. Out of the ordinary."

Pepper Jones looked at me for a long time.

"Yes," she finally said.

"You said she was in some kind of trouble," I reminded her.

She thought about it for a while, and looked away. "I knew something was wrong. She got a telephone call this morning that upset her very much."

"Who called?"

"I don't know. The funny thing is, she didn't know either.

152

She told me it was a—it sounded like a tough guy. I couldn't help but see that she was upset by it. Her hands were shaking. This man—I don't know who he was—said he had some important information he wanted to discuss with her. About her husband. Her husband is in—"

"Mr. Rococco?"

She nodded. "Yes. He's in New York." She looked at me sharply. "Suzanne had this crazy idea, I don't even know if I should say this, she had this crazy idea that someone was trying to—you know—someone was making attempts on Mr. Rococco's life. I've never met him myself. So I don't know. But she believed it."

"She talked to you about it?"

"Yes. Now and then. It bothered her a great deal. She said he was—he was foolhardy, and very brave, and she could never get him to treat it seriously. Macho man. I believe he's quite a bit older than she is."

"What time did the telephone call come through this morning?"

"A little after eight-thirty. We'd just come back up from breakfast, that's how I know. She wanted to be here when Mr. Rococco called."

"Rococco called her this morning, too?"

"Of course! He calls from New York every morning at nine. He's devoted to her. Obviously. She's a beautiful woman. I usually take the paper and go into the bathroom. Sometimes they bill and coo for half an hour. I mean, I'm out of high school. I don't need it. Bernie called this morning and Suzy told him all about it. The other call. Mr. Rococco, I'm sorry. She calls him Bernie, I call him Bernie. He apparently encouraged her to forget about it. Not to go see this man. But I could see she was going to go. She told him she wouldn't, but I knew she would. She was upset."

"Where was she supposed to meet this man?"

Pepper Jones shook her head and ground the cigarette out in the ashtray.

"Got me. I don't know. I don't even think she knew. She would have told me. I'm sure of it. But she didn't. All I know is that this man, the tough guy, wanted to talk to her about Bernie. Someone came by for her and picked her up." She leaned forward. "Listen—you said this was an accident—"

"He came here and picked her up?"

"Some guy did. I watched from the window. He waited downstairs in the car, she was supposed to watch for him, and when he came she went down."

"What kind of car?"

She thought a moment, rubbing her face. "A little one," she said finally. "White. I think it was a Camaro. I didn't see the driver. Not until Suzy got in the car and he made a U-turn."

Pepper Jones reached for her pack of cigarettes.

"You want me to describe him?"

"Yes."

"I can describe what I saw," she said. "He was wearing a blue T-shirt. He had one arm resting out the window. He looked like the kind of joe who'd kick sand in your face at the beach. You know what I mean. I didn't see his face, though. So I'm no help, am I?"

"You have no idea, Pepper."

"Is that the car? Is that the guy?"

"Pretty close."

"I knew it. Did she ever talk to the—tough guy?"

"Maybe the one who picked her up was the tough guy. He's dead, too, as I said. So we'll never know. What time did they leave?"

"It was five after ten. She said she'd be back by two. The show's at three but we have to be over at the theater by two. She didn't make it, did she?"

I stood up.

"Maybe her boyfriend knows something," Pepper added. "He's a cop, too. You probably know him. Talk to him. Maybe he can help."

"She had a boyfriend?"

Pepper finally got around to lighting the cigarette she'd been playing with. She waved the smoke away from the front of her face, and spit something into the ashtray.

"You bet. He was a fan of Harry Warren. So was she. I can't tell you his name. Tall. Skinny. He must be one of those plainclothes guys. Never wore a uniform or anything. Just real plain clothes."

"*He* was her *boyfriend?*"

"You bet," Pepper answered. "You must know him. They were a real number, honey. They were together every night for the past week, maybe longer. I mean *all* night. A couple of times right here in this room. They played the most godawful records. Real old-fashioned stuff. You know what *that* meant, don't you?"

"No."

"When they were here, it meant *I* had to go spend the night with *George*. And *that* meant poor *James* had to go spend the night with someone else!" She put her hand to her mouth again. "Oh, Christ! What if he shows up again tonight? I'll have to break the news to him—"

"I thought she was crazy about her husband. Talked on the phone every day. Billed and cooed."

Pepper Jones smiled at me. It was the first time she'd smiled, and I didn't like it. It was the kind of smile that said hello sucker.

"She was crazy about him, honey. But she wasn't *that* crazy."

# 18

Darkness was falling by the time I hit the street. Something was different, something in the air, and it took me a while to realize what it was. The smell of rain. I looked up. There were no stars. The wind had shifted to the west, and clouds were coming in over the mountains for the first time in weeks. The heat wave was breaking.

I got in the car, took a turn around the block, decided no one was going my way, and headed east. The lights were on at the Paramount and people were already standing around on the sidewalk out in front. I stopped at the first gas station I saw—it was closed—and fed a few coins into the pay phone. Dr. Lew Diamond answered on the first ring.

"It's going to rain," I stated.

"I'll believe it when I get wet."

"I'm on my way over to the Arnold Hotel," I announced. "Don't worry, I'm not going to make waves. Not yet. The only guy I have to look out for is Max Sinclair. I still can't believe he showed up. Yesterday he was a basket case. Today he's just another old soldier. It doesn't figure. One of Harry Gallagher's pals tends bar at the Arnold. I thought I'd get acquainted. It might help to have a friend in low places. I'm also starved.

I've seen enough Bar None Beefburgers today to keep me away from food for a week, but my stomach begs to differ. So I'm going to have supper. I just want to let you know what I'm doing. Then I'm on my way out to the airport, because it suddenly—"

"Wait a minute," Diamond said. "You're at the Arnold?" His mouth was full. He was eating again, at his desk.

"I'm on my way. Good-bye."

"Everyone's there. Richter and Sinclair checked in earlier today. I mentioned that. The others checked in about an hour ago. McDonald, Anthony O. Nevada, and Louis Lemaire. They're early birds, Nick. They're looking for a worm. So am I. Bernie Rococco's missing in action. I've tried his New York apartment four times. No answer. And he hasn't checked in here."

"Maybe he went for a walk with Honey Mellon."

"The two-timing sonofabitch."

I let it pass.

"Something very funny is going on," Diamond said.

"Sure," I agreed. "Everyone shows up for the reunion two days early. Everyone except Rococco."

"You see what I'm driving at. I've been sitting here eating another beefburger and thinking. Maybe Bernie Rococco wasn't invited, Nick. Maybe the others know something Bernie doesn't know—something about the man of glass."

"The whole thing was Bernie's idea. He's the one who wanted to flush the rat out of the wall."

Diamond was chewing. And thinking.

"Maybe the whole thing was Bernie's mistake," he finally said. "That's the way Suzy saw it. She didn't want him taken out by his own—I was going to say monster. I don't know. He unleashed it, that's for sure. All I know is what I see. These bastards are going to hold a little reunion of their very own. Without Bernie Rococco. I'd like to know why."

I considered it.

Then I filled him in on what I'd learned from Pepper Jones,

not all of it but most of it, and he found it interesting. I could tell from the tone of his voice that he'd managed to do something to himself, he'd put the badge on, and he was treating Suzanne's death as though he was the chief of homicide, which he was, and not as part of a hot number, which he also was.

"I have one question," I said.

"Shoot."

"Let's say you wanted to run someone off the road. What kind of car would you do it in?"

Silence.

"A Berlinetta?" I asked.

Silence.

I didn't take no answer for an answer.

"It sticks out like a sore thumb, Lew. Even a college kid would notice a Berlinetta."

"I'll ask him," Diamond said. "I'm going to see him right now. I'd like to know if he saw anything else out there on Copper Peak Road. Maybe something he forgot to tell the county police."

"Then what?"

"Then I come back here and keep dialing Bernie's number. Bad news. It goes with the badge."

"I'll check with you later."

"Why the airport?" he asked.

It proved he was listening. But by then the phone was already halfway to the hook.

The doorman at the Arnold Hotel wore a green and gold jacket, green trousers with a gold stripe, and a look on his mug that said he had plenty of pomp no matter what the circumstance. "Your fly's open," I said to him confidentially as I walked past. The color drained from his face but he didn't flinch.

I pushed my way through the revolving doors and looked the place over. The lobby went on as far as the eye could see, which wasn't very far because the joint was a greenhouse of potted and hanging plants. Three salesmen stood together over at one side of the jungle, telling one another jokes that I'd heard before. I recognized two of them—Diamond's men. He was covering all of his bases.

I crossed the lobby without being panhandled, you see what I mean about class, and opened one of the swinging doors to Wicker's Celebrated Bar & Grill.

Wicker's was a long, dark, and narrow room with a high, ornate bar running halfway down one side. It had plenty of cut glass and plenty of—you guessed it—wicker. Wicker tables, wicker chairs, wicker shelves on the wall, wicker seats on the bar stools. I counted the house and stopped when I got to four. Two men sat apart at the bar. Two couples shared a table in the darkness at the rear of the room. Another man sat alone at a table to my left. Obviously I stopped counting too soon. But it didn't matter. Business was slow. And the clientele didn't include any has-been artists with itchy .38s.

"Make it a double," I said to the bartender when he walked over. I pointed to one of the bottles behind him. "I'll need some food to accompany it. Then I'll need something to wash it down."

"It's been like that all summer," he laughed.

He was a big guy, well-balanced, deft movements. He had black curly hair and a dark craggy face with a few reddish pimples left over as a reminder of tough times in front of the mirror as a teenager. He looked like he'd been poured into his black suit and left to harden. When he wanted to get out of it, all he had to do was take a deep breath. It would snap right off. He'd probably worked his way up from bouncer to bartender.

"Also," I added, "I have a question."

"The Yankees," he answered. "They have the horses. Their bullpen's pretty good. They're winners."

"That's not it. Wicker's Celebrated Bar & Grill," I pointed out. "What's celebrated about it?"

'The wicker," he said. "You notice the wicker?" He waved his hand. "We got more wicker here than Tampa, St. Pete, and Miami put together."

"Oh," I confessed. "I thought maybe Harry Gallagher mentioned this joint in his column. That would make it celebrated."

The bartender's face lit up.

"You know Gallagher?" he asked.

"Joe Scruffiato," I declared.

"You *do* know Gallagher. How is that sonofabitch? I miss him."

"We all do."

I introduced myself and gave him a paw. He was glad to meet me.

I told him Gallagher's mind was going, a result of his long confinement, he was becoming forgetful, but his free-throw percentage had improved dramatically. Scruffiato drank it up. He knotted his face into a grimace of concern. He liked Harry Gallagher because Harry Gallagher was famous. Joe Scruffiato put one giant hairy hand down on the bar in front of me, put one foot on something under the bar, took a deep breath, nearly popped a button on his white shirt, and started telling Harry Gallagher stories. He was very earnest.

I finally had to remind him that I was still waiting for my first meal of the day, if you didn't count the black olives, and the day was going fast. He got the idea. By the time he came back from the kitchen with my supper, something with green peppers around the edges and a side order of onion rings, the joint was starting to fill up. Joe Scruffiato got busy and left me alone. I voted for that. I didn't want to marry him, he wasn't my type. I just wanted him to remember me.

People wandered in and out of Wicker's, anonymous faces, laughing young women. Some of them even ordered food, not realizing that the bar was more celebrated than the grill. One of Diamond's men came in and sat next to me. He had a quick beer, said nothing, and left.

I had plenty of time to think it over; what bothered me was the Berlinetta, and I decided it was too easy. The man of glass was one thing. The Berlinetta was another. He'd made it so easy a schoolboy could figure it out and I didn't like it.

Two hours later, when I called it quits, I left Joe Scruffiato a tip that cleared up his complexion. He remembered me.

I crossed the lobby and used one of the phones by the bank of glass-walled elevators. Diamond answered on the first ring again. Obviously he was getting jumpy.

"You were right," he said. "The kid's positive. It was a Berlinetta. He's got a picture of one on the wall above his desk, with all the centerfolds. He drives a Volkswagen himself, but a guy can dream, can't he? That's all he knew. I talked to Rococco."

Diamond paused a moment, waiting for me to say something. I did.

"How'd he take it?"

"A half hour ago. At his apartment. He'd just walked in."

"How'd he take it?"

"He's catching the first plane out of New York in the morning. He'll be here in the morning. Early."

"How'd he take it?"

Diamond's voice thickened. "He started to cry. Nick?"

"Yes."

"This is a lousy business. I'm going to quit."

"What about Canetti?"

"Yeah. Canetti was right, too. I locked him in a room with a videotape machine and the vice squad's tape collection. He just came up for air. Listen to this." I could hear Diamond shuffling through some papers on his desk. "*Swinging in the Rain,*" he finally said. "*Bum Rap. Sweet Roll and Coffee. Over Easy. Godiva Was No Lady. Made in Japan. Charity Begins at Home.* He's a star, all right. The guy was in seven of those little movies. The trouble is, he used four different names. Probably all phony. I don't know. The county might beat me to it. I put through the forms. I went through the motions. I'm

**161**

checking each of the names out. But I won't get anything tonight. It's too late. Normal people are all home in bed. There's only one thing I want to know."

Diamond's voice grew grim.

"What the hell was Suzy doing with him?"

"Go home, Lew. Get some sleep."

"Yeah," he agreed. "I'll be here for a couple hours. Just in case."

His voice trailed off as he hung up the phone.

I was at the airport twenty minutes later, walking across the fluorescent, antiseptic lobby toward the gaudy booth of Vegas Rentacars. I knew it was going to be easy. Too easy.

The young man at the counter squinted at me.

"You need glasses," I said. "I need a car."

"Stutz Bearcat. Alfa-Romeo. Isotta-Fraschini. Deusey," he droned. "Have we got a car for you. Vegas puts the fun back in renting a car."

"Berlinetta," I suggested.

The kid's hand went to his tie. He wiggled the knot.

"We've got one. But it's out," he said.

"When was it rented?"

He reached for the file box on the left side of the little counter and started going through it. He finally found what he was looking for—a yellow form. He pulled it out and laid it on the countertop.

"I'm sorry," he said. "It's not out. It's in. But it's in the garage." He shook his head. "Sorry."

"When was it rented?" I repeated.

He squinted at the yellow sheet.

"Ten o'clock this morning."

"When was it returned?"

The kid looked up at me, startled. "You a cop or something?"

"Something."

"Three-thirty this afternoon," he gulped. "I don't know what the problem was. Wait—left front fender." He looked up at me. "It's funny the way people treat these cars. Last month a guy ran the Stutz into a telephone pole."

"You've only got one Berlinetta?"

"The garage has it," he corrected me.

"Where else can I rent one?"

"You're looking at it. Unless some cowboy up in Aspen has one."

"Who wrecked yours?"

"Insurance covers it," he said. "Insurance covers everything." He squinted at the form in front of him. "Can't make it out." He turned the sheet around so I could see it, and put his finger on the line at the bottom.

It was all carbon, blue and scratchy, but I could make it out because I'd seen the name before. And I didn't even have to squint.

The Berlinetta had been rented by someone named Bradley Saltonstall.

# 19

It didn't end with a bang. It ended with a gentle northwest wind and a slow rain falling in the night. The heat wave was over. Whatever had been bottled up all summer and gnawing at people's lives—grief, guilt, greed, helplessness—was dissolving in the darkness.

It's the way the world works. Everything has its season.

I took the long way home from the airport, thinking about Bernie Rococco and the Berlinetta and the good old soldiers who had come to market a day early. Even a dead man. They were all dead men in a way—trapped in their own dry season, propped up against one another like dry sticks.

Everyone had lost something he would never get back again.

The Berlinetta I could handle. It was an old trick, I'd used it dozens of times myself, I saw through it right away. Bernie Rococco was another story. He was a long way away, holed up in his fashionable New York apartment. The man someone had tried three times to kill, but couldn't. The man who laughed everything off, because he was so brave and good. I wondered what he was thinking. I wondered whether he already missed Suzanne and whether it mattered and why he cried.

There was more than one way to kill a man, and the man of glass knew it. He was the true survivor of a war that had nothing to do with war. It had to do with life.

The streets were all but empty. I drove slowly. Here and there I saw young couples walking along the sidewalks, faces turned up to the gentle rain, ready to embrace whatever the darkness would bring. They held hands. They seemed happy.

But the windshield wipers were a metronome to murder.

I wondered about the others, the men I'd never met—Ted Richter, Louis Lemaire, Anthony O. Nevada, Sty McDonald. Survivors. But of what? Maybe they were all men of glass.

They were invisible. They were figments of someone's fear. I could see right through them and I didn't like what I saw: Dominick Iceone, Peter DeHooch, a kind of darkness that never lifted from the soul, a man dying on my front steps with half his face blown away.

Saltonstall was right, something he'd told me in that telephone call in the middle of the night when time was running out and it was already too late. It was only a small confession, but it came from a man who never made a mistake: he had overestimated the power of guilt.

That was his mistake.

I had the feeling, somewhere along the back of my neck, that she'd be waiting.

Delgany Street was dark and empty, except for the fluorescent glow of the Pee Wee Lounge down at the other end of the block. They still hadn't fixed the sign. Part of the tubing was still burned out. The pavement glistened in the soft rain. I parked the car, killed the engine, got out, locked up, walked across the street, and went quickly up the steps. I was reaching back into my pocket for the keys when the voice behind me said:

"Caine."

I took one step to the right and spun around. The orange glow from the streetlight at the corner glanced off the steady barrel of the Margolin Special.

"Caine!" she said again.

This time there was a little jump to it, as though she was surprised. She was surprised. I could see it in her sleepy violet eyes. They were opened wide and they were fixed on the barrel of the gun. She stood on the sidewalk, at the bottom of the steps, and I suddenly realized she had come out of the dark alley alongside the building. She was dressed for a heat wave—a light blue cotton blouse that had darkened to match her eyes, a pair of jeans, open sandals, a thin beige coat that was soaked through from the rain. Her hair was wet and fell in knots and dark curls alongside her face. It gave her a slightly drowned look.

She was shivering.

"I should put my hands up?"

Her eyes narrowed. They flashed with something close to anger, but not quite. She was only shivering on the outside. Inside, she was still the same Barbara Sinclair. I slid the Margolin Special back into my jacket and changed my tune.

"Hello," I declared. "Are you busy tonight? Your place or mine? What's your sign? Any more at home like you? What's a nice girl like you doing on a street like this? Lovely weather. Nice legs. Now or later? Bryn Mawr or Barnard? Horizontal or vertical? Hi, there."

"Get lost, Caine," she snapped.

"You're the one who looks lost."

"You said if I changed my mind—" She left it unfinished. I didn't remember saying it.

"Sorry."

"I haven't changed my mind," she said forcefully. "But—"

She left that unfinished, too. There was something strong and confident in her face, a certain force of character that I'd seen the day before when she'd stood beside my rented car on the Coast Highway and looked into the dying California sun and told me she was going to cast her lot with Max Sinclair. But her eyes were trapdoors to trouble.

I unlocked the door and pushed it open.

She came up the steps quickly and walked past me into the

darkened house. Her hair smelled rich and clean, as though it were already spring. It wasn't. And I knew it. I shut the door behind us, turned the lock, flipped the lights on, and gave her a good close look.

Her chin was up. Her high cheekbones glistened. It dawned on me that there was probably Indian blood in her veins. Her lips trembled. She was chilled to the bone.

"You could have done that yesterday, couldn't you?" she asked softly. She wasn't looking for an answer. She already had it.

"Pulled the gun on him," she said to herself. "Just that fast. You could have killed him."

She followed me up the stairs at the end of the hall. I showed her where the bathroom was and I warned her about the water. "Count to a hundred," I said, "it'll be luke. If you're lucky. Two hundred might get you warm." I found some dry clothes in one of the spare bedrooms—there were plenty of spare bedrooms in the old house on Delgany Street—and I left them in a neat pile on the floor outside the bathroom door. I could hear the water running. If she was counting, she was up to about a hundred and fifty.

Then I went downstairs, turned on the stove under the teakettle, and tried the telephone. It worked.

"Diamond," he croaked. His voice told me how tired he was.

"Caine," I observed.

"I'm going, I'm going," he said quickly. "You're right. Nothing can be done. Everyone's home in bed. I need some sleep. Don't worry, I'm going—"

"I found the Berlinetta."

He was silent a moment. He was collecting his thoughts. It made a nice collection.

"Vegas Rentacar?" he asked finally.

I confirmed it.

"I figured it out," Dr. Lew Diamond announced. "After you hung up on me. It's the only place in town you can rent a car like that. I'll send a couple of boys over."

"It's in their garage, Lew. Banged up a bit. I told you it was too damn easy."

"Too *easy*?" he sputtered. "*I* figured it out. Nothing easy about it."

"It's a setup," I explained. "Whoever took the Berlinetta wanted to make sure we knew it. He wanted to make sure we found it. I suppose you'd like to know who rented it?"

"I'll have the boys find out."

"Someone who wanted us to think that Bradley Saltonstall is still alive."

Diamond considered it.

"Saltonstall signed the papers?" he asked.

"Somebody did. Saltonstall's dead."

"Maybe not."

"He's dead, Lew."

"Yeah. Maybe. Maybe not. Hard for a dead man to stay on the right side of the road. I think I'll just hang around here for a little while yet. See what they come up with. Prints, maybe."

I hung up. I looked at the phone for a long time after I hung up. I didn't want to think about it.

I didn't have to. Not right then. When Barbara Sinclair came back downstairs, the red and black wool shirt reached to her knees. The khaki pants were rolled up around her ankles. She was barefooted. She wasn't cold anymore. She looked like a clown in some sad circus. A very beautiful clown.

She gravitated to the recliner, spotted the wool blanket, and covered herself with it. Her feet found a warm spot. She rested her forearms on her knees and tucked them under her chin. Then she noticed the steaming mug I'd placed on the table next to the chair.

"Hot chocolate?"

"Somewhat stronger."

She sipped it. Her eyes lit up.

"You're very hospitable, Caine. Except for your gangster tendency to wave that big gun at innocent people. I think I've finally warmed up. At least I've stopped shaking. I was out there for about an hour in the rain. I waited in the cab for a while, but the meter kept running. I was afraid I was going to run out of money. This is a nice house, by the way. Big. And old. I love old houses. You had a visitor."

"A visitor?"

"Yes. A funny little man in a long gray overcoat. I don't think he saw me. I was in the alley. I stayed in the shadows. He pounded on the door, nobody answered, he left."

She smiled, and brushed the hair back from the side of her face. The smile didn't affect her eyes. They were still troubled.

"Caine?"

"Yes."

"Somebody's trying to blackmail my father."

She waited for it to sink in. It didn't take very long.

"What makes you think so?"

She leaned forward. "Does the name Richter mean anything to you?"

"Ted Richter?"

"Maybe so. I don't know. But he called my father last night, a couple hours after you left. I took the call. I was in the kitchen doing dishes. Father wouldn't come to the phone—not at first. He was downstairs in his little gym, working out. Caine, I know it's foolish the way he acted—holding that pistol on you and shooting at the door. But he's not well." She paused a moment. She knew I didn't buy it. "He calls it exercising," she said finally. "I call it exorcising. I don't know what ghosts he has. I'm sure his second wife is one of them. I think Mr. Richter is one of them, too. I told Mr. Richter that Father couldn't come to the phone, but he told me—Mr. Richter said I should tell Father that the man of glass was calling, and wanted desperately to talk to him. That's what he said. Desperately."

"The man of glass?"

She nodded. Her jaw was set firmly. "Yes. Then he laughed—sort of chuckled to himself. When I told Father, he came upstairs right away. He came right to the phone. He looked terrible. He waved me away—he wanted privacy—so I went outside."

"Did you hear any of the conversation?"

"Only the beginning. Father took the phone from my hand and said hello. The man must have said something, because Father said, 'Richter?' By then I was on my way outside."

"The man on the phone didn't identify himself?"

"No. Not to me. Except to say he was the man of glass."

"It could have been anyone," I said. "He could have said Richter died. Richter's daughter married the center for UCLA. The IRS finally caught up with Richter. Richter?"

Barbara Sinclair lowered her eyes.

"I see what you mean," she said. "It could have been anyone."

"Including Richter. You heard nothing else?"

"No," she said softly. "I didn't try to listen. The conversation was very short. Perhaps two or three minutes. I don't think Father said much. He listened. When he came to the door and called me in, the phone was on the hook. He said he was flying here today. Which we did. We got in around noon. He was very upset, I could see that. He didn't object when I told him I was coming with him. He's right at the edge, Caine. I *had* to come with him. He's got no one else."

"Why is he here?"

Barbara Sinclair pulled her hands apart and tugged the blanket up to her chin. Maybe I was wrong. Maybe she was still cold. I heard a car cruise slowly down Delgany Street and made a note of it. I didn't like it. I didn't like the way things were turning out. Max Sinclair was a sick old man, a stick of dynamite primed and ready to be detonated, and somebody knew it. Not necessarily Ted Richter.

"That's the funny thing," Barbara said. "I asked him the very same question. Why? At first he said business. But it was almost like it—slipped out. He seemed surprised by it. Then he said it wasn't business at all, it was a reunion of his old

Army buddies. That's why I think he's being blackmailed. Or *something*! He never leaves home. He doesn't *care* about any old Army buddies. And he sold out. Isn't that what he said? He's out of it. But something made him come here. Something that man said on the telephone last night. I knew I had to come, too. Caine?"

"Yes."

"I care about the old guy. He's in some kind of trouble. I want to know what it is. Caine? It's funny. I trust you. I don't know why. I think it's—I think it's because you didn't kill him, Caine. He tried to kill you. Will you help me?"

She said it very slowly.

I didn't answer. I looked at her. Then I got up and went into the kitchen. I poured another cup of something somewhat stronger than hot chocolate for her, and brewed a cup of tea for myself, and thought about it. Barbara Sinclair carried the past around on her back, too. The past that said she had to care about a man who was beyond caring about. I knew the feeling. I had one of those monkeys on my back myself.

I was on my way back into the other room when there was a loud and persistent knock on the front door. Whoever it was, was in a hurry. He waited a moment and then started in again. He could have rung the bell, if there was a bell, which there wasn't, and he didn't.

"Caine!" Barbara said in a small voice from the study.

I put the mugs down on the counter, placed a finger to my lips, and reached for my jacket. It was heavy. I slipped it on, headed down the hallway toward the front of the house, and pulled open the door. I had one hand inside the jacket, fingering the cool steel handle of the Margolin Special. I didn't need it.

"I'm Square. You're Caine. You keep odd hours, Caine. So do I. Call me Harold."

"Okay, Harold."

He was an old guy, he needed a shave, he chewed on the stub of a cigar, and he was wearing a long gray overcoat that his grandfather must have slept in at Waterloo. It had stopped raining.

"Here's the goods," he said gruffly. He thrust a large manila envelope toward me. I took it.

"Send me a bill," I advised.

He grabbed the package out of my hand.

"Send me a check, pal." The cigar did a little dance along his lower lip.

I dug down into my pants pocket, pulled out some bills, and paid him off. He seemed to appreciate it. The package of photographs went under his arm, he counted the bills with one hand, liked what he saw, jammed them into his overcoat pocket, and handed over the package again.

"You understand. I'm a businessman," he said. "It's nothing personal."

"Did you get all of them?"

"All except Rococco. He ain't here. At least he ain't checked in at the Arnold yet. Don't worry. I'll nail him. He's from New York, right? He'll stop and pose, unless he's keeping company with company he shouldn't keep. Follow?" He winked. "I already know where they're gonna put him. Room one-seventeen. One thing I got to mention, Caine. Watch out for this guy Richter. Gray hair. Brushcut. Looks mean as a rat with his tail in a trap. I had to chase him outside. The sonofabitch took a swing at me."

"I'll remember that, Square."

"Call me Harold. You don't know it, but the wife and me, we honeymooned at the Arnold. Forty-two years ago."

He peered past me into the empty hallway.

"You don't want to come in," I stated.

"Naw. No thanks, Caine. Just checking the light. I never drink while I'm working."

He suddenly flipped back the left side of his overcoat, whipped an old black Speed Graphic camera up to his eye, it looked like it weighed about forty pounds, and snapped. The flash went off in my face.

"Never know when I'll need that," he said.

He turned and went down the stairs toward his car, leaving only the faint aroma of a stale cigar.

I stood in the doorway and thumbed through the glossy photographs. They were all there: Richter, Lemaire, Sty McDonald, Nevada, Max Sinclair. Only the sixth man was missing. The background of bare walls and carpeted hallways told me that all the photographs had been made at the hotel except one. Ted Richter was turned halfway around at a streetcorner, snarling at the lens. Behind him a group of kids were standing at the curb with portable radios pressed to their ears. They were a blur. Other people were crossing the street behind them, heads turned toward the photographer.

In this racket, you never know what your advantage is. You take what you can get. What Harold Square got were the faces of a bunch of heroes who'd gone over the hill and never come back. And they didn't have mine. I stuffed the prints back into the envelope, closed the door, locked it, and returned to the kitchen. I left the envelope on the counter and went back into the study with my hands full.

Barbara Sinclair was still there, curled up in the big recliner, watching me with those quiet violet eyes. They held the same question.

"Yes," I answered. "No promises. I need someone on the inside. You're going to need someone with a gangster tendency to wave a gun at innocent people."

She smiled. It was enough.

It was long after midnight when we finished talking. The rain had started to fall again, harder than before. The wind had picked up.

We covered the ground we'd been over before: her father's career, Georgia Sinclair's death, Max Sinclair's search for oblivion, the sudden trip to Denver. She looked through the photographs and recognized only one face: her father's. They'd been given separate rooms at the Arnold Hotel, on opposite ends of the second floor. She hadn't seen Max since about a half hour after they checked in. They were supposed to have met for dinner. Max never showed. Barbara went down the block, found a Bar None Beefburger joint, and tried to enjoy being alone. When she went back to her room she was still alone and wasn't enjoying it. Her father's room was empty. That was when she decided to obey her instincts and head for Delgany Street. She had good instincts.

"I can call a cab, or I can drive you back," I said.

She bunched up the blanket and dropped it on the floor next to the chair.

"Like this?"

The shirt still came to her knees. The pants legs were still rolled up around her ankles. She was still barefooted. A clown in a sad circus.

"Or," I said, "there's a spare bedroom upstairs."

"There are nine spare bedrooms upstairs," she corrected me. "I counted them."

A half hour later I was lying alone in bed. The house was quiet. I left the drapes in the bedroom open. A smudge of orange light hit the far wall, from the streetlight at the corner. The rain drummed on the roof over my head. It streamed down the window. In the darkness, I could feel the earth turning, the slow erosion of rock and water, my own hesitant progress through the long, blind night. What once was true, no longer is.

Her footsteps in the hallway were very quiet.

She stood a moment in the doorway, and then crossed silently toward me.

"Caine?"

"Yes."

"Don't think I'm being grateful."

"Of course not. You're a very unusual woman."

"In what way, Caine?"

"That's a good question," I said. "Let's find out."

# 20

"Caine?"

"Yes."

"Are you awake?"

"Yes."

She ran her fingers gently across my chest, tracing something she alone saw.

"You're a very unusual man, Caine."

"In what way?"

"That's a good question," she whispered. "Let's find out—again."

It was morning. The rain had stopped during the night. From the window I could see that the sky was like stretched muslin: taut, off-white, soiled by the remembrance of a summer filled with yellow dust. A few gray and sullen clouds were belly-up along the horizon. It was going to be the kind of day in which everything turned its own particular shade of gray.

An hour later it was still morning. The sky was brighter. But I wasn't paying attention. I was looking up into the sleepy violet eyes of Barbara Sinclair.

"Caine?"

"Yes."

"What do you think will happen to him?"

"It'll catch up with him."

"What will?"

"The ghosts. They always do."

"I hope not. He never hurt anyone in his life. It woke me up."

"What did?"

"The silence. It stopped raining. About three o'clock."

"I didn't hear it."

"You were asleep."

"Sorry."

"Poor boy." Her face slowly descended toward mine.

"Caine?"

"You have my attention."

"I was wondering—"

"Yes?"

"Whose car was that parked across the street at three o'clock?"

"What kind of car?"

"Black. A Cadillac."

"Her name is Snow White. She works the Pee Wee now and then. It's her office."

"What an unusual neighborhood. I'm not surprised."

"Neither am I."

"You're supposed to ask why." She pressed a fingertip into the cleft in my chin and started to fool around.

"Why?"

"Because you're a very unusual man."

"Sorry. I heard that one before."

"Caine?"

"Yes."

"I mean it. Do you remember the question?"

She reminded me.

An hour later it was still morning. The high clouds were starting to break up. I could see faint patches of blue through the upper half of the window. Barbara Sinclair's head was resting gently on my chest. Her hair was like silk. Her bare foot was doing something interesting to my legs.

Maybe there was something to it after all. He would give me the answer. And let me try to find the question.

"Caine?"

"Yes."

"Why do you have so many bedrooms in this house?"

"People tell me I'm hospitable. Except for certain gangster habits."

"Do you know the phone's been ringing for the past hour?"

"Ignore it. It'll go away."

"It could be important."

"Forget it. Close the door if you wish. I have enough storm windows. The basement's full of storm windows. Hell, I don't need any more storm windows."

"Caine?"

"Yes."

"Do you always sleep with the drapes pulled back from the window like that? And the curtains pulled back?"

"Yes."

"Why?"

I couldn't tell her. When you live half your life in a place without windows, you appreciate windows.

"I think it's unusual," she said.

"I don't think it's so unusual."

"I think it's unusual."

"I don't think it's unusual."

"I think it's unusual," she persisted. She started to laugh, and looked at me expectantly.

"In what way?" I asked.

"Good question, Caine. Let's find out."

An hour later it was still morning. I glanced at the window. The sky was scrubbed clean. It was brilliant, an innocent blue. Barbara Sinclair was sprawled carelessly on her back. Her head was on my shoulder. Somehow she'd managed to get both sheets and the blanket wadded up on the floor beside

177

the bed. She must have been double-jointed. The telephone resumed its insistent ringing downstairs, pleading for an answer.

The answer was Roger Penrod. The answer was Bradley Saltonstall III. The answer was Suzanne Leeds. The answer was the man of glass. That much was easy.

"Caine?"

"Yes."

"I'm glad I came."

"Likewise."

"Who's the man of glass? What does it mean?"

"Don't you know?"

"No. Do you?"

"Yes. I think so."

"Can't you tell me?"

"No."

"Does it have to do with Max?"

"It has to do with everyone."

She rolled over. Her hair brushed against my face like a thought that had flickered a moment and couldn't be caught. She was a happy accident at the end of a bad summer, a pliable hope at the end of a long dry spell. She knew about the darkness but she fought against it in the only way she knew. With life. With light.

"Caine?"

"Yes?"

"That's some scar. Where'd you get it?"

She traced her fingers across my chest again.

"Along the way."

"War?" she asked.

"Along the way."

"That's it? Along the way?"

"Yes."

"You're a very unusual man, Caine."

I closed my eyes.

"Don't you remember the question, Caine?"

She placed her thumbs gently on my eyes and forced them open. I looked up at her face. Her sleepy violet eyes weren't very sleepy at all.

"Caine?"

"Yes."

"What is the question?"

"Not that unusual."

"You're avoiding the question."

"Not that unusual," I begged.

"Want to bet?"

She started to laugh. I started to laugh. That made two of us. The phone was ringing again, far away. She had closed the door. We ignored it. Light filled the room from the window. The phone stopped abruptly. Silence flooded over us. I listened to the sharp ebb and flow of her breathing. It sounded good.

The darkness was gone.

There were plenty of answers. But there was only one question.

The question was Bernie Rococco.

An hour later it was still morning. I'd showered, shaved, answered the phone, made breakfast, driven her back to the Arnold Hotel, and found my way unassisted to Room 117. I'm good with numbers. Very unusual in my own way.

The light was blinding. It came in through the big double windows, bounced off the white walls, and slapped him square in the face. I looked at him.

He was wearing a Palm Springs suit, a Palm Springs hat, a Palm Springs tan, and tears in his eyes. His name was Bernie Rococco and I was very pleased to meet him. Slick black hair, fleshy round face, a rough nose that looked like it had gone through the meat grinder and been patted back together again. It matched his silk burgundy shirt. In color, not texture. He put some kind of pill on his tongue and washed it down with something very fancy. One of his eyes had a very slight tic—it didn't ruin his looks, he was nothing to write home about to begin with, but it was enough to tell me he was wound up tight as a spring and under tension, and he didn't look like he could do very much about it at the moment. Maybe the pill would help.

He looked wearily from Dr. Lew Diamond to me and then back to Lew Diamond. He screwed the good eye shut and let the other one twitch. His face dropped into his hands again.

"I'm sorry," he sobbed.

"That's okay," Diamond said.

"I'm very sorry."

"That's all right."

Diamond walked over to the window and stood next to me. I glanced over at him. His face told me nothing except that he'd gone without sleep for a long time.

Rococco's hands waved helplessly in the air. "She was a beautiful woman," he sobbed. "I loved her. She was my dumpling. My valentine. She was the girl of my dreams. My plum pie—"

"That's okay," Diamond said to the window. "You can take your hat off, Rococco."

Rococco yanked a maroon handkerchief from his shirt pocket and covered his nose. It was a real large handkerchief. He made a loud, obnoxious noise, like something coming out of a whipped-cream can when there was no whipped cream left. He closed his fist around the handkerchief and jammed it back into his shirt pocket.

I counted the rings on his fingers. Six. All gold.

"Take your time. Control yourself," Diamond said. "Can you talk?"

Rococco's head wobbled. He made a little squealing noise, like a pig. The small room was oppressive with the scent of bay rum. It emanated from Bernie Rococco like heat waves from a potbellied stove. His leather valise, very expensive, lay opened on the bed. A pearl-handled revolver lay in plain sight atop a neat little stack of maroon boxer shorts.

I looked closely at Rococco. He didn't look color-coded to me, but he was.

Diamond turned away from the bright light of the window. "We've already been through most of it," he said to me. "Before you came."

"But you haven't found the Berlinetta?" Rococco interrupted. He sniffled.

"No. I told you we've had no luck along that line," Diamond said abruptly. He looked at me again. "He wanted you here. Apparently his wife had some kindly feelings about you."

"Yes," Rococco agreed. "I feel as though I know both of you personally. Suzanne spoke to me about both of you."

"Both of us?" Diamond said. He cleared his throat.

"I talked to her every day," he said. He stiffened in his chair. There were still tears on his cheeks, but he had the bad eye under control. "I'm sorry my emotions got the better of me. I've been through worse than this. Believe me. You're not seeing me under the best circumstances."

"You talked to her every day?" Diamond asked.

"Yes. I called her from New York."

"Did you call her yesterday?"

"Yes. From New York."

Diamond spun around. "Where the hell else would you call from? Peoria?"

Rococco winced.

"I'm sorry," Diamond said.

"That's okay," Rococco answered.

"What did she tell you?"

"She said she loved me." He sniffled.

"Did she tell you about receiving another call earlier? From an unidentified male, informing her that there was some information to be had about yourself?"

"Yes."

"Who was this man?"

"I don't know."

181

"What sort of information could he have had about you?"

"I don't know that either."

"Could it have been detrimental?"

"Detrimental? I don't understand the question."

"Detrimental is like shit, Rococco." Diamond peered down his nose at the man in the chair. "Do you know what shit is?"

Rococco looked away a moment. "I know what shit is," he said. He raised his head and stared straight at Diamond.

"You're ducking the question, Rococco."

"I don't understand the question, Diamond."

"Wait a minute," I suggested.

Something cold and hard had come into Bernie Rococco's voice. I glanced at Dr. Lew Diamond. Something cold and hard had come into Diamond's face. They were even.

There was silence in the room.

"You told her not to go?" Diamond asked finally.

"She said the man wanted to see her. Yes. I told her not to go."

"What were you afraid of?"

"Afraid?"

"Afraid is like fear, Rococco."

There was more silence in the room.

"She was a wonderful girl," Rococco said. His voice was thick. "Much younger than I am, a lovely girl, but she adored me. She doted on me. And she was afraid for me. I was afraid for her. I admit it. That's why I told her not to go. I'm an emotional man, but that's an emotion I don't often feel. Fear. She told you about the man of glass? Of course she did. She knew how I felt about it. She knew my dreams of—I've dreamt of vengeance. I admit it. There are some things a man can't forget, Diamond. That's one of them. Cowardice by itself is a sickness. Cowardice that takes the lives of others—that's murder."

Rococco was riding the silences like they were a roller coaster.

"This was no accident, no matter how it might appear," he said. "It was murder. She was murdered. He tried to kill me three times, and failed. So he killed *her*. Don't you see? He tried to get me through *her*. The man of glass."

Rococco's big brown eyes swam in a sea of pink. He looked first at Diamond, then at me.

"Find him," he said. "I want you to find him. Tell me his name. I don't want him arrested. All I want is his name. From there, I'll do what needs to be done. These were the bravest bunch of boys I ever knew. All except one. I want to know who he is. I know this is against regulations, but I'm ready to make it worth your while. Both of you."

"This is obviously against regulations," Diamond declared.

"How much worth my while?" I added.

"Ten thousand dollars, Mr. Caine."

"This is against regulations," Diamond repeated. "You're trying to buy private vengeance. You're circumventing the process of law. You're attempting to bribe—"

"As I understand it," Rococco said coldly, "Caine here has no regulations. I'm offering a reward for certain information. I'm willing to pay for it. All I need is a name. The name of the man of glass. You know about tomorrow's reunion. I need that name by tomorrow. He's going to be here. Right here in this hotel."

"This is against regulations," Diamond said. "Take your hat off. I have some questions."

Rococco smiled at me.

"Mr. Caine?"

"No," Diamond insisted.

There was a quizzical look on Rococco's puss. "Caine appreciates the value of money," he said. "I see it in his eyes. Most people dream of wealth, but they know nothing of stakes and gambles. They lack—courage. Caine? My main business is futures. I play the market. I put my money where my dreams are. You look like a man with a future."

"Who is Dominick Iceone?" Diamond asked sharply.

I watched Rococco. He blinked. His face was like a lightbulb that suddenly went out. The smile melted away.

"Wait a minute," I suggested.

I could feel it coming. Dr. Lew Diamond didn't like Bernard Rococco. Bernard Rococco didn't like Dr. Lew Diamond. Neither one of them was very good at keeping it a secret.

"Iceone's a pal of yours?" Diamond asked. "Take your hat off."

"No pal of mine," Rococco said softly. "If you're interested in Mr. Iceone, why don't you check with the attorney general, State of New York? You're not interested in finding the man of glass. That's obvious. You're not interested in ten thousand dollars. That's obvious. You should have plenty of time to pursue your other interests."

Bernie Rococco was trying to be agreeable. The sneer on his face showed just how agreeable he was trying to be.

"I *have* checked with the attorney general, State of New York," Diamond said drily. "This morning."

Rococco's thick eyebrows did a half-gainer and never did hit the water. They stuck in the up position.

"Iceone is a crumb," Diamond said. "He's a criminal. Do I need to refresh your memory? Take your hat off."

"Scum," Rococco said. "He's scum. But Mr. Iceone has no criminal record that I know of."

"A lot of criminals have no record," Diamond answered. "Look around you."

He hesitated a moment.

"I don't mean *immediately* around you," he added quickly. "I mean look around." Dr. Lew Diamond's long neck was turning red. He glared at Rococco. "Iceone was a principal in the founding of Seven Sisters Productions. Along with yourself, and Mr. Sinclair, and Mr. McDonald, and Mr. Lemaire, and Mr. Richter, and Mr. Anthony O. Nevada. Does that refresh your memory, Bernie? Dominick Iceone is your partner."

"Former partner," Rococco said sourly. "Former principal. I told you, he's scum."

Diamond began to pace nervously up and down along the little patch of carpeting between Bernie Rococco and the bed.

"What *is* Seven Sisters Productions, Bernie?"

Rococco smiled. "I've just lost my wife. What's the purpose of this?"

Diamond stopped in his tracks and spun around. His back was to the window. His arms were folded tightly across his chest. He answered his own question: "Pornography. Seven Sisters. Who is Toby Kinser, Bernie? Also known as Tod Kinsey? Also known as Jack Rabbitt? Also known as Harry Rock. Also known by a dozen other names. A pal of yours? Or is he scum, too? Wait a minute—if he's a pal of yours, he's automatically scum."

Rococco's head wobbled again. "Never heard of him. By any means—I mean, by any name."

The redness in Diamond's neck was flooding upward toward his scalp. His fingers had ambitions. They wanted to become fists.

"Take off that goddamned hat!" Diamond barked.

Rococco didn't move.

"Wait a second," I proposed again.

I had to hand it to Lew Diamond. He'd been up all night, he never did get away from his desk, and he hadn't spent all his time eating Bar None Beefburgers. He'd hit some pay dirt. If it wasn't pay dirt, at least it was dirt. Of course, he also had a vested interest in Suzanne Leeds. He knew it and I knew it, even if Bernie Rococco didn't know it, and it looked to me like maybe Bernie Rococco did know it.

Dr. Lew Diamond glared at Rococco.

"Toby Kinser," he said, "was the man with Suzanne when she took that detour on Copper Peak Road at twenty minutes past one yesterday afternoon. What were you trying to do, Bernie? Drag her down in the mud with you? You wanted her to crawl in the slime, too? Is that it? You wanted her to—"

I stepped in front of Dr. Lew Diamond and looked back at Rococco. "I've got an idea," I announced. "I haven't mentioned it before, because I didn't want to interfere in police business. But here's my idea: Wait a minute. Calm down. Cool off."

"He's looking for a lawsuit," Rococco said grimly. "He'll

get one." His face was pale. So were his eyes. They looked like they were concentrated on something far away.

"You don't know the man who called Suzanne?" I asked.

"No."

"You have no idea what he wanted?"

"No."

"You don't know where he called from?"

Rococco shook his head.

"You don't know why she went to Copper Peak?"

"No."

"What's the gun for, Bernie? Figure someone's going to steal your underwear?"

He looked up at me, a little surprised.

"I've got a permit. Dick Tracy here saw it. It's clean."

The same gentle smile began to play around the corners of his mouth. I imagine it was there at Anzio, when he looked deep into the darkness from the edge of the Mussolini Canal.

"I'm going to catch me a killer," Rococco said.

"Kiss my Kate!" Diamond snarled. He pushed his way around me and stormed toward the door. On the way, he reached out and flipped Rococco's hat from his head. Bald spot. "All you're gonna catch is your ass in the wringer, Rococco!"

I was at the door myself when Rococco stopped me. His voice was calm and surprisingly pleasant.

"Caine?"

"Yes?"

"She meant everything to me. I want this man's name. Find the Berlinetta. There's five grand in it for you."

I looked at him. His bad eye was twitching again.

I caught up with Lew Diamond at the end of the hall. The veins were standing out at attention from the side of his neck. His teeth were clenched.

"I shouldn't have done that. I know I shouldn't have done that. I don't know why I did that. Why in the name of God did I do that?"

"You shouldn't have done that," I said.

"I know."

"You'll be back on the banquet circuit."

"I know."

"You need some sleep."

Diamond turned his head away from me. He was holding the wall up with one shoulder.

"I look at it this way," he said softly. It was a whisper. "I'm a cop. I gotta work. If Saltonstall's alive, we have to watch out for him. He's a clever sonofabitch. Okay? If Saltonstall's dead, it's a new ballgame. You can take your pick. It's one of the others. One of them rented the Berlinetta and used it to force Suzy off the road and he wants us to find it. I'm with you there, Nick. A hundred percent. What I mean is—don't worry. I'm okay. I can still think straight. If he wants us to find it, it means Saltonstall's dead—"

"We have found it, Lew."

"I know, I know," he said. "I know that."

"No prints?"

He shrugged. "Clean as a whistle. The crime lab boys came up empty. That's the point, Nick. That's why we can't let anyone know we've found it. Don't you see? The man of glass *wants* us to find it. We have to play dumb."

I stared at him.

"How dumb?" I asked.

# 21

Dr. Lew Diamond's face hovered over what appeared to be a plate of scrambled eggs on the bar at Wicker's Celebrated Bar & Grill. I could see he was having second thoughts. He pushed the plate away, reached for the full glass of whisky, and cleared his throat with it. All of it.

"She didn't know," I said. "Suzanne didn't know about Seven Sisters. She had nothing to do with it. She didn't know Bernie was up to his three chins in that kind of stuff."

I hit the nail on the head.

Diamond swiveled around to look at me. His eyes were bleary. "I didn't think so. I don't think she *did* know. You're right." He shook his head sadly. Suddenly he said, "I never touched her, Nick. I'm a cop."

"You should have."

"I did."

The jukebox started up from the back of Wicker's, something slow and full of tears. The joint was almost deserted. A couple of serious late-morning drinkers sat at tables in the back. There was a window there, looking out on the street. Joe Scruffiato was busy minding his own business at the other end of the long bar with a blonde wearing a tight red skirt and white boots. An urban cowgirl, looking for a buckeroo. Two bellboys sat at a table off to the side, chairs turned around, watching the girl with their round, blank faces. They spoke softly to each other in Tex-Mex. They were very polite. They kept their hands in their laps.

Bernie Rococco had done a lot for me. He was the question, all right. He was the question Saltonstall would have wanted me to ask.

Dr. Lew Diamond was another story. His head was down. He stared for a long time at the little ring of water that had been left behind on the top of the bar by the glass of whisky. He slowly reached out his right hand and erased it with his thumb.

If only it were that easy, I thought.

"You were up all night," I declared. "Never went home."

He nodded.

"The old procedure?"

He nodded.

"I wait," he explained. "That's all there is to it. I simply wait."

"There were only seven of them?"

He nodded.

"Saltonstall wasn't in on it?"

"Not Seven Sisters," Diamond said. "But he still found out the war wasn't over. He was a casualty thirty years late."

"Everyone's a casualty," I said.

"Not everyone. Lemaire hasn't lost anything. Richter's in the clear."

"How'd you find Seven Sisters, Lew?"

"They found me," he admitted. "I called Albany. That's where I originally got the sheet on Iceone, the fact that he has no sheet. The usual great police work—I asked them to dig a little deeper. If you ask, sometimes you receive."

"And Kinser?"

"A local boy who made good," Diamond said. "Thank God for Ribs Malone. He's missing something. A brain. I put him on a retainer—ten dollars a day—and the dummy called me back an hour later with a lead on Kinser."

"Ribs works for ten bucks a day?"

"He's nothing but skin and bones. It doesn't take much to fill him up. But I figured he'd milk it for a day or two at least. Maybe three."

"He must be back in the rackets. Stealing cars or something."

"You're absolutely right. We fed Kinser to the computer for breakfast. He had a record. The usual stuff for a rich kid who gets too big for his britches. Petty theft—a sporting goods store, a couple of Jap radios, some recording tape. That sort of thing. The essentials. He was nailed on a couple of assault charges, too—he must have had a temper—but it never went to court. Why bother a judge? His old man's in plastics, you know."

"The county never came through with an ID on him?"

"The county—*au contraire*—the county came in this morning with the prints. Kinser's prints. I had the pleasure of saying, 'Oh? Really?' I called you on that, Nick. Around seven or eight o'clock. I called you on the stuff from Albany, too. Seven Sisters. You didn't answer your phone."

"That's very unusual."

"The hell it is," he laughed.

He stood up and stretched. He was a pillar of the community but I wouldn't describe him as a Rock of Gibraltar. He looked more like a scarecrow with a severe straw problem. His shirt started to pop out of his trousers. His tie was yanked apart. When he sat back down on the wicker barstool, he wasn't quite together. He used both hands and both feet to steady himself. Then he waved to Joe Scruffiato and ordered a ham sandwich on whole wheat with a couple of big dills on the side and a glass of milk and a glass of beer. And in the meantime, another glass of whisky.

"Milk *and* beer?" Scruffiato asked.

"My stomach's upset," Diamond explained.

"Bernie Rococco," he said to me. "What do you think?" He drank only half of the second glass of whisky and left the rest for later.

I told him: "Bernie packs a lady's revolver. I don't like his underwear. I never was big on bay rum. The tears were real. I don't know why, but they were. Also, he wants you to find the Berlinetta."

"I found it," Diamond said. He wasn't listening.

"I'm gonna tell you something, Caine. I'm a sap. I know I'm a sap. But I feel sorry for him. He's vain, right? You noticed the bald spot? I embarrassed him. I feel bad about it. But no matter how you feel about it—let me explain this to you, I'm trying to be subjective, I think he's a *shit*—Bernie's a victim, too. Like the others. Like Max Sinclair and Sty McDonald and Anthony O. Nevada, who, by the way, has a record. I checked it out. A violent man when it comes to police officers. Saltonstall as well. You might as well add Saltonstall. I don't know about the tears, Nick. I'm only an off-duty cop. But Bernie Rococco lost something in this little game, too. No matter how he felt about Suzy, he lost her. Thanks to the man of glass."

"I agree."

Diamond smiled to himself.

"You *are* a sap."

He dropped one foot to the floor with a thud and turned to face me.

"You bet he's lost something," I said. "Five of the Seven Sisters come to the class reunion a day early and they don't bother to invite Bernie? Why not? My guess is that what he's lost is control over Seven Sisters Productions. Or he's in the process of losing control. When Max Sinclair sold out, it wasn't Bernie he sold out to. You saw Bernie. He's in a buying mood. But Sinclair went elsewhere. Maybe the others are going elsewhere, too."

"Iceone?"

"Why not? He's a founding father of Seven Sisters. Bernie kicked him out of bed—or vice versa. Figure it this way, Lew. What can Dominick Iceone get out of control of Seven Sisters Productions? A gold mine. The same goes for Bernie. The same gold mine."

Dr. Lew Diamond's face screwed itself into a snarl. "Then I was right!" He reached for the rest of the whisky and drank it quickly. "He's a sonofabitch!"

"Everything okay?" Scruffiato hollered from down at the end of the bar.

I shrugged. "He says he's going to shoot the place up if he doesn't get his sandwich in the next hour and a half."

Joe Scruffiato jumped off his perch like somebody had turned the current on. He disappeared toward the kitchen. When he came out he was carrying the ham sandwich and the big dills and the glass of milk. He put them on the bar, turned around, drew a glass of beer from the tap, and put it down on the counter in front of Lew Diamond.

Scruffiato looked at me. "He's got a gun?"

"I don't think so. He's just hungry."

"He don't want the eggs?"

"No. He changes his mind real fast."

Diamond was already chewing his way through the ham sandwich.

Joe Scruffiato wiped his hands on a towel. "I wouldn't recommend the milk," he said. "In fact, I definitely advise against it."

"It's his life," I explained.

"Yeah. But I'm the guy that has to clean up."

He took two or three quick steps backward, eyed Dr. Lew Diamond suspiciously, and returned to his post at the end of the bar. I drank the milk myself. Diamond didn't even notice. He was busy.

"The county police were going to check out the lodges on Copper Peak Road," I reminded him.

"Dead end," he croaked. "Nobody saw her."

He shifted his sandwich to the other hand, reached in his jacket, and pulled out a long sheet of paper. It was folded in half. It looked like someone had done the Texas Trot on it with ballpoint pens attached to his toes. Diamond's notes. I recognized his style.

He stared at them and stopped chewing.

"The Abbey—that's where the kid was applying for work. They remembered the kid but they never saw Suzy. You know why? She was never there." He started to chew, then stopped. "Mountain View Ranch is at the other end of Copper Peak Road, where it hits the interstate. They talked to the owner. Someone named Amurao. Mrs. Amurao. Filipino lady. Not good English. She never saw Suzy. You know why? Suzy wasn't there."

Diamond rubbed his face. "I'm tired." He reached for his beer and washed down the rest of the sandwich.

"You know what I think?" he asked. "Where's the milk? I ordered milk. They were somewhere else—out on the interstate somewhere. And he was taking a shortcut to get her back to town for the matinee. Copper Peak Road. They could have been tailed for miles on the interstate. See what I mean? It's a dead end. That's all it is—a dead end. Just like the other lodge up there. Little Bearskin Lodge. Out of business. Been closed down for months. They talked to the caretaker."

He tilted back on his stool, caught himself, and leaned forward. He peered at his notes. He shook his head.

"A guy named DeHooch," he said. He looked into the air, searching. "He never saw Suzy. He never saw the Berlinetta. He never saw the Camaro." Diamond's face wrestled with it but it was no contest. The whisky was getting to him. He held on to the bar with both hands. "You know why, Nick? She was never there. You know what I mean?"

"It's a dead end?"

He stared at me. His eyes started to close. A smile began to inch across his face.

"I'm with you there, Caine. One hundred and ten percent. You really are a clever sonofabitch. That's exactly what it is—nothing but a dead end!"

He started to wobble on the barstool again. I turned him around.

"Where's Canetti?" I said. "What's his number?"

193

# 22

Sergeant Canetti showed up in six and a half minutes, plaid slacks, a solid green shirt, and sunglasses. He walked into Wicker's Celebrated Bar & Grill with the sunglasses in his hand. He was wiping them with his shirt, trying to appear casual.

Dr. Lew Diamond didn't even have to try. He was slumped over toward the bar. His long legs were wrapped around the stool. He was humming a smash Broadway tune that no one had ever heard of.

Canetti sized up the situation right away.

"Drunk and disorderly," he announced. He glanced at his wristwatch to note the time.

"He's not disorderly," I pointed out. "It's a catchy tune."

Canetti put his arm around his boss and helped him off the barstool. Diamond was smiling. He was doing something funny with his lips, and smiling didn't make it any easier. It took me a second, I'm not as quick as Canetti, but I finally figured it out. Diamond was trying to whistle. As Canetti led him out, Diamond kept twisting around in Canetti's arms and looking back at the blonde in the tight red skirt and white boots.

I left a little something on the bar for Joe Scruffiato, it was more than enough, and went outside to help Canetti squeeze Diamond into the front seat of the command car.

I told Canetti across the top of the car:

"Take him home, Canetti. Stay with him, Canetti. Is there a ballgame on TV? Make sure that he sleeps, Canetti."

"I'm sure as hell not going to take him back to headquarters," Canetti said.

Diamond was tapping on the window with his knuckles. I motioned for him to roll down the window—he was in no condition to think of that himself—and he did. I could see how red his eyes were. He shook his head, but his voice still caught in his throat.

"She didn't know, Nick. She had nothing to do with it. She didn't know anything about it."

He was close to tears.

Canetti pulled into traffic with his lights flashing. Diamond's head snapped back. The last I saw of him, he had forced his face to the open window and was looking back at me as Canetti pushed the accelerator to the floor. His mouth was wide open. There was something helpless in his eyes. It had finally caught up with him. He'd lost something he couldn't talk about, he was falling backwards into the darkness, and he couldn't do anything about it.

I'd let go of Bradley Saltonstall long ago. I hadn't known Max Sinclair's bicycling wife. Suzanne Leeds was just another pretty face to me, with a couple of very average gams and a fairy tale for tough guys rattling around in her head—but not to everyone. Not to Dr Lew Diamond.

I didn't have long and I knew it. The reunion was one day away. Suzanne Leeds was one day dead. I had the feeling that Dominick Iceone was getting ready to make his move.

An hour later I shoved the gearshift into second and took the last hundred-yard rise on the yellow dirt road that crossed the flank of Copper Peak Mountain. I didn't have any company, except in the shoulder holster under my arm. I checked the mirror. The window was open. The air was cold.

The entrance to the Abbey Ranch slid past on my left: a ramshackle fence, a wooden sign board, and two well-traveled tracks turning off into the trees. I wasn't interested.

Little Bearskin Lodge was a half-mile up the road: a ramshackle fence, a wooden sign board, and no tracks turning off into the trees. A chain-link fence blocked the entrance. I turned the car around, parked off the road, and went over the fence.

It's a good question, who saw whom first. He came out of a large and rustic redwood cabin half hidden in the trees and started walking down the sandy path toward me.

I didn't like the way he walked.

I didn't like the way he dressed.

I didn't like the way he looked.

He was a short, muscular little man, immaculate, with quick nervous movements and a head that got stuck on the wrong body. His head made him top-heavy. High forehead, blond hair combed straight back, amber aviator glasses that hid his eyes. His skin was so white I figured he spent most of his time in a box on the closet shelf, with a .45 and a few slugs. He looked like a little boy who had grown old before his time, a cretin, a formaldehyde baby. Sunken cheeks, bone, sinew. The closer he got, the less I liked the way he looked. He had nothing to smile about, and he didn't. He looked like he never heard of words. You can tell by the mouth. His was puckered together. It looked like it had been sewn shut. He looked like the kind of guy who communicated with a twist of the lip, a subtle movement of his hand toward the inside of his jacket, a bullet in the face on a summer morning.

I knew in an instant it must be DeHooch.

He pulled off his glasses. There was a little yellow flicker of recognition in his eyes. He remembered me from somewhere. Of course he did. He was the guy who'd followed me from Penrod's house. He was the guy who'd picked up Saltonstall on the morning Penrod was gunned down and tried to finger him at the airport. No wonder he got so close to Penrod. They knew each other. He was Mr. Ice's accountant.

I had an account I wanted to settle.

"Get out of here!" he yelled. "You can't come in here!"

His lips weren't sewn shut after all. They should have been.

He'd started to slip his glasses inside his coat when I gave him my best Sunday smile and a punch of the same persuasion. It caught him square on the side of the face. It didn't hurt as much as the left did, coming up from nowhere and catching him flush on the chin. It snapped his head back. It crossed his eyes and dotted his teeth. It introduced his nose to my right fist, coming back for seconds. They hit it off right away. His little yellow mustache began to fill with blood. His hand came out of his jacket. It was empty. He folded in half. If I'd wanted a counterfeit bill I could have slipped him right in my money pouch. Something told him to stand up straight. It told him wrong. I gave him a left in the rib cage, stepped forward, and connected with another right. I watched the blood spurt from my knuckles and felt sorry for his dry cleaner. His eyes started to close. His head rolled back. I rounded him off to the nearest tenth. He spun around helplessly on the sandy path, arms flopping out from his sides, and I hooked my arm around his neck from behind.

"I'd like to see Mr. Ice," I said politely.

I reached inside his coat, came up with a .45, and stuck it in my back pocket. Then I grabbed one of his arms and had him shake hands with his shoulder blades. His mouth opened wide. He scared the birds right out of the trees.

"Let's go, Tootsie," I advised.

It was good advice. He took it. We moved down the path toward the cabin.

Dominick Iceone stood alone on the porch, looking out through the dark screen. He'd watched the whole thing without moving. He was wearing white shoes, a white suit, and a gray fedora. The gray fedora was so people would know he wasn't all bad. His arms were folded across his chest, and he cupped his pointed chin thoughtfully in one hand. A faint smile played around the corners of his thin lips.

"Mr. Ice," I said.

"Iceone."

I stood corrected.

I encouraged Peter DeHooch to ascend the porch steps, gave him a shove as Iceone reached out to open the screen door, and sent him flying. He found his own level. His level was on the porch floor at the feet of Mr. Ice.

Iceone looked down at him and wrinkled his nose. "Clean yourself up," he said. "You look uncivilized." He stepped carefully over DeHooch's back and went into the cabin. I followed. DeHooch let out another scream. Someone had stepped on his fingers.

The interior of the cabin was a single large room, dominated by a massive fieldstone fireplace and Iceone's big walnut desk, cluttered with papers, mailing envelopes, and stacks of invoices. Rustic furniture lined one wall. Mr. Ice went to an ornate little liquor cabinet in the corner behind his desk and turned around with a glassful of something in his hand.

"Yes?" he said as he placed the glass on the desk.

"No," I said.

He looked at me.

"I don't believe we've met."

"Caine," DeHooch said from the porch doorway. "Nick Caine."

Peter DeHooch had figured out the difference between his hands and his feet, and was standing up. He had both hands on the door frame, making sure it didn't move. I glanced over at him. Mr. Ice was right. DeHooch didn't look very civilized. Not with the blood all over his mouth and shirt.

I ignored him.

"You're a businessman," I told Iceone.

"Yes?"

"So am I. But my business is my business. A man made me a very interesting proposition this morning. I'm open to alternatives. You need help. I've got excellent references." I reached in my back pocket and placed DeHooch's .45 down carefully on the big desk. "There's one of them," I added.

"What kind of help?" Iceone asked cautiously.

"Ask DeHooch."

"What kind of references?"

"DeHooch is my reference."

"I see," Iceone said. "DeHooch is your reference."

He turned his back on me and looked out the window at the afternoon. There was no sound in the room except for the soft whirring of the overhead fan. "Peter," Iceone said finally. "You look pathetic. Go straighten your tie. Change your shirt. I'll call you if I need you."

DeHooch took the hint.

He limped across the room and went through a doorway in the far corner. That left me alone with Iceone.

"I'm very impressed," Iceone said when he turned around. "Peter is an accountant, and a good one. But his talents far exceed the ability to tabulate columns of very large numbers. I've never known anyone to get the jump on him. Much less—"

A broad grin split Iceone's face.

"The drink is for you, Caine," he said. "I abstain."

"No, thanks."

"Yes?" Iceone said. He shook his head. "I should have anticipated as much. I know something about you, Caine. It might interest you. Miss Leeds spoke very highly of you. She spoke a great deal, indeed between tears. About yourself. The man of glass. Her beloved Bernie. She seemed to think that you were going to find this man of glass? Yes?"

He didn't wait for an answer.

"I wish you would," he said. "Her death was a very unfortunate accident, which I assure you I had nothing to do with. It surprised me as much as I'm sure it surprised her. And, of course, it confounded my predicament. Yes? The loss of Kinser is even more unfortunate."

Mr. Ice pulled back his chair and sat down at the desk. He

rested one elbow on a stack of papers and began lightly stroking the line of his lips with his fingers. His eyes didn't leave mine.

"So we have something in common," he said to himself. He reached out and fondled DeHooch's .45. "There's no question about your talents, Mr. Caine. The question is—what sort of assistance do I appear to be in need of?"

"The question is—how much do I know? I told you, my business is my business. Since this morning, your business is my business, too. You want control of Seven Sisters Productions. You have Sinclair. My guess is you have Richter. That makes three. You need one more."

Iceone's eyes narrowed. He locked his hands behind his head.

"Go on," he suggested.

"You'll never get Rococco," I said. "He's a—"

"He's a very florid and tasteless little man," Iceone interrupted.

"He loves you, too. He offered me ten grand to put you on ice."

"Ice?" Iceone's eyes popped open. "Only ten grand?"

"We started at fifteen hundred," I said.

Iceone's feelings were hurt. I could tell by the look on his face. "Fifteen hundred," he muttered to himself. "Marriages for money rarely last."

"You may have a chance with the others. McDonald and Anthony Nevada—they're both down and out. I don't know about Lemaire. But a push in the right direction? It might be worth money to you. It's you or Bernie. I can help them decide."

He looked at me.

"There's an alternative," I pointed out.

"Yes?"

"Six Sisters. Five Sisters."

Iceone was silent for a long time.

"And how would you propose to help them decide?" he finally asked. I could see he was interested.

"Ask DeHooch," I recommended.

But Iceone was shaking his head vigorously from side to side. The faint little smile didn't come off.

"No, no, no, no, Caine. You don't understand. You people all think alike. You've got it wrong. These boys are stubborn. They're cagey and they're tough. They don't respond to pushes in one direction or another. Life is more subtle than that. The two men you mention? They're down, Caine. They're not out. These are stubborn bastards."

Iceone agreed with himself. He reached for the glass of something on the desk and emptied it. "Your loss, my gain," he said as he placed the glass back down. I watched his eyes wander over to the doorway. DeHooch had come back into the room, very quietly. I didn't turn around to see how civilized he looked with another gun in his hand.

Mr. Ice wiped his lips with his fingers.

"Caine, I give you credit. But I'm confident that they've already decided. You're quite right. I've invested a great deal of money—my own, and that of some people I happen to know—in these facilities. The lease of this property runs into thousands of dollars a year. The capital investment in the buildings in back, the production facilities, runs into tens of thousands of dollars. This is an investment I'm obligated to recover. Tenfold. You're absolutely right, Caine. I can't do it with a minority interest in an enterprise over which I have no control. It's my nature, I'm afraid, to want control. I was never one of Bernie's bunch. I knew him in New York, I had some connections that proved useful to him in establishing Seven Sisters Productions. We arrived at an agreement. Forty percent for me. Forty percent for him. Four percent for each of the others. Their investment was far less than mine."

Iceone pushed back his chair and stood up. He reached for a cigarette and tapped it lightly against the desk. But he didn't light it. He probably abstained from cigarettes, too.

"My business is making people vulnerable," Iceone said. "You're right about Richter. Mr. Richter has a very poor temperament. I would say he's a dangerous man—unpredictable, except in one regard. He made the mistake of performing in a Los Angeles motel room with a nice young man from UCLA. Of course, he's very embarrassed about it. Especially since I have it on tape. He's very concerned that his tastes not become well known.

"Bernie's tastes are far more conventional," he continued. "I spoke to Bernie on the phone, only two or three days ago. I hadn't spoken to him for months. I explained to him what I had—an excellent videotape of him in bed with a young lady of my acquaintance, Ms. Honey Mellon. Color. The lighting was excellent. And with full sound, of course. He makes the most disgusting little noises, you know. Like a pig. I gave him a choice. Deliver Seven Sisters over to me, or I'd have his dear wife up here for a private screening. It comes as no surprise to me that he would hire you to kill me. Do you know what his reaction was, Caine?"

"He dared you."

Iceone put down the cigarette and walked halfway around the desk.

"You understand Bernie," he smiled. "You understand my position. These men have something in common, too. They don't respond to a demonstration of strength. I anticipated his reaction. But perhaps—I thought perhaps he might be made vulnerable in other ways."

"People might get hurt in the head," DeHooch said from the corner behind me.

"Shut up," Iceone snapped. He looked back at me. But I beat him to the punch.

"Did you make her vulnerable?" I asked.

"She collapsed, Caine. Of course, she was not the point of my exercise. She was merely a means to the end. But she collapsed under the weight of the evidence. I showed her first one of our most successful productions. It's called *Charity Begins at Home*. She wanted to leave. She was incensed. But I encouraged her to remain for Bernie's inept performance with Ms. Mellon. My God, she was devastated."

Iceone smiled to himself. He spread his palms upward.

"As for Bernie himself?" he asked. "All of that takes time. And time, I'm afraid, is a commodity I'm fast running out of."

"Forty-five minutes," DeHooch said.

"Miss Leeds is dead," Iceone said. "I assure you, I had nothing to do with that. It was certainly against my interests. But perhaps the man of glass will succeed where my plans have been disturbed. I have to be down there in forty-five minutes. I've made an excellent offer to each of them. I expect an answer. All I need is a single affirmative decision, and I have no doubt that I'll get it. Peter?"

DeHooch grunted.

Iceone waved a hand at him. I turned around just in time to see DeHooch slide his right hand inside his jacket. He was putting it away.

"One thing I don't abide, Caine. People working both sides of the fence. The grass on my side of the fence is greener, so long as you don't go near the fence. You have already demonstrated extraordinary prudence by coming to me and giving me this opportunity to triple Rococco's offer."

"Thirty grand," I said.

Iceone laughed. "Of course! What did you think? Forty-five hundred? I assure you, I have a much higher regard for your abilities than Mr. Rococco has. I've seen them demonstrated." He nodded to himself. "I'm intrigued by your alternative, Caine. It never would have occurred to me. I'm a nonviolent man. Six Sisters. Five Sisters. I like the ring to it. It may be needed. I fully expect a satisfactory resolution this afternoon, but one never knows. It may indeed be necessary. In that case, I would prefer not to be connected with it. Nor to have Peter connected with it. Do you understand?"

"I do."

We were married. Iceone reached down and opened a desk drawer.

"Would ten thousand in your pocket be satisfactory? Considering it as a retainer? Yes?"

He held out a green wad of hundreds, wrapped in a white paper band. I took it. The marriage was consummated.

"Very well," he said. He looked at his watch. "Since you'll be carrying my money, I would like you to come with us. Yes?" He smiled.

"I thought this was my money."

He shrugged. "Of course it is."

"I've been on Delgany Street," DeHooch blurted out.

"Peter!" Mr. Ice said. "Be civilized!"

# 23

Dominick Iceone played both sides of the fence, both sides of the street, and both sides of his mouth. It was a setup and I knew it. He didn't have to spell it out for me. If the boys in the band said no, Mr. Ice had hired a hit man. If any one of them wound up playing his tune, he had control of Seven Sisters Productions and it would be my turn to solo. Peter DeHooch would be happy to see me swap that stack of greenbacks for a bullet hole in my jacket pocket. Or in the back of my head. It wouldn't matter to him. One thing I was convinced of: Dominick Iceone had nothing to do with the death of Suzanne Leeds. He wanted to bend her a little, not break her. She was his way of getting through to Bernie Rococco. Somebody else got through to Bernie for him, or wanted to make it look as if he had. Somebody else wanted her broken in half.

We walked out to the front of the property together while DeHooch went down back to get the car.

I said, "I've got to hand it to you, Ice."

He pretended to hear only half of it. "Yes?"

"He's a real disciplined accountant."

Iceone smiled. "Doesn't make mistakes. He's an excellent accountant, Caine. He follows orders very well." Then he added, "And he's the most remarkable shadow man I've ever met."

"Ditto."

"Caine?"

"Yes."

"It's a real pleasure doing business with you. I like the way you move. You got my attention. You're fast. You're tough, that's obvious. You've got plenty of nerve. Nobody's going to pull the wool over your eyes. I think we've got a deal. I look forward to a long and profitable relationship. For both of us." He stuck out his hand and I took it.

"You're looking in the right direction."

"You married, Caine?"

"No."

"Need a broad?"

"Not this afternoon. I have a track meet tonight."

It was already late in the afternoon. The air was lazy, and turning red. There was silence between us for a few moments. Dominick Iceone seemed almost human, standing there beside Copper Peak Road with no one around except me. His face was dark. There was a certain sadness in it. You see it in the faces of men on trains or sitting in the airport or going home from their high-rise offices after dark, when their faces suddenly go blank. I remembered that he'd abandoned Madison Avenue to run with the mob. I wondered what he'd done on Madison Avenue. Sweep it?

"I was married once," he said softly.

I had nothing to add.

"Right out of high school. Brooklyn. She helped put me through school." He looked off into the distance. "She ran away with a cop. She was in a traffic accident and met this— cop—and ran away with him."

"It's been a lousy summer."

"No. This was long ago."

I watched the midges and gnats rise up from the long grass where the sunlight slanted through the trees at the side of the road.

"How did Bernie find you?" Iceone said.

"Where's DeHooch?"

"It's quite a walk. He's got to come all the way around."

"I found Bernie," I said finally. "I know a cop, too. But he's not a bad guy. Albany, New York. Detailed to the attorney general's office. We were in the Navy. He calls me now and then. He knows I like night work. The police here have been asking a lot of questions in Albany about Seven Sisters. He thought there might be some money in it for me. He was right. He knows something about money."

I watched Iceone's eyes shift toward me.

"Talk about a profitable relationship," I said casually. "Two boats, a summer place somewhere up north, drives a Berlinetta, and he gets to Vegas at least one weekend a month." I kicked at the gravel alongside the road.

Iceone tilted back the brim of his gray fedora. He looked me straight in the eye.

"That's a lot of living for a cop," he said.

I looked straight back. And I smiled. That's all. Just smiled.

"Congratulations, Caine," he said suddenly. He reached out for my hand and really pumped it. "You're going to be a valuable addition to our little team. Yes?"

It was a wonderful honeymoon. Very civilized. We lied a lot, but we both enjoyed it.

DeHooch came over the rise in Copper Peak Road a couple of minutes later. He was behind the wheel of a white Lincoln. Iceone tightened up.

"You lead. We'll follow," he snapped. He wanted to keep an eye on me.

I shook my head. "Sorry. I meant to tell you. I don't like being followed. Ask DeHooch."

Peter DeHooch lowered his head and looked up at me through the open door on the passenger side of the Lincoln. He was missing his yellow aviator glasses, but his mustache was cleaned up. And he had a real nice shirt on. He looked like he had a lot of muscle on the left side of his chest, under his jacket.

"Very well," Iceone said.

He got into the Lincoln. I heard him tell DeHooch to step on it. DeHooch did. I followed the yellow dust cloud down the mountain.

The mask goes on. The mask comes off. Who's good? Who's evil? Who's the victim? Who's the victimizer? I thought about it. There was no answer. The answer was locked up somewhere in the heart of Dominick Iceone, and the man of glass, and Bernie Rococco, and all the rest of them. Somewhere along the line, the key had been lost. And would never be found.

The Sunset Motor Lodge was located on the outskirts of town. The parking lot was only half full. The red neon sun that glowed over the entrance said there were no vacancies. We didn't bother to check. We had reservations.

We went into the motel through a side door, with DeHooch leading the way. He carried a slim attache case in his left hand. That left his right hand free. He walked briskly.

The motel smelled of chlorine and dust and dampness. We took a right and walked down a long carpeted hallway, nearly to the end. DeHooch knew where we were going. He should have. He'd set it up.

He paused for a moment before an unnumbered door and glanced up at Mr. Ice. Then he opened the door and strutted in.

It was somebody's office. The manager's, perhaps. There were no windows. The desk had been cleaned off. The air was thick with stale cigarette smoke.

I looked them over.

Three of them sat on a long blue sofa against the wall straight across from the desk. Lemaire, Nevada, Richter. I'd seen their mugs before, thanks to Harold Square. He was right about Ted Richter: closely cropped gray hair, pinched face, a martinet. He held himself rigid, even when he had to sit on an uncomfortable couch. He held himself above everyone else.

Anthony O. Nevada was in the middle, and he needed a shave. The stubble of his beard was gray, his face was baked, he wore wire spectacles wedged on top of his flat nose. Louie Lemaire's square face was dominated by his eyebrows: big, black, and bushy. His bright eyes glared out from beneath them. One look and I knew he was a little man with a big man inside.

The mountain in the corner was too big to climb. He was a big man with an even bigger man inside. He weighed close to three hundred pounds, and even then his thin gray suit was draped over his massive frame in loose folds, as though he'd lost a lot of weight. He hadn't lost it from his face: pink cheeks, hairline headed north, warm good-natured eyes swimming around in a sea of crow's feet. I said hello to Sty McDonald without opening my mouth.

The little stick figure sitting on a wooden folding chair next to McDonald didn't open his mouth, either. Max Sinclair's face was still red and blotchy, maybe something didn't agree with him, and his nervous eyes got a little dizzy when he spotted me. He started to stand up, but he sat back down very quickly when DeHooch said:

"Keep it on the chair."

DeHooch walked around behind the desk, put his attache case down, and opened it up. Iceone pulled the desk chair out and sat in it. He cupped his chin in one hand. His other hand reached out and picked up a pencil from the desk. He started to play with it. I stayed on my feet, flat against the wall next to the door. I could feel the light switch pressing against my back. Just in case.

DeHooch waved his hand around the room like he was delivering a blessing. Or a benediction. "McDonald, Sinclair, Lemaire, Nevada," he said quickly. "You know Richter. This is Mr. Iceone."

It dawned on me that most of them had never met Mr. Ice.

"Very good, boy," McDonald said. "And who are you, suh?" His voice had a churchly resonance. He was looking right at me.

**209**

"His name's Caine, he works for us, he's the driver," DeHooch snapped. His mouth was like a machine gun. "We're late. We're sorry. We'd like to get right down to business."

"Well, I'd like to say something before you get started, suh."

DeHooch looked at Mr. Ice. McDonald was standing up—standing still—but he seemed to be moving. There was a lot of him.

"My thought is, this is highly irregular," he said. He looked at the faces in the room. "It's unseemly. Bernie's woman died yesterday. You all know that. We ought to have some small respect for human life. We ought to draw together, not pull apart. We ought to have Bernie here with us, as I declared before these gentlemen arrived. We ought not to be—"

I don't know where he trained, on a stump somewhere in Missouri, but he was winding up.

"Can it," Lemaire said. "This ain't life or death, Sty. It's money. There'll be plenty of time for tears tomorrow."

DeHooch saw his chance and took it. "I'll be brief. I'll be very brief. You've all had a chance to consider Mr. Iceone's offer. I'm very pleased to be able to say that Mr. Sinclair and Mr. Richter have agreed to Mr. Iceone's terms, for a very substantial consideration."

"What's that, suh? What's that, Max?"

The room started to get warm. Iceone smiled. He twirled the yellow pencil in his fingers.

DeHooch pointed at Max Sinclair. "Why don't you tell your friends here why you decided to accept the offer, Mr. Sinclair?"

It was testimonial time. Sinclair looked at the floor. He wiped his mouth and ran his hand through his hair. "I—it was a great offer—I needed the—I needed a lot of money—" His face turned even redder.

"Bernie said he'd match any offer, from anyone," Anthony Nevada said. He had sand in his throat.

McDonald had honey. "That's right, Max," he said gently. "I don't understand this. Bernie's offer's been on the table for a year now. There for you to take. If you needed the money, God knows we all need the money, you should have given Bernie the opportunity. We been through the war together, Max. Same goes for you, Ted. One way or another, we been through life together. And we been together in this little enterprise that Bernie started up."

"It was *my* idea," Richter said. His nose was out of joint. If it wasn't out of joint, at least it was pointed up in the air.

"Let Sinclair finish what he had to say," DeHooch said.

"I'm finished," Sinclair stammered. "I mean—uh—" His lips were working overtime, but nothing was coming out.

"Did you recover your investment?" DeHooch asked.
Sinclair nodded.

"Were the arrangements satisfactory?"

"Yes."

"What I want to ask you, Mr. Sinclair, is this. Will the payments allow you to resume your painting? To pick up your life and carry it forward? Are you happy with it?"

"Yes, sir," Sinclair said very quietly.

DeHooch turned toward Ted Richter. Richter was a contrast to Sinclair. His chin was up. It held a faint sneer on his face. His eyes were half closed and steady.

"The point is, Max, these are hard times for all of us," Sty McDonald was saying. He didn't look like he was going to let go. "I lost my farm, Max. It's hardscrabble, as you know. Tony lost his business, a very fine one. You lost your wife, Max, for which we're all deeply sorry. The lieutenant lost his life. And now Bernie has lost his lady. Whom you might remember, Max, was a fine woman. You had the pleasure to meet her last year."

He was going to plow another furrow, but Louie Lemaire slapped his hands on his knees and said, "Thanks to the man of glass." No one needed reminding.

"Mr. Richter?" DeHooch said.

"The point is, Max," McDonald continued, "hard times we damn well ought to pull together. Four mules make a better team than one horse's ass. We've stuck together before, ain't that close to right?" His voice floated around the room like a tune no one wanted to hear.

"All but one of us," Lemaire said.

He looked around the room.

"Mr. Richter?" DeHooch said.

"Just a moment, suh. You're right, Louie. All but one of us. You tell me which one." McDonald wriggled his fingers. They itched to be around someone's neck.

Lemaire's eyebrows descended half an inch. "You know damn well, Sty."

"Do you mean to tell me the lieutenant?"

"He wasn't one of us, was he?" Lemaire's nostrils were spread wide. He was itching for a fight, too. It was too bad it was just a meeting of old friends and buddies.

McDonald tilted back on his feet. His little mouth turned down at the corners. He stared silently at Lemaire. He breathed very slowly.

Mr. Ice interrupted the silence.

"Let me make a suggestion," he said. His voice was pleasant. His dark eyes took in everyone. "I'm a businessman. I'm not a fortune-teller. I'm not a psychiatrist. I'm merely a businessman, and my position has been made very clear to all of you by Mr. DeHooch—"

"I most definitely will not sell, suh," Sty McDonald said. "I've stated that previous to your little man here. My position is very clear."

Iceone ignored him.

"We haven't heard from Ted. Why don't we hear from Ted?" Mr. Ice asked calmly. "And then, perhaps, I can sweeten the pot? Yes?" He smiled.

"Gladly," Richter said hastily. "I want to say this. I've known Mr. Iceone for some time now. He's an honorable man. He's an excellent businessman. He has a great deal of experience in the line of production. My feeling is, the future of Seven Sisters Productions is in very good hands—with Mr.

Iceone. I'm very happy with the price I was paid for my four shares. I've never made a great deal of money from them. I'm only—we're all only very minority shareholders. But I made a *great* deal of money by selling them. Thank you."

He hardly got the thank you out of his mouth when Sty McDonald started up:

"Well, my God, Ted! Tie me up! We live on hope. I put hope on my table every supper. This little company's on the edge of making a bushel of money. You've heard Bernie say it. This is dirty movies. You know it. It don't suit my taste. I'm just an old hog farmer from Peace Valley in Missouri. But what does suit my taste is the keen prospect of making a bushel of money. I'm a country boy, but I'm not a rube. I think you're a horse's ass to sell yourself out of such a prospect. I'm obliged to say I also think you are a traitor, suh, to what we are. And what we were."

Richter twisted about on the couch and hissed, "You fat sonofabitch!"

"Gentlemen!" Mr. Ice said sternly. He drummed his pencil on the desk. "You've chosen the wrong time for this. Save it. I don't care about the man of glass. I don't care who's a horse's ass and who's not. What I care about is the very fine offer I've made to each of you. You're reasonable men. Some of you are in need. I'm adding ten thousand dollars to my offer—to each of you—as an encouragement to bring this matter to a conclusion."

He looked at Louie Lemaire.

"Mr. Lemaire?"

"It's a good offer," Lemaire said. "No." He looked at McDonald.

Iceone sighed. He turned toward Anthony O. Nevada and moved one eyebrow toward the roof.

Nevada looked at his hands. "I'll stick with the others. I need the money, but I'll stick."

"Your answer is no, I presume?"

"That's my answer," he said hoarsely.

DeHooch snapped his attache case shut.

"My answer, suh, is a most definite and emphatic no," came the voice from the corner. Iceone didn't even have to ask.

Mr. Ice got to his feet.

"Very well, gentlemen. It's your life," he said. "That's the way business works. The good with the bad. Sometimes you make a mistake. The bad gets worse." He looked at DeHooch. "Let's go," he said.

"We're *all* making a mistake," Max Sinclair squeaked. "A terrible mistake." He'd gotten to his feet, too. You could tell because the wooden folding chair fell over. Everyone turned to look at him. His legs shook, but not as badly as his hands. His voice was worse. He was looking at me.

"This man Caine," he stammered. "He doesn't work for Iceone. You're being fooled. You're *all* being fooled." He shook his head, like he was trying to dislodge a bad dream. His voice rose, and I watched that dizzy look come back into his eyes. "He works for Lieutenant Saltonstall! He told me that himself! That's who he's with! I'm telling you—he's with the lieutenant!"

"Saltonstall's dead," someone said.

"They never recovered his body," came a gravelly answer.

"Don't be ridiculous, suh! Get Max here a drink."

There was silence in the room.

Sinclair stared at Mr. Ice. Mr. Ice looked at Peter DeHooch. I heard the pencil snap in half.

DeHooch looked at me.

He smiled.

# 24

I opened the door and stepped into the hall. Mr. Ice and Peter DeHooch followed me out. DeHooch slammed the door behind him. Inside, voices started to rise.

Dominick Iceone stared at me. The gray fedora was tilted back on his head. The corners of his mouth were turned down like a claw. I was ready for anything. Mr. Ice was just about to speak when I said:

"I'm not a fortune-teller. I'm not a psychiatrist. I'm merely a businessman. And a very good shot."

"Animals," he said. "They belong in the zoo." He spat the words out.

He turned on his heel and headed up the hall. When we got outside, he stopped again.

"Tomorrow morning, Caine. Seven o'clock. Let's get it over with. I want you up at Little Bearskin Lodge."

I headed for my car.

"Oh, Caine?"

"Yes?"

"We do understand each other. We have an excellent working relationship."

I agreed.

"Make sure it works," he said. "Be there at seven."

I got in the car, started it up, and headed out into a long line of late-afternoon traffic. It was a short trip: around the block. When I got around to the main drag again I turned left and cruised slowly past the Sunset Motor Lodge just in time to see a man in a white suit and gray fedora slipping into a taxicab under the canopy over the entrance. I checked the rearview mirror and said hello to a white Lincoln right on my tail, two cars back. I thought maybe DeHooch would stick his arm out the window and wave, but he didn't.

The honeymoon was already over.

DeHooch was good and I knew it, but he could have been bad and it wouldn't have made any difference. I didn't push him. I drove slowly. I stopped on yellow. I didn't make any fast turns or sudden lane changes. I signalled everything. He stayed two cars back. I don't imagine he was crazy about the idea, tailing me in a white Lincoln, but he couldn't do anything about it.

I sorted it out on the way across town.

Iceone knew it wouldn't work. He'd been nice enough about it, he hadn't raised his voice, he hadn't called anyone a horse's ass, he'd made a simple proposition and he had no takers. Not with Sty McDonald standing in the corner and brooding over the whole bunch of them from his stump. Ice had found the two soft spots, Richter and Max Sinclair, and he'd gone after them like they were bad teeth. I had the feeling he wanted to go to work on Louie Lemaire likewise, but Lemaire stuck with the others. The others didn't necessarily like one another, that was obvious. They were afraid of something, that was obvious, too. But in the end, blood turned out to be thicker than money. They'd spilled a lot of blood together, once upon a time in Italy.

They didn't know it, but Mr. Ice's proposition ended with a sentence of death. Some more blood was going to be spilled: somebody innocent. It didn't matter who. It was dealer's choice, making it Six Sisters or Five Sisters. Iceone had only one problem: finding somebody innocent.

My problem was different.

It wasn't figuring out who'd killed Suzanne Leeds and Max Sinclair's young wife to make Bernie and Max vulnerable, or who'd pulled the rug out from under Sty McDonald and Anthony O. Nevada, or why. It wasn't finding the man of glass. It wasn't that at all.

The problem was nailing the hammer before I got nailed.

I picked up a bite to eat at a little German restaurant near the heart of town, Schlogel's. Two slabs of ribs. When I finished I called Canetti. Dr. Lew Diamond was still asleep on the living room floor of his apartment, Canetti had tried to make him comfortable, it looked like he was good for another twenty-four hours or payday, whichever came first. Canetti wanted to know why he'd bothered going to the police academy and whether he'd get paid overtime for baby-sitting or would have to take it in time due. "I don't know the answer to either of those questions," I said. "I'm not your boss." He sniffed: "You act like it sometimes."

Everybody's feelings were getting hurt.

When I left the restaurant, the white Lincoln was parked down at the corner. I walked down there, gave DeHooch a friendly smile, and tossed the doggy bag through the open window into his lap. It was full of bones.

"You're a real wise sonofabitch, Caine."

"You've got a short memory. Keep your distance," I said. "I don't like this. It's a breach of trust. Don't press it."

DeHooch looked straight ahead and didn't say anything. He was a real disciplined accountant, all right, but everyone was getting a little touchy.

Ten minutes later I was parking the car along the street about half a block from the Arnold Hotel. DeHooch's distance was two spaces back. He was pressing it.

I got out, slammed the car door, and headed into the hotel. DeHooch stayed where he was.

I cut across the lobby, walked past the registration desk, took a right at the hallway, stopped for a moment before the door to Room 117, it was closed, and then went up the stairs to the second floor. The hallway up there was empty. She'd given me her room number and I remembered it. I knocked three times and whispered low. There was no answer. I tried it again, without the whisper. The answer remained the same.

I was about to leave when I spotted the little slip of blue hotel stationery sticking out from underneath the door.

"To whom I hope it may concern," it said. "I'm taking myself out to dinner. Excellent company. Then I'm going to see *Kickin' Up a Storm*. My sentiments exactly! I found Father—he seems okay—don't worry. Doesn't want to be here, I can tell. But no worse than normal. I'll be back by ten. That's very unusual!"

It wasn't signed. It didn't need to be.

I turned around, put the note in my pocket, went back down the stairs, and knocked on Bernie Rococco's door. His answer was the same as hers. I went out into the lobby. The man behind the counter was meditating. I hated to do it, but I broke his trance.

"Hey, you."

"Yes, sir?"

"Mr. Rococco's expecting me. Room one-seventeen. Will you give him a ring?"

He reached for the house phone and dialed. Thirty seconds later he hung up.

"I'm sorry. He doesn't answer."

"He hasn't checked out?"

He thumbed through his book.

"No. He's still registered. Through tomorrow. Perhaps he's late. What time was he expecting you?"

"Listen, pal," I said confidentially. I leaned across the counter. "I was in his room this morning. I left my glasses in there. I'm blind as a bat without my glasses. Can I get in there and fetch my specs?" I put my hands out in front of me like a blind man. "Otherwise I'm a goner."

He shook his head. "I'm sorry, sir. That's against regulations. You can certainly understand why. He may be out to dinner. I'm sure he'll return shortly. Why don't you have a seat over there? Or try Wicker's. Excellent food. What time was he expecting you?"

It was a good question but there was no one around to answer it. I was already on my way to Delgany Street. So was my shadow.

It was starting to get dark when I let myself in the house. I closed the door behind me, went to the window, and watched Peter DeHooch drive gingerly across the crushed-brick parking lot across the street. He turned the Lincoln around and backed himself into a corner. It gave him a nice view of my front door.

The house was very quiet.

I went upstairs, showered, and shaved. I had the feeling that all the dirt didn't come off. When I looked in the mirror, he didn't look back. He's that way. Tries to mind his own business, stay out of harm's way. I remembered a telephone call in the middle of the night.

You haven't forgotten everything, Caine.

This is a confession, Caine.

I'd recognize your voice anywhere, Caine.

My back's against the wall, Caine.

Do you still have that little number—the Margolin Special?

I was on my way downstairs, two at a time, when I heard the thunderous knock at the front door. Somebody with a two-by-four. I still had that little number, strapped to my side. I slipped my jacket on to cover it, unsnapped the safety, checked the window, saw the Lincoln still across the street, noticed the cab at the curb right in front of the house, and opened the door.

It surprised me a little. Not a lot, but a little. Something very large was darkening my doorway.

"Good evening, suh."

He was alone. If he wasn't alone, they were all standing behind him and I couldn't see them. The thin gray suit still hung loosely over his massive frame. His eyes had the same friendly twinkle.

"All right, I'll bite," I said. "How'd you find it?"

"Well, suh, it's not in the telephone directory, of that you may be assured. I inquired of the others, but they professed ignorance. Even Sinclair. So I telephoned Mr. Iceone himself. I declared to him that I was in the process of considering reconsidering my previous position, but that first I was desirous, do you understand, of discussing a matter of mutual interest with yourself, suh. He was kind enough to provide me with your address, and I availed myself of that gentleman down there to drive me over here. I presume, suh, you are aware that this residence is under surveillance by a man with a yellow mustache, pale white skin, brown eyes, blue shirt, red tie loosened at the throat, sitting in a Lincoln Continental of white color parked directly across the street?"

He smiled. He didn't talk like a pig farmer.

"Why don't you tell your cabbie to be on his way, McDonald?"

"That won't be necessary, suh." He squeezed through the door and surveyed the hallway. Then he looked at me.

"I speculate that you worked for Mr. Bradley Saltonstall, suh. A great inspiration on the battlefield in war and a great American in peace."

"You speculate wrong."

"I surmise," Sty McDonald said slowly, "that you *knew* Saltonstall?" His thin eyebrows made sharp little semicircles above his eyes.

"You surmise right, suh."

"Very well, then!" He clapped me on the shoulder and broke into a wide grin. "I hasten to add that I am a great admirer of Bradley Saltonstall."

McDonald patted his belly.

"I can offer you sour milk, tepid water, or some bourbon from a bottle with no label on it. The houseboy isn't home with the groceries yet."

"I will accept the bourbon from the bottle with no label on it. I worked for Bradley Saltonstall, suh," he announced. "I have the highest regard for him." He eyed me kindly.

I went into the kitchen, matched the glass to the man, and filled it. When I went into the study, Sty McDonald had already found the recliner and wedged himself into it.

"May I sit down, suh?"

"Don't try to get up."

He took a swallow—not a sip, a swallow. "Yes, suh," he declared, "I worked for Bradley Saltonstall for two years, some years after the war, and I came to the reluctant conclusion that the sun don't shine in Washington, and I carried myself direct back to Peace Valley and resumed the raising of hogs. However, suh, Bradley and myself have kept in regular communication throughout all these years. You understand, suh, that Bradley is dead?"

"Yes. Of course he is."

"Well, suh, Max Sinclair is not of that persuasion. And I believe Louie Lemaire has certain suspicions along that line. But we know better. Neither one of them, suh, cottoned very much to Lieutenant Saltonstall. They were of the feeling that he was an outsider. I was of the opinion, in opposition to that, that he was a remarkable man. Most understanding of people. I often remarked to him that he would have made a very fine hog farmer."

McDonald put a palm to his forehead. Maybe he wanted to see whether he had a fever. He certainly sounded like he did. He took another swallow of bourbon.

"Indeed, Max would not attend the funeral," he continued. "The others of us were obliged to attend. And my obligation, suh, was of a very special nature. It was on my responsibility that Bradley is dead. It was I, suh, who encouraged him to look into this extraordinary reemergence of the man of glass."

He fell silent. His chest heaved when he took a breath and slowly exhaled.

"Bradley Saltonstall had the most wonderful facility for playing upon the hearts and minds of men. I'm an old man, suh. So is he. Our powers wane. The glories are forgotten. We had anticipated when he retired from the government service that he would spend some time at Peace Valley. Now that cannot be. But when I heard Max's outburst this afternoon, suh, I was struck by the faintest hope that my perceptions could in some manner have become clouded over by my feeling of responsibility for Bradley's death. I perceived that Bradley might yet be alive."

"Pardon me?"

"I say, suh, are you now in the employ of Bradley Saltonstall?"

The loose flesh in Sty McDonald's jowls tightened around his mouth. A kind of bewilderment came into his eyes.

"No," I said. "I'm not. I'm sorry to disappoint you."

"I disappoint myself, suh. I'm a forgiving man. I understand that fear is the root of courage, and that the bud does not always flower. We all bear guilt, suh, in our own measure. I feel it myself. And I'm obliged to say that by resurrecting this—this spirit of the past, Bernie also has suffered the burden. He has lost his lady to the power of guilt."

McDonald paused. He pawed the air with one hand, as though he could not continue.

"She was run off the road by a man in a rented car," I corrected him. "You overestimate the power of guilt."

Sty McDonald suddenly seemed to relax. A smile spread across his round face.

"Oh, Mr. Caine, that is what I hoped to hear you say. That is what I came to hear you say, suh!" He drained his glass and struggled in the chair, trying to get to his feet. His face turned red. "You confirm every kind word that Bradley ever related to me."

He looked like a giant frog on the edge of the recliner, ready to pounce. I heard the screech of brakes outside on the street.

"We all have our work to do, suh, whether it be raising hogs or raising hell. I wish you well with yours."

I was already on my feet, looking out the window. Another cab had pulled up in front of the house behind McDonald's taxi. Delgany Street was having a traffic jam. Harold Square emerged from the second cab, looked up and down the sidewalk, and headed for the steps.

"Stay here," I told McDonald. I headed for the door, and got it just as he started to knock.

"Caine? Square. You're never here. Here it is. Bernie Rococco. Let me in."

"Sorry," I said. I took the manila envelope from his hand and pulled out a glossy photograph of Bernie Rococco.

"Let me in," Harold Square said. He looked like he was going to insist.

"The house isn't clean, Harold. Thanks a million, though. I paid you, didn't I?"

Harold Square looked like he had to go to the bathroom. "My transmission's shot, or I wouldn't have taken a cab," he said. "I have to see the other one, Caine. Don't you understand? The shot of Richter. I pitched the neg."

He pushed his way into the hall.

"Don't move," I suggested. I pointed to an imaginary spot on the hallway floor.

"You notice that he posed," he called after me as I went to get the photos. "I told you he would. Goddamn peacocks. They're all the same!"

He grabbed the stack of photos out of my hand when I returned and started shuffling through them. He was in a big hurry. He pulled out the shot of Ted Richter on the street, and slapped it down on the table next to the door. I turned on the light for him, and he put his eye very close to the photograph. I didn't even notice he had a magnifying glass until he came up for air. His head started bobbing up and down with excitement. His face turned up toward me.

"I was right! Goddamn, I was right! Look at this, Caine!"

I looked. Harold Square had his dirty finger pressed down on the middle of the photograph. In the background, behind the snarling face of Ted Richter, several people were crossing the street. One of them was standing still—he had stopped when he saw the photographer—and he was staring right at the camera. Looked like a Palm Springs suit, a Palm Springs hat, and a Palm Springs tan.

It wasn't the best likeness in the world, but it was close enough.

"Rococco!" Harold Square said triumphantly. "The sonofabitch!" he added. He turned to face me. "I shot him this afternoon, Caine, in the hotel lobby. I thought I recognized him. I noticed that yesterday, Caine. I noticed the guy who stopped in the middle of the street. I thought to myself, that guy's from New York. If I had the neg I could blow this thing up, you know that? Maybe I can find the neg. It's enough to be right, but maybe I can find the neg. I told him I'd caught him yesterday, crossing the street, in the background of another picture. He denied it!"

"He denied it?"

Harold Square scratched his head. "He was a sweetheart until then. Real obliging. Look—he posed for the big one, didn't he? All smiles. Macho, macho. The lousy sonofabitch!" Square was shaking his finger at me. "I knew he was there! I knew I was right! What an eye!"

"Where did he claim he was yesterday?"

"New York. New York! The brass of that guy! Said he just flew into town this morning. You know what? He's got a cookie here. He's got a cookie in the jar. Let me have the print, Caine. He wants to see it. He wants me to prove it. I can make another neg and blow it up. I told him I'd get it from you!"

"Wait a minute, Square."

"Call me Harold. What an eye, huh?" he beamed.

"You gave him my name?"

"Listen, was that okay? This some kind of secret or something? The guy challenged my veracity. He accused me of lying."

I took the photographs, shoved them into the envelope, and handed them to Harold Square. He was still talking to himself as I pushed him out the door.

So was I.

# 25

Sty McDonald made it to his feet by himself. He was standing in the hallway when I turned around.

"I'll be taking my leave, suh. I thank you for lifting a mighty weight from my shoulders." He looked like he was going to say more, but he didn't. He'd already said more than enough.

He patted his huge belly and walked past me. I reached for the door, opened it, and watched him go down the steps. He walked with a slight limp. His taxi was still waiting.

The big eight-by-ten photograph of Bernie Rococco was sitting on the table, where Harold Square had forgotten it in his haste. I picked it up and looked at him. He was posing, all right. There was a faint smile on his face, and the look in his eye let you know that he was a man who lived by appearance alone.

"Nice trick, Bernie," I said. "Being in two places at the same time."

He didn't change his expression.

I folded him in half and stuck him in my pocket. Then I grabbed my tan raincoat from the hook, locked the front door, killed the lights, checked the safety on the Margolin Special, it was still off, and headed for the back of the house.

The weather was changing again. The night was turning cold. Darkness was everywhere.

Somewhere, Dominick Iceone was waiting for morning. Somewhere, Suzanne Leeds was dead. Somewhere, Lew Diamond was dying by inches. Somewhere, Bernie Rococco was on the run. It had been a lousy summer. It was getting worse.

I slipped the raincoat on as I ran down the alley in the darkness. I turned left at the cross alley and came back to Delgany Street on the side street. My car was parked near the corner. I got in and turned the key in the ignition.

Someone had popped the light at the corner. All it delivered was darkness. Down at the other end of the block, the neon sign of the Pee Wee Lounge gave a soft, gaudy glow to the night. Sty McDonald's taxi was still sitting in front of the house on Delgany Street. Its engine was running. Its lights were out.

I put the car in gear and crept forward. Then I gunned it. There was an ear-splitting screech of tires on Delgany Street.

DeHooch suddenly turned on the lights of the Lincoln. They were blinding. They leaped forward through the darkness from the corner of the parking lot, like a hound loose from its chains. I turned my head away just in time to see the highbeams sweep Sty McDonald's taxi. The driver had the face of an old man. An old man put together with slabs of granite and no clay but patience. Short white hair. Burning black eyes. It was the face of a man without fear. He looked directly into the light.

DeHooch wheeled across the crushed bricks to come after me, and the taxi was once again swallowed by the darkness.

I took the corner at the Pee Wee on two wheels. It was a short block. Halfway down I spun the wheel again and shot down an alley to the right. I spotted a loading-dock apron and swerved into it. I killed the lights. I rolled down the window. The Margolin Special rested its chin on the sill.

It was very dark. There was no sound except the low steady

throb of the car's engine. Nobody came. Not friend, not enemy. I was alone.

I waited a couple of minutes and then pulled out. At the end of the alley I turned and went around the block. When I got to the main drag I stopped. Cars were parked along both sides of the street. There was no traffic. Streetlights burned through the night in both directions. I turned to the right and headed for the heart of town.

I looked up at the rearview mirror and saw his lights go on behind me. He pulled away from the curb. A moment later he was right on my tail, two car lengths back. A white Lincoln Continental with a Peter DeHooch behind the wheel.

It was going to be a long night, a sharp descent into the darkness. I was going to have company whether I wanted it or not. I picked the Margolin Special up from the seat beside me and slipped it back into the holster.

Then I headed for the Arnold Hotel.

Wicker's Celebrated Bar & Grill was jammed with people. I pushed my way through the crowd, split up a couple of lovers at the bar, and got Joe Scruffiato's attention.

"I'm here to inspect the kitchen," I announced.

He said, "Huh?"

I went around the end of the bar and through the swinging doors into the kitchen. Scruffiato came after me. I got him alone in the corner by the cooler, reached into my pocket, and put a couple of tens in his hand. He closed his fingers around them like he was used to it.

"Remember me?"

"You bet. Gallagher's pal. Caine. You were here—"

"I need to get into a room."

"What's her name?"

"It's not a her, it's a number. One-seventeen. End of the hall."

Joe Scruffiato's eyebrows knitted themselves together.

"Nobody in there, pal," he said. "Save your money." He started to give it back.

"How do you know?"

"Take a number. I was in there myself an hour or two ago. The room's empty. The guy's stuff is there, but he's not. Rococco. Isn't that it? I looked it up. A fat guy wanted to take a peek in the same room. Gray suit. Walks with a limp. It was worth fifty smackers to him."

"Okay," I said. "I'm taking a number. One-seventeen."

Scruffiato shrugged. "It's your money, pal." He led the way out a side door that opened directly into the hallway. As we walked past the lobby entrance I looked through the arch and saw Peter DeHooch standing next to what I think was a coconut tree. They looked real good together. Down at the end of the hall, Scruffiato used the master on the door to Bernie's room and flipped on the lights. He didn't even knock.

Not much had changed since morning.

The bed was made. The drapes were still pulled back from the window. There was a strong aroma of bay rum in the room. Bernie Rococco's fancy leather valise was still sitting open on the bed, with its stack of maroon boxer shorts. He was traveling light.

All that was missing was the pearl-handled revolver. That and Bernie Rococco.

"The fat man take anything?"

"No. He didn't step more than two feet inside the room. I watched him. He was a very courtly old gentleman. He just looked around, sniffed the air, made a face, and left."

Scruffiato scratched his head.

"Rococco left in a hurry, huh?"

"Joe," I said. "You catch on real fast. Here. Buy yourself a drink."

I gave him another ten.

"Where'd he go?" Scruffiato asked.

It was a good feeling. I finally had a question I could answer.

The plane touched down in New York at ten minutes after two in the morning. I was traveling light, too. All I had with me was the Margolin Special and my shadow.

DeHooch had class. He went over and bought flight insurance when I approached the Vegas Rentacar booth in the Denver airport.

"You rent a Berlinetta," I told the girl behind the booth.

"Not anymore we don't. It's been impounded."

Then she added, "I rented it, though. I rented it to the man the police are looking for."

"Bradley Saltonstall?"

"That's it. I looked it up."

I pulled the photograph of Bernie Rococco out of my pocket, unfolded it, and put it on the counter.

"That's him," she said.

"Keep it."

On the flight east, DeHooch hadn't pushed his luck. He sat two seats behind me. And when we got to New York he waited discreetly against a wall while I reclaimed the Margolin Special. Then he went and reclaimed his .45.

The cabbie didn't have much to say. He was a Jamaican, he liked soccer, he was studying law, he'd been married three times, he wondered if I knew the words to "Cara Mia," and he sold dope, so we didn't have much in common. He put himself on automatic pilot when I told him:

"Times Square."

There wasn't much traffic at that hour. Just the glow of lights from the center of the universe, where all the atoms and molecules of dreams were being crushed together under great pressure, getting ready for the start of something big: the next regular working day. The clouds over the city were streaked with a red glow, as though they were hovering over open furnaces. We were still on the Long Island Expressway when I suggested to the driver that he use the next exit ramp. He did. "Now let's get right back on," I said, before he came to a stop. We did.

Then he looked in the mirror.

He tapped a crooked finger to the side of his head. "I get it, mister. That other cab follow us."

He twisted around in his seat and looked me over carefully.

I must have passed. "I take him for a ride?" he asked.

"No," I said. "I have the feeling he take me for a ride."

I sat back and didn't enjoy it. But it gave me time to go over it again in my head. Mr. Ice calls Suzanne at 8:30 in the morning. Bernie calls Suzanne a half hour later. She figures he's in New York, because New York is where he usually is. But he isn't. He's in Denver. He's already given Iceone the back of his hand and he knows what Iceone will do. When Toby Kinser shows up at the Drovers Hotel in the Camaro, Bernie's ready. In the rented Berlinetta.

It was his misfortune that Harold Square had had to chase Ted Richter out to the street. If Bernie had turned his face the other way, if Bernie had kept right on hoofing it across the street, he'd have been nothing but a blur of black and white in the background of Harold's picture. But that wasn't Bernie's style. He saw the camera and he stopped. Then he hightailed it back to New York. It took a while, because it was real late when Dr. Lew Diamond finally got through to him and burst his bag of tears.

Bernie Rococco was a high-stakes dealer, and the cards he was turning faceup on the table all had the same picture on them: the man of glass.

I don't want to make it sound easy. It wasn't.

It meant standing on steamy platforms in the middle of nowhere, waiting for the next Eighth Avenue Express to come screaming at me out of the night, with Peter DeHooch leaning against the tile wall twenty feet from me on the same platform. It meant cold coffee. It meant upstairs and downstairs. It meant the smell of cabbage and onions. It meant forcing my way between cars while the train was in motion. It meant peering in windows coated with grease and dirt and tiny droplets of human blood. It meant looking at rubber faces and bloodshot eyes and sleeping beauties with something ugly running down their chins.

"I don't know, you know?"

"I don't know, either."

"I know."

"You know?"

It meant flashing red and green lights, and darkness, and the smell of death deep in the subways, the lingering scent of herds that had passed that way. It meant watching the minutes tick by, and feeling the concrete and steel tremble beneath my feet, and noticing suddenly that it was an hour later than it had been only ten minutes before.

It meant that at 4:32 in the morning, at a stop called Lafayette Avenue in Brooklyn, I stepped through the rear door of a Manhattan-bound A train, looked up, and saw a Palm Springs hat, slick black hair, and the top third of a Palm Springs suit scrunched low into the seat near the front of the car.

He was sitting on the aisle. His topcoat was thrown over the back of the seat next to him.

No one was near him.

I felt DeHooch slip behind me and swing around into the seat next to the rear door.

The train started to roll.

# 26

Caine, Rococco, Peter DeHooch. We were three pawns in a game none of us could win. It was a fairy tale for tough guys, and it didn't have a happy ending.

I walked forward in the swaying car, tossed my coat on top of his, and sat sideways in the seat behind him.

He squirmed a little.

His chin was slumped down on his chest. His Palm Springs hat was pitched back at a rakish angle. He looked like he'd been to the track and lost big. He was a sad little man from Cold Lake, and somewhere in Italy, and an indifferent New York high-rise. He dealt in fear and futures, but his future had run out. All he had left was the fear. He was a hero who'd outlived the need for heroes. He was back where he'd begun, looking for courage in the long darkness beneath the streets.

"Bernie," I whispered.

The hairs got restless on the back of his neck. His head snapped up.

"Caine? Is it Caine?"

He was expecting me.

He tried to clear his throat. He shifted uncomfortably in his seat. His pudgy little hand found its way up to his neck. He loosened his silk tie. His hand was trembling. His nerves were shot.

I leaned forward.

"Relax, Bernie. Don't turn around. I have a little shadow named DeHooch. He works for Iceone. He's sitting by himself in back. With a gun. He knows how to use it, Bernie. He's already plugged a guy named Penrod. Now he wants to punch somebody else's ticket. Let's not find out whose."

Rococco turned his head around suddenly and looked past me. His bad eye was doing a wild dance. When he faced the front of the car again, he knew what he was up against. I picked up the faint scent of bay rum. He was sweating.

"Who's paying your bills, Caine?"

"You've got it all wrong, Bernie. We all had it wrong."

"I'll double it."

Rococco's head wobbled from side to side.

"She told you," he rasped. "She told you where to look."

"You didn't have to kill her, Bernie."

He was quiet for a long time before he said, "It was an accident. I didn't mean to, Caine. All I wanted was a little accident."

"There are no accidents, Bernie."

I could barely hear him. There was something caught in his throat. A little hook of panic. He was trying to tough it out, but it made it hard for him to breathe. I watched the muscles pulsate in and out along the side of his neck.

The train stopped, then started up again. I scanned the platform. It was empty.

"You were a dead giveaway, Bernie."

His chin floated up from his chest.

"Bernie, I figured it out a long time ago, but I figured it wrong. The way you wanted the cops to find the Berlinetta. The way you insisted that you called her from New York. It was too much of a good thing, Bernie."

"I got plenty of money, Caine. I'll make it worth your while.

I know this line. I know every stop. Believe me. If you get to DeHooch—"

"She believed you, Bernie. Even the dry runs—the car that tried to run you down in the parking garage, the accident in Connecticut, the fire on your boat I saw through that, too. It didn't go with the rest of it. McDonald's farm, Sinclair's wife, Nevada's business—you worked around the edges, Bernie. Never went for the jugular. You couldn't do it. You boys had too much in common. You just wanted to shake them loose from the money tree. Right, Bernie? Scare them a little. Make them vulnerable. In order to cover your own tracks, you had to appear vulnerable, too. You had to look like a victim of the man of glass. That's why you started the whole thing. You know something, Bernie? You *are* a victim of the man of glass. We all are."

The train thundered on toward Forty-second Street.

Rococco squirmed in his seat again. He turned and looked at his reflection. What he saw was an old man who'd stayed out in the sun too long, looking for something he'd lost and would never find. He'd already started to shrivel up. But he was a man who liked to be a winner, even in a game where there were no winners.

"I'll tell you what, Caine. There's money in it. We can cut a deal. Whatever he's paying you, I'll triple it. Triple, Caine. Who's paying you? Iceone?"

"You're not listening, Bernie. You figured wrong. We all figured wrong. You thought it was just between you and Dominick Iceone. A battle for control of Seven Sisters. A chance to stand at the well with a very big bucket. The well's empty, Bernie."

"Not Iceone?"

"No, Bernie. Not Iceone."

I let him think about it for a while. His shoulders sloped off to nowhere.

At every stop his head turned slightly toward the door. He watched it open. He watched it close. His hands fidgeted nervously. Maybe he was thinking the same thing. He needed people. He needed night people, and morning people, and afternoon people who were confused about what time it was. All coming in through the doors to the subway car at the same time, so he could get out. It was his only chance and it was no chance at all. It was the only thing that would stop DeHooch, and DeHooch wouldn't be stopped.

The doors opened, the doors closed. The platforms were empty. There were no people.

No one moved.

The train rattled on, a mole beneath the land of dreams. It rocked back and forth. It made its stops on schedule. It sang its own little lullaby of darkness and of death.

I watched the skin shiver along Bernie's cheekbone. I couldn't see the front of his face, but I knew his eye was still going crazy. He was thinking about it. He was beginning to catch on.

"You mean it's not Iceone?"

I could barely hear his voice above the noise of the train.

"You resurrected the wrong man, Bernie. The man of glass. He's not dead. He's alive. I don't think he was afraid. Not after all those years. I don't think he knew what fear was. Not anymore. He spent too many years in the dark, trying to live with it. But once you raised that bad memory from the dead, it was between you and him. He had too much at stake to let you off the hook. He had the advantage. You could look right at him and you couldn't see him. When his boat went down in Chesapeake Bay, that wasn't the start of it. Not by a long shot. The start of it was when he called me in the middle of the night and said his back was against the wall. All I saw was the wall. And an old bear of a man in a wheelchair."

Rococco took a sharp breath and held it.

The twitching stopped.

"The man of glass?" he whispered. "Saltonstall?"

"We all read each other wrong, Bernie. All of us except him. He knew himself. He knew what happened back there on the other side of the Mussolini Canal. And he knew me. He knew I'd find you."

"He's dead," Rococco said. "I saw his casket. I saw his widow."

"You married a dancer, Bernie. He married an actress. She knows something about appearances, too. Everybody betrayed everybody else. Bernie? He told me not to overemphasize the power of guilt. That was the key to it. He didn't want me looking for the man of glass. He didn't want me looking for him. He wanted me to find you. And Dominick Iceone. And Seven Sisters. That way, when I found you—Peter DeHooch would be right on my tail. And the man of glass would be home free. Everybody got used in this one, Bernie. All the tough guys."

Bernie Rococco sucked in another sharp breath. When he finally let it out, it sounded like a scream—something from so deep inside him that it had to tear its way through the flesh to get out. It was only the brakes going on as the train started to slow. Something mechanical, masquerading as human.

I saw faces flash by the windows. Then I saw the sign: "42nd Street." People were running along the platform toward the train.

I leaned toward him so he could hear me.

"Who's the victim, Bernie?"

He didn't answer.

"You're right, Bernie. We all are—"

I didn't get to finish.

The train slammed to a stop. Bernie jackknifed forward. He reached for the post to steady himself. The front doors hissed open, and people started to push their way into the car. Night people with old tired faces, hookers on their way home from a hard night at the office, kids with nowhere to go, salesmen with dull eyes who hadn't made it home, married men who spent the night telling people they were single, morning people with brains of cotton, afternoon people who were confused about what time it was.

Rococco's right hand swung around toward me. He was holding my coat as though it were a whip. I turned my face just as it lashed my head. Then I was out of the seat and on my feet, pushing my way toward the rear of the car past the people who were coming in through the rear doors.

"Watch it!"

"Hey!"

"Easy, man!"

I was almost to the rear door when I got a good look at the chest of a guy who didn't believe in shirts. He wore turquoise beads under his jacket, he was so big he had to stoop to stand up, and when I gave him a shove he took my shirt in his fist.

I glanced down. He did likewise. The calm black eye of the Margolin Special stared him in the face.

His fist relaxed.

We communicated real well. I looked around his shoulder. Peter DeHooch was gone. I twisted around and looked back toward the front of the car. Somebody else was sitting in Rococco's seat. She had a Palm Springs tan but she wasn't wearing a Palm Springs hat.

It was all over and I knew it.

I made it through the rear doors just as they slammed shut. The train started to move behind me. It had somewhere else to go, but this was the end of the line for Bernie Rococco.

The platform was deserted. Down near the end, an old man shuffled along toward the stairs. Baby steps. At the foot of the stairs, three kids stood looking upwards. They were frozen. There was a cold, musty odor in the air. It wasn't bay rum. It was worse.

"I wouldn't do it, man," one of the kids said when I reached the stairs. "There's a guy with a gun. Chasing someone."

"I'm not going up," another kid said.

I moved past them and walked up to the concourse. It was empty. I looked it over, went through the turnstile, and took the last set of stairs up to the street. There was no hurry.

Out of the darkness, into the darkness.

There was a hint of a breeze on the dark street. Faint luminous streaks of red light lined the sky between the buildings, like vessels of blood about to burst. I turned the other way and looked into a blur of lights. The air seemed incandescent.

Two shadowy figures moved quickly past me on the sidewalk. They were headed for the bright lights.

"Check it out," I heard someone say. "Check it out."

Another shape separated itself from a doorway and headed in the same direction. Behind me, a cabbie started hitting his horn.

Bernie Rococco was down near the end of the block. A small group of people hovered over him—whores, hustlers, all the lost and forgotten. They hovered over him like flies around a carcass. Looking down at him, moving closer, making little gnawing noises with their burnt-out throats, falling back when they had their fill and letting someone else take their place.

In the distance I could hear the high, frantic cry of an ambulance racing toward us in the night.

I moved up, staying in the shadows.

He was a lump at the edge of the sidewalk and he didn't move. His hat was gone. So was his bald spot. He was wearing my coat. His toes were turned awkwardly in. One pudgy hand hung limply over the curb, its fingers dangling in a dark pool that had started to form in the gutter.

Somebody reached down and started wrestling with Bernie Rococco's rings.

The sound of the ambulance crawled up the back of my neck. It was in a hurry. I looked back toward the subway and saw the ambulance shoot out from between two dark buildings. It paused a moment while the driver checked traffic. Then it accelerated quickly through the intersection.

It kept on going.

The siren began to fade.

They were on the wrong street. Or they were going somewhere else. Or they got paid by the mile. Or they had something better to do. Or they didn't care.

I looked back at the lump on the sidewalk at the other end of the block. He was alone. The whores and the pimps and the hustlers had started to walk away. The brilliant lights flashed on and off in the glistening pool of blood, like a heartbeat, and didn't stop.

Nobody was coming for the hero.

# 27

The bouquet of flowers arrived two days later. I opened the door of the house on Delgany Street. A young man stood on the steps. He was wearing a light blue uniform, his truck was parked at the curb, and he stuck the flowers out toward me. They were wrapped in green paper.

"What is it?"

"A bouquet, sir."

"Who sent it?"

"There's no name, sir."

"What are they?"

"Forget-me-nots."

"You've got a girlfriend?"

"Yes, sir. Three."

"Pick one of the above. Give her the flowers."

I slammed the door.

Dr. Lew Diamond stopped by a couple of times.

The first time I was able to tell him where he could find the .45 that had killed Roger Penrod and Bernie Rococco.

The second time he was able to tell me they'd found it. It had fallen out of DeHooch's coat pocket while he was riding a roller coaster in Anaheim, California, with his arms around a blonde by the name of Honey Mellon.

"There are no accidents," I said.

"Too many tears," Diamond said. "Why do I dream those dreams?"

I knew he was over it.

I found the check on top of the refrigerator, where I'd left it. Two grand, made out to me, signed by Suzy Leeds. All I had to do was find the man of glass. I turned it over to Diamond, he turned it over to the police widows' fund.

They never did find Dominick Iceone. When the cops went up to Little Bearskin Lodge, all they found were an abandoned log cabin, a couple of empty production buildings on the other side of the hill, and a lot of heavy-duty truck tracks in the dirt. There was a winner after all. He was it.

Michael Moro dropped in and offered me a couple of free tickets to a new show in town. Song and dance. He was the front man. I declined. The lights finally went out for good on the Pee Wee. Somebody put a sign in the window: "Lost Our Lease." Harry Gallagher sent me a postcard from prison: "Wish you were here."

But I wasn't. By then I wasn't even on Delgany Street.

I was standing in the stream-side trees along a little run called Cobb's Fork in the Trinity Mountains, northern California, not far from a one-hospital town called Cedars, and I was dropping a #10 winged Black Ant very gently onto the water below a riffle near the shore. The sky was so blue it hurt. It was the blue that comes just before the dark. The sun was already down.

I had company.

"So you were the man in the middle," she said.

For some questions there are no answers. For some answers there are no questions. I looked over at her. The tent was pitched behind her, in the cool blue shadows. Her black hair flowed down from beneath the red bandana. She'd already slipped into a down jacket, but she was still wearing shorts.

Her sleepy violet eyes were waiting for an answer.

"No matter what side you're on, you're in the middle," I

said. "You're a painter's daughter. Put all the colors together and what do you get?"

I lifted the Black Ant into the wind, and watched it drop.

"Caine?"

"Yes."

"Maybe he was a hero after all."

The Black Ant landed softly on the water, and started to ride down toward me.

"He took your coat, didn't he? Maybe he thought DeHooch was after you. Maybe he sacrificed himself."

I looked over at her. She wasn't kidding. She was an unusual woman.

"You never found the man of glass," she said.

"No."

"Does he know you're looking for him?"

"I'm not looking for him."

"Will he try to kill you?"

I watched the water. I was listening for the wind.

A few hours later, the fire had gone out. The air was calm. We sat on the ground in front of the tent. The mountain silence reached all the way to the stars.

"Caine?"

"Yes."

"I know how you feel."

"How would you?"

"Lost."

I had nothing to add.

"You left your heart somewhere, Caine. I don't know where."

I looked at her. She leaned toward me in the darkness.

"You need something to hold on to," she said.

"A four-pound rainbow."

"Try me instead," she added.

I did.